Beyond The Bright Lights

A Reverse Age Gap, Plus-Size Romance
Settle Myer

Cover design by: Y'all That Graphic

Photographer: Mitzie Gibson - Bold Bodies Collective

Models: Hazel Hellcat & David Kurti

Edited By: Owl Eyes Proofs & Edits

Author's Note

Content Warning

This book deals with a lot of tough topics which you will find listed below. Some may include spoilers.

Grief, the death of a loved one, terminal illness, sexual assault, domestic abuse of a child and spouse, drug and alcohol abuse, suicidal thoughts, depression, miscarriage, fatphobia, and homophobia.

Help is available

Suicide & Crisis Lifeline — Call or Text: 988

https://988lifeline.org/

https://afsp.org/

https://nami.org/Home

National Domestic Violence Hotline: 800-799-7233 or **Text** START to 88788

https://www.thehotline.org/

SAMHSA:

https://www.samhsa.gov/find-help/national-helpline

Please consider donating to St. Jude:

https://www.stjude.org/

Table Of Contents

Playlist

1. Bittersweet Symphony – The Verve

2. Starting Over – Chris Stapleton

3. Wonderwall – Oasis

4. The Heart Of Life – John Mayer

5. Turn Me On – Norah Jones

6. Tennessee Whiskey – Chris Stapleton

7. Two Step – Dave Matthews Band

8. Sparks – Coldplay

9. I Found (Acoustic) – Amber Run

To those who have lost loved ones to addiction as I have.

Chapter 1 – Mylan

I toss up both middle fingers as I walk out of Forest Ridge Rehabilitation Center in the backcountry of Northwestern Washington.

"And I'm not coming back."

"You said that the last two stints," the discharge counselor yells right before the heavy glass doors close behind me.

A black Range Rover waits in the circular paved driveway. The driver, an older man with stark white hair and too many wrinkles, exits as I approach. My bodyguard, Bruno, walks towards me—his dark blond hair tied at the nape of his neck like always. I'm tall, six-foot-four, but Bruno has a few inches on me. More muscle too. Despite the terrifyingly intimidating mask he wears in public, in private, he's more teddy bear than grizzly as he offers me a smile and opens his massive arms. I fall into them, and he gives me three rough slaps on the back before releasing me.

"Miss me?" I smirk, combing my fingers through my shoulder-length hair. It grew too long as I sank deeper into my addiction. My self-neglect amplified in the months leading to rehab, and I stopped showering, stopped grooming, stopped caring.

First thing tomorrow morning I'll head to my favorite barber, Allan, for a trim. I'll probably have him shave this beard too. Though women love men with beards and soon mine will reach lumberjack status.

"Miss you? Hell, no," Bruno says in his thick German accent, with a chuckle rumbling through his hefty chest.

He holds out his hand for my bag. Before giving it to him, I take out the manila envelope containing my phone, Patek watch, keys, and wallet—items I had to turn in thirty days ago when I checked in.

Bruno swings the duffle into the trunk, and the driver pushes a button to close the door. By the time both men are done, I'm inside the vehicle, my head leaned back, and my eyes closed.

"I know this was a tough one, Boss. You okay?" Bruno asks, his voice softening.

I answer with a nod and a long stream of breath. He doesn't push me to talk about it. He knows I'll talk when I'm ready. Instead, he taps his calloused palm on my jean-covered knee, his silent way of telling me he's there for me.

He's always there for me.

The drive from the rehabilitation center to the private airport is thirty minutes, which is long enough that I doze off. If I had a superpower, it'd be falling asleep fast and anywhere. I've slept standing up while in between filming scenes on movie sets. I've slept like a baby during loud parties in my hotel room. I even slept at the MTV Movie Awards. My drooling face was turned into a meme that people still tag me in on social media despite it happening two years ago.

Sleeping fast and hard may be my unimpressive superpower, yet I tossed and turned every night in rehab. Sleep was my villain, winning the war my body waged. Because this time was different.

Because this time, I hit rock bottom, and they tried to keep me longer.

Bruno shakes my shoulder, waking me. I wipe drool off my chin and crawl out of the massive back seat. My private jet is parked on the tarmac, being prepped for the flight back to L.A. I wait, leaned up against the vehicle as the driver hands my duffle bag to an airport worker.

The sun sets in a wonderful display of pastels cast over mountainous land. A breeze washed over me, offering a welcome relief while standing in this dry heat. I savor this peace and quiet, knowing it will all go away the moment I return to the limelight and my disappointment of a life.

A deep chuckle pulls my attention to the two male pilots, who look like they moonlight as models, walking toward the jet. My chest tightens with jealousy as the men joke and talk about weekend plans. I yearn for that type of friendship. How pathetic is that? I mean, yeah, Bruno is my friend, but he's also my protector. He rarely loosens up when we're out because he's on alert, keeping fans and paparazzi away.

In private, Bruno helps me run lines. I vent to him or tell him about the women I fuck. Sometimes we gossip about the asshole actors and directors I work with. Bruno has seen me at my darkest. He's seen me cry and not the manufactured tears I use during scenes. Real fucking tears.

Bruno is my friend until we're in public, then he's just an employee doing his job.

I've had friends, but they always fuck me over. I can't trust anyone anymore. They'll share my secrets with the tabloids for a fat paycheck or take candid pictures of me looking my worst to sell to the highest bidder. I had one alleged friend steal my underwear to sell to my stalker. Most of the people who are in my entourage are only there for the fame, the pussy that tends to gravitate towards me, or the free trips on my jet.

Poor rich white boy, right?

I tuck away my self-loathing thoughts when I spot the gorgeous redheaded flight attendant strutting by. She turns to me, grinning her ruby lips and winks. I run my eyes down her body, appreciating her curves. Not curvy enough, if I'm honest. I love women of all sizes, ages, and colors, but I *love* my women thick. The thicker, the better.

I'm about to follow this fiery woman up the plane stairs when my phone rings.

My manager, Tony.

"Tell me I got the role."

He sighs and my heart sinks. Fuck. I needed this job.

"Yeah, yeah. You got it."

Wait. What?

"But you're on a short leash, Mylan. No drinking, no drugs, no sex."

"No sex? Come on, man!"

"Mylan," Tony warns. "You know what I mean. You don't need any distractions and that includes sex. Go to set, say your lines, and go back to the hotel. You hear me?"

I roll my eyes. Tony's been my manager since I started acting at age five. He knows me better than anyone else. He was more of a father to me than Aaron Andrews ever was. That fucker barely lived past my tenth birthday.

If you don't stop, you'll end up just like him.

I remind myself that Tony's *not* my father because, like Bruno, at the end of the day, he's still a man paid to deal with my shit.

"Yeah, I hear you."

The flight attendant pokes her head out of the door and waves, informing us the plane is ready for departure. Bruno slaps me on the shoulder and walks ahead.

"When do I need to be there?"

"You're not going to like this." He pauses as if working up the courage to say it. "They start filming in two weeks."

"Are you kidding me?"

"They're trying to stay on schedule and on budget." He exhales loudly, and I briefly wonder if he's seconds from quitting after finally reaching a breaking point. "You should know that the only reason you got this role is because the lead had a family emergency. You're not their second choice. Fuck, Mylan, you're not even their last choice because no one in their right mind would hire an actor who can't stay out of rehab."

Ouch. That stings.

I collapse into one of the massive leather seats in the plane's cabin, covering the phone to tell Red my drink order. I scowl at Bruno when he cancels the whiskey on the rocks and tells the flight attendant to bring me water instead.

"Okay. Then how the hell did my agent book this role?"

"*She* didn't. *I* got you this role. *I* was the one who called in favors. A lot of favors. Favors that will end my career if you fuck this up."

"Okay, I get it."

"Do you? 'Cause I just heard you try to order a whiskey on the rocks."

My comfort drink when I'm stressed. Tony knows that, so I don't even try to defend myself.

"This is it, Mylan. For you and me both. If you want to continue acting, then be ready to film in two weeks, lines memorized, in character."

I curse and lean over, elbows on my knees as I rub my palms over my face. Learning the lines is not an issue. Becoming the character, however, is something I typically take pride in—at least, I do when I'm not lost in my addiction. Transforming into a character is a process, one that I try to spend months perfecting. Especially for a role like this one.

Red returns with a bottled water and a glass of ice. She smiles, no longer that sexy, flirty smile, but one full of pity.

I *hate* being pitied.

"Look, son. Go to this small redneck town, tonight if you can, and win over those hillbilly hearts. Find people who knew the real person this character is based off. Forget Mylan Andrews. You need to become Tyler Taylor."

I grunt a response that Tony accepts as compliance and he rambles off more instructions that I tune out, not even worried I'll forget because he always sends a million follow-up emails. When I hang up, I open the water and forego the ice, sucking half the bottle down and wishing it was that whiskey instead.

I need the whiskey to forget. I need it to mute my overactive brain. I need it to dull my sharpened nerves because I'm about to reunite with the last person I want to see.

The director of this movie. My former best friend.

Red's contagious laughter brings me back to reality as she flirts with Bruno. I'm too numb to care that she's moved on from me.

"Hey B.," I say the moment their conversation ends, and she disappears behind a curtain. "Want to go to Arkansas?"

He rubs his hands together like he's about to dine at the finest restaurant in the world. "God gave us women, but the Devil gave us Southern women. Let's go sin, brother."

I choke out a quiet laugh and shake my head. Bruno has lived in the U.S. for six years now, he's been my bodyguard for five of those, and his English has improved tremendously. Still, sometimes his phrases get lost in translation and make no sense. Other times he makes them up and pretends it's gospel.

I call them Brunoisms.

M y assistant handled all the travel arrangements. As much as Tony wanted me to leave last night, there was no way. I literally just walked out of rehab. Shit, I didn't even want to go today, but he's right. I need to research this character, and I'm running out of time.

I can't fuck this up.

We landed in L.A. late, so I spent the rest of last night at my Beverly Hills home, packing enough clothes to last the entire three months filming on location. This morning, I called Allan and told him I was coming by for a shave and haircut.

The old-fashioned barbershop, with its red, white, and blue swirling pole out front, is located in a touristy area of Hollywood. I remember the first time I walked through the doors. I was six years old, clutching my mother's hand tight.

"How much to fix my son's hair? I . . . I messed it up."

Allan takes one look at my mother's bruised eye, at my red nose and puffy face, and waves us to the chair.

"I'll tell you what," Allan begins. He leans over, hands on his knees, and smiles at me. His dark brown skin creases around his brown eyes and mouth. "I could really use a street team. You walk out of here with your new haircut and stop the first ten people you walk by. Show them how great I did and point them my way. If you do that, I'll cut your hair for free."

I shake the memory from my head.

Entertainment Tonight did a feature about the small-time barber with his high-profile client, but *that* part of the story wasn't reported. No one knows the real reason Allan still cuts my hair, nearly twenty years later.

Once I no longer look like a lumberjack-in-training, Bruno and I head to the airport and hop on my jet.

By the time we're landing at a regional airport a few miles outside of Silo Springs, Arkansas, population 2,234, the sun is setting. I step out of the jet and stretch my arms high above my head. I take in the view, appreciating the show mother nature is putting on.

Not bad, Arkansas. Not bad at all.

A spectacular ombre of reds, purples, pinks, and oranges paint the sky behind brush strokes of feathery clouds. I breathe in deeply and fill my lungs with scents of oak trees, fresh air, and something else. Something . . . I can't describe it, but whatever it is, my body relaxes in response.

Maybe it's the sounds pulsing from the thick forest beyond the worn-down tarmac. A chorus of bugs singing their goodnight songs, animals responding with their calls of prey. Or maybe it's the heat. Damn it's hot. No, humid. A sauna. I'm already sweating through my clothes.

A black SUV takes us to a hideous two-story building made of tan bricks and rust red trimmings that most certainly hasn't been renovated since the eighties. Potholes and trash litter the paved parking lot. I blanch at the rancid odor that hits my nose and wish I were back at the airport, breathing in the oak trees and untainted air.

"Hungry?" Bruno points over his shoulder at the dead deer at the side of the road.

So that's what reeks.

I cover my mouth and nose with my shirt and ignore the smartass.

He thinks he's hilarious and full-belly laughs as he unloads the vehicle. He hands me my duffle and two other suitcases, one of which is full of books. There's something nostalgic about holding a physical book in my hands. When I was young, my mother would take me to the library. I'd choose as many books as they'd allow and take them to set to read during the hours of downtime between scenes.

At home, I'd lock myself in my room and escape to fictional lands while my father berated my mother in the real world.

Reading saved my sanity.

With the driver's help, we haul our luggage into the lobby where my assistant, Eloise, waits with a luggage cart. I'm surprised this hotel had that 'luxury' item.

"Great, you made it."

Eloise is a few years older than me and stunning with her long blonde hair braided and swung over her shoulder.

She's wearing a power suit and high heels, making her all of five-foot-five. I hired her two years ago, and she's the only assistant of mine to last more than a month. Entirely my fault, of course. Between fucking them, or me going all male diva, they either quit or I fire them. Eloise is different because from the moment we met, she put me in my place—and that doesn't happen often.

"This is the hotel?" I ask putting my bags on the cart.

"Only one in town." She's not as horrified as I am. Likely because she's used to the small-town life. Eloise moved to L.A. five years ago from some Podunk Midwestern town, which is where she's been for the past thirty days, visiting her family while her pathetic boss got his life together. "The whole place is booked for the cast and crew. We're getting the rooms the previous lead and his entourage booked. Which worked out perfectly because there weren't *enough* rooms, so some people opted to book an Airbnb."

"I think I'd prefer an Airbnb to . . . this."

"You'll live." She hands over my room card. "They don't have suites, Prince Mylan, but your room has a king bed and a view of a pond. That's as good as it gets."

I frown at her calling me Prince Mylan like I'm some sort of spoiled royal brat.

Maybe I am.

Eloise hands another card to Bruno. "You'll be in the connecting room next to Mylan."

We follow her to the elevator. After ascending one floor, she takes us to the end of a long hallway and points at door 220.

"Your room, Mylan. I'm across the hall. Bruno, you're one room down."

Bruno walks past with his bags and tosses them in his room before coming back to help me.

I nod to Eloise. "Did you miss me?"

"Hell no." She rolls her green eyes but still manages a grin.

"I know I've already said this, like, a million times but I really am sorry."

She turns her head away fast but not before I caught that grin falter. She sighs. "Goodnight, asshole."

By the time Eloise disappears into her room, and flips the bolt to lock the door, Bruno has already dumped my bags and is heading down the hallway to return the luggage cart downstairs.

I unpack then walk around the small space, inspecting the horribly cheap-looking paintings on the equally horrible wallpaper. The room is the size of a small studio apartment with a king bed, an awful brown and tan stripped couch, a chipped coffee table, and an outdated smart TV. There's even a tiny kitchen space with a refrigerator as tall as my chest, a stove top with two burners, and a microwave.

No minibar, though there's an empty space for one. Of course, they removed it from the alcoholic's room.

I collapse onto the hard, uncomfortable couch and check the time on my phone. Only eight? I wasted thirty minutes and now I'm bored as fuck. I'm too anxious to read. I pull up Google, typing in words I shouldn't.

Jumping up, I knock on the door connecting my room with Bruno's. He opens it within seconds, still wearing his bodyguard uniform of a black t-shirt and black jeans.

"Want to go out?"

By the scowl he gives me, his answer is 'no,' but I *am* his boss, so he has to do what I say.

Tony said no distractions. He also said to go out and meet the people of this town. I'm sure I can find someone who knew Tyler Taylor at the only bar in town.

Chapter 2 – Lana

"**A**nd I'm not coming back," slurs a wasted woman. She crosses her arms over a heavy chest and wobbles where she stands. Her bleach blonde hair falls halfway out of her ponytail, her eyeliner and mascara smeared beyond repair.

"Tonight is wild," my best friend, Ginger, says in her honey-sweet southern twang. She shakes her head of tight coiled curls and sets a tall glass in front of the drunk woman who stops pouting to take a big gulp . . . then spits it out, all over the bar.

"What the fuck? I didn't ask for water!"

"You didn't?" Ginger laughs, wiping away the mess. "How strange."

"Let's call that one a ride." I nod my chin at the woman who is now resting her head on the bar.

"You got it, Boss."

"Stop calling me that," I say and fan myself. It feels like an oven in here tonight. How is Ginger not dying like me? Despite the heat, my bestie is flawless. Her dark brown skin glows with sweat, and I don't miss the way the men here gawk at her beauty. She's a big beautiful woman, like me, but she's better at using her hips, tits, and rolls to charm people.

"But you *are* my boss, Lana Banana."

I scrunch my nose at my nickname, turning my head to hide a smile after Ginger winks and blows me a kiss. Technically, I own Lilies Bar & Grill, but Ginger helps me run the place. She knows her job is just as important as mine. I'd be lost without her.

Ginger holds her cell phone between her ear and shoulder to call Frankie. We don't have cabs in Silo Springs, but Frankie and her wife Helen are two recovering alcoholics who offer to pick up drunk patrons for me. I pay them with free food and a stipend I set aside from part of the profits from sales.

I scan the Friday night crowd. My bar has never been this packed before—not even during tourist season, which technically begins in a month. Something is going on, but I've been too busy the last few hours to pause and check text messages or listen in on conversations from the excited mouths rambling throughout the crowd.

Same with Ginger. She knows everything. She sees everything. Tonight, however, neither of us has barely had time to take a bathroom break let alone stop to gossip.

Folks who've never stepped a foot inside my bar are sitting at the red booths that outline the room, or at the matching red tables in the middle, drinking their weight in liquor. The kitchen has been inundated with orders as well. To be fair, Lilies serves some of the best food in town, aside from the old-fashioned diner off Main Street.

I know all these people aren't here for the band playing tonight. Jerry and the Jerry Boys (yes, that's really their name) perform here all the time, but they never have *this* many fans. Still, a horde of young girls crowd around the stage at the back, dancing and having the time of their lives. What's weirder? They all poured in an hour or so ago.

Strangers. They're all strangers.

I *definitely* don't recognize the handsome Goliath and the unbelievably hot man who just walked in. My bouncer Aaron is taking a piss, so I toss the towel I'm holding on the counter and walk around to greet them.

"Keys and identification, please," I say, plastering on a smile while holding out my palm.

Unbelievably Hot Man hesitates before reaching an arm behind him to retrieve his wallet from his too tight jeans. "Um, my keys?"

He extracts his driver's license with ease and hands it to me between two fingers, which shouldn't have been sexy, but was. I locate the date of birth first. Twenty-five? Seriously? My eyes travel up and down his body as he scopes out the place. There's no way this dude is twenty-five. He towers over me by nearly a foot. Besides the too tight jeans, he also wears a too tight black t-shirt stretched deliciously over his muscular chest and thick biceps. His messy raven hair falls in adorable curls. His eyes are *wild*. I swear there are different shades of blue to them—darker at the edges then fading to a lighter blue around his pupils.

Men this fine don't live in Silo Springs. They don't just show up here all of a sudden.

I force myself to look away and swipe the ID in the fancy scanner I bought after too many people were trying to use fakes to get in.

I point to a sign over my shoulder explaining the rules. "Everyone who comes into my bar hands over their car keys. At the end of the night, you blow into a breathalyzer to determine if you're sober enough to drive yourself home."

"Is that legal?"

I shrug. "Don't know. Don't care. No one has tried to stop me."

He smirks and it sends my heart fluttering. What the hell is wrong with me?

"Guess it doesn't matter because I'm not driving."

I hold out my palm in front of Goliath, and he happily puts his identification on top.

Unbelievably Hot Man points his thumb at his friend. "He's not driving either."

I don't look away as I repeat the entrance ritual. "How'd you get here? Walk? Ride a bike?"

"We have a driver."

I huff a sarcastic laugh. "Aren't you fancy. You two, like, celebrities or something?"

"Yeah."

I roll my eyes, already annoyed at these two. Well, not the big one. Just this brat. "Right, well, I won't hesitate to call the police if I catch you lying and you drive off drunk as a skunk."

"Skunks get drunk?"

I narrow my eyes at him. "That's strike one, Kid."

"Kid?"

This time *his* eyes travel up and down my body. He's not subtle about it. Shit, maybe I wasn't either. He swipes his thumb over his lower lip, his eyes darkening with . . . something. He takes a deeper step into my personal bubble. I can smell his musk—sweaty and expensive with hints of spicy citrus and cedar, maybe? Hell, whatever it is, I want to bathe in it.

"What happens when I get to strike three?"

I raise my chin high. Is he trying to intimidate me? Flirt with me? Whatever game he's playing, he's about to lose.

"I kick you out." I step back and wave my hand, indicating for the two men to enter.

Unbelievably Hot Man leans down before passing by. "I love your accent," he says next to my ear, low and seductively.

I barely stop myself from biting my lip when his breath fans across my neck. His voice weaves around the strings controlling my lust, tugging ever so gently. I've lived in Arkansas my entire life, and no one ever told me they loved my accent. No one that mattered, at least, and certainly no one who can make me hotter than Satan's armpit with just their words.

The Goliath, whose name is Bruno according to his ID, chuckles and shakes his head before slapping his friend on the shoulder.

Mylan.

That's the kid's name. Ugh. He's not a kid though. He's far from it. Still, he's too young for me. I'm a forty-year-old woman with a rule to never hookup with, or date, anyone more than ten years younger than me. I made that rule because I don't want to waste my time with men who are still trying to figure out their life, who don't know who they are let alone what they want for their future.

Not that I've allowed myself to date or fuck anyone lately. To be fair, I'm a hard person to love. Which is why I've been in dozens of failed relationships and why I'm still single.

Maybe I'll amend the rule tonight for this man. Who says I can't have a little fun?

No. I am *not* a cougar.

Mylan and Bruno sit in a corner at the bar, out of view from everyone there. I wonder if that was intentional because there are seats available where plenty of women could walk by and give them all their attention. Wait, are they a couple? A pang of jealousy rips through me. What the hell is wrong with me? I have no right to get jealous over a man I just met.

Mylan's blue eyes follow me as I walk back behind the counter. My stomach clenches and a part of my body I've neglected for years stirs to life. I fan myself, positive my chest, neck, and face flare red.

"Are you serving us tonight?" A simple question, if it weren't for the way Mylan's voice dropped on the word *serving*, deep and smooth and laced with desire.

Fuck me.

I search for Ginger, but she's running around waiting tables tonight since we're swamped, and my other servers are overwhelmed. My bartender Zack is on a smoke break and my barback Max is busy restocking bottles of beer and liquor.

Of course, I'm the only one left to serve the so-called celebrities.

I set a napkin in front of Mylan, then Bruno.

"What are y'all drinking tonight?"

Mylan regards Bruno with a raised brow. They have an entire silent conversation before Bruno clenches his jaw, muscles rippling like waves.

"He'll have a Coke," Mylan says, pointing his thumb at his friend. He peers over my shoulder. "You have any craft beers?"

I smile wide. "We sure do. It's what I mostly keep in stock. What's your taste?"

"IPA?"

"Hazy or west coast?"

"West coast, obviously."

I don't know what he means by 'obviously,' so I ignore it and open the fridge behind me. I select a pale ale with a Sasquatch on the label.

"This one is made in the Ozarks. My best-seller. It's strong."

Mylan takes a swig and nods his approval.

I glance at Bruno; his eyes are lowered as he traces a finger-tip over a name carved on the countertop. Those carvings are a staple of Lilies. Something I started myself. Now everyone who sits down finds a spot to carve their name. I'm almost out of room on the bar itself, so people started leaving their names elsewhere: the wooden poles, the wooden walls, the chairs, and even the floors in some spots.

"You sure you don't want anything harder than a Coke?" I ask the big man.

He looks up and replaces his scowl with kind eyes. Kind but pained. "I am sure, miss."

An accent. I wonder where he's from.

"Not while on the job."

Again, I'm not sure what that means but it only makes me more curious about these two. I walk off and grab a glass, filling it with Bruno's drink order.

"Thanks," he mutters as I set it down in front of him.

Mylan pushes his empty bottle towards me.

Damn that was fast.

"Want another?"

He shakes his head and Bruno relaxes his tense shoulders.

"I think I want something harder. Whiskey on the rocks please."

Before I can turn away to make Mylan's drink, Bruno slams his fist down on the bar. I jump and look around, but no curious heads turn our way. Either because the noise level masked the sound or because the two men are hidden in this corner behind a large pole where prying eyes can't see.

I have so many questions about what just happened, but instead, I force myself to walk away and fetch Mylan's order. By the time I return, both men are sitting, fists clenched as if they've had a fight, and neither will call truce.

Mylan peels open his hand to take the drink I hand him, and he swallows the dark gold liquid down in one gulp.

"Another," he grits out, slamming the empty glass on the bar. I narrow my eyes and mount a hand on my hip. He grimaces. "Sorry. I'd like another one please."

I have the overwhelming urge to cut him off right now, not only because that was rude as fuck, but also because this is not the same man who walked through those doors moments ago. This man has demons. Owning a bar, I've seen it far too many times. The way he grips the glass as if the moment he lets go, he'll lose his sanity. No, this man is facing an endless battle, one he doesn't believe he can win.

He's an alcoholic.

Why the hell is he at a bar?

Also, why is his friend letting him drink? Though, Bruno did try to dissuade him through their silent staring contest.

I return with Mylan's drink and this time he savors the taste, letting it soak his tongue, his throat, before settling in his stomach. I sigh because it's disheartening to see, especially in someone so young.

I want the other version of Mylan to return. The one who entered this bar with confidence and challenged me. I want him back to keep pushing my buttons because that confidence, and the way he looked at me, was exciting. Now, he's so withdrawn into a state of denial, a wall of stubbornness built tall, he might as well be invisible.

"Oh em geeeee." The sing-song voice of Cara Calloway barging through the door distracts me from the troubled young man. "Did y'all hear?"

Ginger returns from dropping off a plate of nachos at a rowdy table of guys and leans her round hip against the bar, arms crossed while Cara hands her keys over to Aaron. Ginger and I lock eyes and smile, both of us knowing, as the Gossip Queen of Silo Springs, Cara is about to share news that is none of her goddamn business.

She fluffs her straight brown hair, adjusts the fitted red top she's wearing, and walks over to where Ginger and I stand.

"No, but I bet you're about to tell us," Ginger taunts.

"Did none of y'all get my texts?"

I wave my hand around the bar. "A bit busy tonight, Cara."

"Whatever." She scoffs and plants her palms on the counter to lean in as if she's about to whisper. She does the exact opposite and raises her voice to speak.

"A movie is going to start filming here in two weeks."

Ginger perks up. "Shut the front door!"

"I swear to God Almighty himself."

I roll my eyes. "How have we not heard about this?"

"The announcement was just made, like, an hour ago while I was at the grocery store. Then I ran into Sarah in the parking lot who heard from Jess, whose cousin Amber Lee works at City Hall and confirmed it's happening."

"Again, how have we not heard about this?" I repeat.

Cara sighs dramatically. "Because, Lana, no one wanted to get fired. Amber Lee told Jess who told Sarah that they were given strict orders not to say a word until the official announcement was made. Mayor Truman was worried about the papa rats people showing up—"

"Do you mean paparazzi?" I ask, deadpan.

"—and the entire project was in danger of being delayed or canceled after one of the lead actors had to drop out for a family thing."

"Okay, but what movie?" Ginger asks, elbow on the bar, chin in palm.

My stomach drops to my feet as I begin piecing it all together. Cara Calloway is not only the Gossip Queen of Silo

Springs, she's also a Drama Dog. She loves to start shit and roll around in it until she's dirty and rank.

"Well," she begins while offering me the bitchiest of smiles that I'm tempted to reach across the bar and slap off her face. "It's based on a best-selling book—"

Cara's words are cut off with a gasp from Ginger. Every person sitting or standing in our vicinity stops speaking, all eyes on me.

Ginger starts for me, but I hold up a finger.

"Say the name of the movie, Cara." I spit out the words with venom. She did this on purpose. She barged into my bar, excited and voice raised to grab everyone's attention, just so she could watch my reaction.

Drama. Dog.

"*Tyler's Team,*" she answers, chin high. Cara, a glutton for scandal, feeds off the awkward air, and keeps rambling. "And get this, Mylan Andrews has been cast in one of the roles."

Mylan?

He wasn't lying. He really is a celebrity. Bruno must be his bodyguard. He's big enough. That must have been what he meant by 'on the job.'

I swing my head to where they're sitting, both overhearing this entire exchange. Mylan's dark demeanor is gone, replaced with hesitation. They're on alert. I understand now why they chose to sit in that corner. They're hiding from everyone because he's *famous*, and his cover is moments away from being blown.

"Mylan Andrews? The actor who's constantly in rehab?" Ginger's tiny nose scrunches. "Isn't he there now?"

Mylan winces at Ginger's comment, his hands tightening around the empty glass. His third drink, all within minutes of him being here.

Cara keeps talking. "Yeah, well, I hear he's out, so. What does it matter? He's hotter than Hades, and he's going to be here. In our town!"

"He is pretty hot for a white boy," Ginger laughs.

Great. They're feeding Mylan's ego without knowing it. But instead of his head swelling five times bigger with every compliment like I expected, he lowers his eyes. He's . . . shy? No, not him. He's not the type. He's ashamed.

Because he just got out of rehab and he's at a bar drinking.

"What role, Cara?" I ask, jaw clenched. "What role has Mylan Andrews been cast to play?"

Cara crosses her arms over her tiny chest. She's so fucking proud of herself. Bitch. "He's the new lead. He's going to be playing Tyler Taylor."

"Great." I turn enough to meet Mylan's stare. He gulps, his throat bouncing. "I can't wait to meet the actor who will be portraying my dead fiancé on the big screen."

The blood drains from his face.

I shake my head and walk past Mylan, heading to the closest door, desperate to escape. The moment I'm within his reach, he gently grabs my elbow. I despise the way my body reacts to his touch.

"You're . . . you're Lana Young from the book?" he asks, voice low.

Instead of answering, I rip my arm out of his grip and keep walking. I can feel Mylan at my back, following. I'm about to turn around and beg him to leave me alone. I can't do this right now.

One by one, gasps and squeals of excitement ripple through the air.

"Is that Mylan Andrews?" someone yells.

"Oh my god, that's Mylan Andrews," another confirms.

"He's here already?"

"No way!"

"Mylan! Mylan! Take a picture with me!"

"Mylan, sign my boob."

Seriously?

A mob of young women and a few men go absolute bat shit crazy, spotting Mylan trailing behind me. I manage to push my way through the chaos, but the celebrity stops in his tracks, trapped by the horde. Bruno is there, attempting to fend them off.

I don't stick around to help. I glance over my shoulder and catch Mylan's eyes. I expected to see the pity that's stared back at me far too many times to count.

Instead, he regards me with fascination.

I look away from his heated stare and nod to Ginger and she nods back, knowing I need to escape.

I can't believe it's finally happening. Rebecca's book about the life and death of my fiancé is being made into a movie.

What she failed to tell me is that it's filming here.

Chapter 3 – Mylan

She's absolutely brutal.

She left me for the wolves then snuck out while my fans smothered me with selfies and autographs.

I've never been so turned on.

The news of me coming to this town to film must have been released before I arrived and being that I'm a fucking alcoholic, people ran to the only bar in this godforsaken town.

A bar owned by that beautiful woman. Lana's almost a foot shorter than me with long dark red hair that I was sure is dyed. It cascades over her pale skin in waves. Colorful tattoos paint her left shoulder and down her arm. I want to trace the lines of the bright, detailed flowers with my fingers until it makes her shudder. She's also thick as fuck. Her tits in that blue tank top she wore spilled out generously. Her tight black pants hugged her hips and plump ass like a second skin. My dick twitches remembering how I wanted to reach out to her, touch her, pull her against my body and bury my face between all her glorious curves.

What is wrong with me?

I'm lusting over the woman whose life is about to be turned into a movie. Her story was already featured in a best-selling book. The heartbreak in her eyes the moment that loud woman said the movie's name made me sick to my stomach.

Did Lana not know? She must have.

It took half an hour, but I managed to escape the throng of fans. After taking a piss in the bathroom at the back of the bar, I'm about to let Bruno escort me to my seat when I hear a series of screams. Not screams for help, screams of anger.

Bruno follows me down the bathroom hallway, heading further away from the noise of the crowd, until coming to a door that opens to an outdoor seating area. One that appears to be closed for the night. Lana is out here, tossing an ax at a block of wood. With every throw, she lets out her fury.

The door we exit slams shut and Lana freezes.

"What do you want?" she says without looking our way.

Bruno ducks out, leaving me alone with this pissed off woman, and I'm not sure if that was a good idea. Isn't he supposed to protect me from danger? Lana is holding a weapon. She has murder in her eyes, and I'm most definitely her next victim.

I don't blame Bruno for leaving me. Payback. He's mad at me for drinking tonight.

It was only a few drinks.

I muster the courage to walk to Lana, stuffing my hands in my jeans to hide the shake. I'm shaking because this woman terrifies me in the best way possible.

"I heard you screaming. Wanted to make sure you're okay."

"I'm fine."

"Are you?"

"What the fuck do you care?"

"I do care."

"Yeah, well, if you care then maybe don't do this movie."

"Is that what you want?"

She pauses to think about my question. Her shoulders drop, and she tosses the ax she's holding on the ground then walks to the patio to a picnic table. It has similar carvings on top, like the ones on the counter inside the bar. Lana swings a leg over the bench and drops down with a grunt.

Bruno returns with two glasses of water and the kind gesture nearly has Lana in tears. Or perhaps she's reached her emotional limit with everything that's happened since I walked through the door.

"Thank you," she whispers, and Bruno disappears again.

Lana takes an appreciative sip, then rubs her palms over her face, her hair, her face again before balling her hands into fists and setting them on the table.

"I didn't want any of this," she says after a while. "Rebecca, Tyler's sister, started writing that book five years after his death. I wasn't going to read it, but I did. I had to. Then I grieved all over again. Now I'm going to have to go through it for a third time with this movie."

Her voice breaks, and I instinctively reach for her hand. She pulls it away fast.

"Did you not know it was going to be a movie?"

She sighs. "I did. Of course, I did. The script was written years ago, and the process to get it made took too long. I needed to move on, so I told Rebecca that I was done and no longer wanted to be part of the movie. She was disappointed, but she eventually stopped calling, stopped texting. I was finally getting on with my life. I was *forgetting*."

She turns her head to wipe tears off her cheek as if she's embarrassed to cry in front of me. Why? Does she believe crying will make her appear weak? From what I've learned in the short time I've known this woman, she's incredibly strong. Still, I have a feeling she's showing me a side of herself few others get to see.

Lana turns back to me. The pain in her eyes . . . God, I just want to hold her right now.

"Rebecca emailed me a few months ago saying the movie would be filming soon, but I thought it would be on some sound stage in L.A. She never told me it would be filmed here in the town I call home."

"Would it have made a difference knowing?"

"I . . . I don't know." She lets out a shaky breath and breaks our locked gazes to close her eyes and palm her forehead. "Maybe I could have mentally prepared myself. Or tried to."

I start tracing the carved names on the picnic table, expecting her to keep talking, but she doesn't. Silence stretches between us before I glance up. She's studying me—my face.

"You don't even look like him."

I raise a brow. "Did you want an actor who looks like him?"

She opens her mouth then immediately clamps it shut. She doesn't have an answer for me.

Because she doesn't want any of this.

"Tell me about him."

She huffs out a laugh. "Didn't you read the script?"

"I did, but I want to hear about him from you."

Lana stands as if my words flipped a switch from sorrow to anger. "I'm not doing this. Not with you."

Wait.

An idea pops into my head, and she's not going to like it one bit.

"Why not do this with me?"

She twists her face in confusion. "What?"

I stand up and walk around the edge of the picnic table. Her body tenses when I lean in, her lips pursing as she fights the urge to step away from me.

Her pride won't let her.

"Help me become Tyler."

She shakes her head. "Hell no."

"Lana," I say softly. That tough mask she's putting on falters, but only for a second. I stifle the urge to reach for her again, knowing she'll coil away if I do. "This wouldn't be for me or for you. It would be for Tyler. Don't you want the movie to be a success? To be true to his life? His legacy?"

Her eyes fill with tears and that need to hold her grows stronger.

"Fuck you," she whispers.

I can't help but laugh. She wants to curse me out and call me all the names in the book because she thinks it will make her feel better—a defensive tactic aimed to hide her grief. A move I've used before.

I expected my laughter to infuriate her enough she'd unleash all hell on me. Instead, she laughs too. God, it's a wonderful sound. From here on out, my mission will be to make this woman laugh and smile. It won't be easy. She's going to fight me every step of the way.

Why does that excite me?

Maybe because women always fall at my feet. Maybe because no one ever challenges me. Maybe because pain and heartbreak consume my life, and this woman is broken like me.

Could we help each other heal?

"Say you'll help. Teach me everything about Tyler Taylor. His mannerisms, his accent. Take me to his favorite spots, tell me stories about the two of you."

She bites her lip, considering my offer, and I almost reach out to pull that lip from her teeth.

Almost.

She lets out a long breath and drops her shoulders. "I'm sorry, but I can't."

She walks past me back towards the bar.

Seriously?

I run and catch her before she makes it to the door. She puts up her hands to avoid running into me. Her palms flatten on my chest and her eyes inch up to my face. She releases a breath, her chest rising and falling rapidly. Her body is reacting to mine the same way mine does to hers. She wants me just as badly.

I'm going to claim this woman right here. Right now. I tilt in and sway slightly because drinking that liquor so quickly after being clean for thirty days went right to my head. Lana must have seen that sway and shoves me away with enough force, I stumble back.

She pushes past me, attempting to leave again.

"Please, Lana, I need this."

She whips back around, narrowing her eyes at me. "You need this? *This* is my life, Mylan. You don't care about me or Tyler. So, why? Why do you so desperately need my help?"

"I'm an actor. Taking on a role means learning the character—"

"Bullshit," she barks and crosses her arms. My eyes fall to her pushed up cleavage.

She snaps her fingers at me, and I grimace at being caught staring at her breasts during this intense moment.

I sigh and run my fingers through my hair. She's watching me closely, demanding my truth. I hate this feeling. Vulnerability. If I don't tell her, she's not going to do it. Then if I do tell her, she's still not going to want to do it.

I lose either way.

"What someone said in there about me being an addict? It's true. Alcohol, drugs . . . sex." My eyes pop to hers at that last word, and she tenses. I can only hope naughty visions popped into her head. Focus, Mylan. Stop thinking with your dick. "I checked myself out of rehab yesterday. I landed this role but barely. This is my last chance to save my career."

She scoffs.

"I know. Selfish, right?" I open my arms wide as if telling her this is me, all of me, here and now being vulnerable as fuck. "Fine. I'm selfish, but you know helping me will also benefit the movie."

"You're unbelievable."

"I've been told."

"Fuck off."

"Lana," I close my distance to her with purpose, and she's so fucking defiant, she doesn't budge at my fast movement. She even lets me cup her face. She feels so good, so soft, so irresistible. My eyes dip to her lips and she licks them. I want to lick them too. I want to lick every inch of her body. I don't make a move. Not yet. Instead, I lock eyes with her. "What do you have to lose? Because I will lose everything. *Everything*."

She studies my face again, my eyes, searching for something. Honesty? Pain? Desperation? I am most certainly desperate.

She reaches up and latches on to my wrists, pulling my hands away and letting go. I immediately miss the feel of her.

"You listen here, Mylan Andrews," she begins, poking a finger in my chest. I stagger back and she steps forward, prodding me with that vicious, red-painted nail until we're on the move, me walking backwards. "You come into my bar the day after getting out of rehab, asking me to help you when you can't help yourself?"

"I—"

"You drank."

"Only a few—"

"You're an alcoholic."

"Functional alcoholic, really."

"Functional?" she says, her voice an octave higher. "Are you kidding me?"

"No?"

"How many times have you been in rehab?"

"Well, three, but—"

"Why should I believe that this time will be different?"

The backs of my legs hit a picnic table. Lana is still poking me with her angry little finger being all demanding and controlling and it's hot as fuck. I bite back a groan and try not to think about my cock hardening with every adorably accented word that pours from her luscious mouth.

"It *will* be different this time," I breathe. "I promise."

"Your promises mean nothing to me," Lana says, and I wince at the harsh words.

"You have no reason to trust me. I understand that."

"Do you?"

"Lana."

"Stop saying my name like that."

"Like what?"

"Like you're a friend asking for a favor. You're not my friend."

I clamp my mouth shut. She's too furious. I could beg for my life, and she'd leave me to bleed out and die. She's not going to cave. Not at this point.

"You're right. I'm sorry. I shouldn't have asked. I'm sure I'll figure it out."

She blinks. Blinks some more. Then she breathes as if she'd been holding it in this entire time. She takes a step back and now I can breathe too. Lowering my head in shame, in disappointment, in defeat, I walk around Lana back to the bar.

"You have to stop drinking. Can you do that?"

I freeze at her words, my hand on the doorknob. "I can try."

"I'm not going to be your babysitter."

The heels of her boots click on the patio as she walks to me. I drop my arm and turn to face her. "I don't need a babysitter."

"I'll do it, okay? Not for you. For Tyler."

My face lights up, and I can't help myself. I scoop Lana up in my arms and kiss her. My lips are like a starved animal, sucking her bottom lip and garnering a breathy moan. A moan that begs for me to devour her. The moment she opens her mouth, I slip my tongue in. She tastes so sweet, better than I imagined. I hum and the arm I have wrapped around her tightens. I press into her, my cock hard against her stomach.

Wrong move.

She stills and pulls back.

And slaps me.

I cover the sting where her palm landed.

"The fuck?" she says through clenched teeth.

"I . . . Sorry, um . . . sorry . . ." I stumble over my words, wrecked with confusion.

"I did *not* give you permission to kiss me."

She didn't. I stole that kiss. But her body *liked* that kiss. I wasn't about to say that out loud, though, because I still had no right.

It wasn't right, but I don't regret it.

"Do not. Kiss me. Again." She points her finger at me, beyond pissed, and I smile because it's so damn adorable. My smile only angers her more. "You know what? I changed my mind. This is a bad idea."

Crap. I'm losing her again. I won't even try to butter her up this time.

"Bad idea for who? You? Why is that Lana?"

She pauses, maybe not expecting that response from me.

I shrug. "Maybe you're just not used to doing bad things."

She narrows her eyes. "I never said I was good."

Fuck.

She takes a menacing step to me. "You better listen up, Kid."

There she goes throwing out that word again.

"The moment you fuck up, I'm out. No drinking, no drugs, and don't you go around sticking your dick where it doesn't belong. This is a small town. We are not your playground."

"No sex? Seriously?"

She stares blankly at me. "Is that not one of your vices? Is that not one of the reasons you listed on why you went to rehab?"

I can't help running my eyes up and down her body again. I've done it three or four times now since we've met. She tenses, squeezing her legs together and I chuckle. "Oh, no. I don't want to be rehabilitated for my sex addiction."

"You're a pig." She rolls her eyes and pushes me out of the way to go back inside the bar.

"So, you're saying you didn't enjoy that kiss?"

Bruno is leaning against the hallway wall and jerks his head up, clearly hearing my words. His eyes widen, either at what I said or the look on Lana's face, which I can't see because her back is to me.

I stop walking the moment she whips around and stalks toward me. She's a snake ready to strike, and I'm the helpless prey. I'm the *willing* prey. I'm the smirking man trying to rile the beast.

She pokes her finger in my chest again—the same spot as earlier. It's going to bruise, and I'm not even mad about it. I *want* to be marked by her.

"Stop. Flirting. With. Me. You're about to portray my dead fiancé, remember?" She pauses and glimpses down at my dick straining against my jeans. I'm so fucking hard right now. She trails her eyes back up to mine. "You're going to find a lot of willing cunts in this small town, but I'm warning you, Mylan Andrews. Keep. It. In. Your. Pants."

I can't help myself. "Why? So you can have me all to yourself?"

Her hazel gaze intensifies with a mix of heat and disgust.

"No, you asshole," she seethes. "I just don't want you going around fucking and forgetting and breaking the hearts of these women who will be infatuated with you because you're some stupid celebrity."

I smile wider if possible. "You still didn't answer me. You liked our kiss, didn't you?"

"There's something seriously wrong with you," she says and turns back around, tossing up both middle fingers as she leaves me in the hallway.

Bruno stands there, laughing at me. "Fremdschämen."

"And that means, what, in English?"

"Exterior shame."

"Try again."

"I am embarrassed for you." He shakes his head and slaps my back. "Dummkopf."

That word I know. Bruno's called me it many times.

I snort. "I'm no idiot. She likes me. I can tell."

He barks out another hearty laugh. "She is out of your league."

"You're right." I smile wide. "But I do like a challenge."

Chapter 4 – Lana

W hat the actual fuck am I doing?

I brush my fingertips over my lips. The kiss happened so fast. He was eager, appreciative. I kissed him back, I *wanted* to kiss him back, but I only allowed myself a taste because if I let his tongue worship me like it was begging to do . . .

That quick kiss, the way his hands held my face like they were carved just for me, made me feel things I hadn't felt since, well, since Tyler.

That scares me.

That excites me.

I walk back into Lilies and Ginger immediately spots my red nose and bloodshot eyes.

She points a finger up. "Go."

I purse my lips. "It's too busy. I'm fine."

"You're not. Home, now."

Rude.

I'm too drained of energy to argue with my best friend, and legit guardian angel, as she sends me home for the rest of the night. I retreat upstairs to my apartment above the bar where I collapse into bed and stare at the ceiling while listening to the booming sounds of the band playing below.

An hour passes I'm still here, in the same spot, frozen, numb, lost.

Did Mylan leave? I never gave him my phone number to set up a time to help him with the role.

Ugh.

Why did I agree to this?

Because if I didn't, he'd mess it up and Tyler's legacy would be trashed. It was up to me to prepare him, to make sure he gets it right.

I pull my phone out of my back jean pocket and bring up Google. I search Mylan's name and tons of articles come up. I click on the first one.

Mylan Andrews' Last Hope

Written by: Angela Borrows, *Entertainment Now*

A-list actor Mylan Andrews is fresh out of rehab and in the backwoods of Arkansas to film his new movie, *Tyler's Team*. Twenty-five-year-old Andrews was cast in the lead role of Tyler Taylor after Rey Michaelson dropped out due to a family emergency that he has yet to disclose the details about. Michaelson said he will be taking a break from acting for the foreseeable future.

Andrews has a huge task ahead of him. Sources tell Entertainment Now that his manager, Tony Wadeson called in favors to get Andrews the job. After three stints in rehab, the Oscar-nominated actor's career has tanked. Casting directors refuse to hire him and jobs he's secured are dropping him like flies following several public incidents of drunken behavior. Sources also tell us that during Andrews's last role, he kept flubbing lines, showed up late to set, or didn't show up at all.

This role could be a great comeback for Andrews's career. *Tyler's Team* is already getting Oscar buzz. The movie, directed by Oscar-nominated Jensen Boliver, is an adaptation of the book of the same name. Written by Rebecca Taylor, Tyler Taylor's sister, it tells the inspiring story of the college football star who died of cancer his senior year. Taylor spent his final days advocating for cancer research, as well as creating the nonprofit organization, Tyler's Team, with his fiancée Lana Young, who will be portrayed by model turned actress, Michelle Miller.

In the weeks following Taylor's death, the video he recorded asking for donations went viral on YouTube, raising millions of dollars for his organization.

I stop reading. There's more about me, about the movie, about Mylan. My heart can't take it anymore.

Déjà vu.

When the book was released, it only took a few months for it to become a best-seller—all because some celebrity with a book club chose it as the month's read. The story was heart-breaking, inspiring. It resonated with millions.

Then people found me—the real Lana Young. The fans who were obsessed with our love story found my address and camped outside my home. Same with the media, hoping to get an exclusive interview with me. It was so bad; I had to call the police. I also changed my phone number far too many times. It didn't matter because they always tracked me down. I still receive phone calls or emails asking to be interviewed. All of which I send to voicemail and delete without listening. Same with the emails. I never open them.

It's why I don't have an online presence to this day. No Facebook, no Twitter, no TikTok, no Instagram. I want none of it. Especially now since it's about to happen all over again with this movie.

With Mylan.

Fuck, I'm an idiot. The moment someone snaps a picture of the two of us together, it'll be sold to the highest bidder and plastered all over the internet. The paparazzi will stalk us, capturing our every move, analyzing our every breathing moment.

They'll show up at my bar.

I've only owned this bar for ten years. My throat aches with threatening tears at the thought of having to leave it. The first time around, the attention became too much, so I moved out of the home my parents owned then left to me when they died. I almost changed my name. What will happen this time? Will I have to sell Lilies and move again?

No.

Because this time I'm not some scared twenty-something year old. This time I will stand my ground. It'll be tough as hell, but I've faced far worse for this to scare me.

For *Mylan* to scare me.

Boy, does he. This young man who makes my body do things it hasn't done in years. Never has a man turned me on as quickly as Mylan does. His soft touches and vicious kisses. His cocky smirk that I want to slap off his face, then apologize with my mouth.

His dick.

Good Lord, his dick must be huge. I felt it when he pressed against me. My nipples rise remembering, my skin heats with desire, aching for this stranger. I need to wash away his smell, his touch. I need to release the built-up pleasure before I explode.

Grabbing my vibrator from the nightstand drawer next to my bed, I head to the bathroom. I start my John Mayer playlist on Spotify and fill the tub with water, pouring in vanilla and berry bubble bath.

Once halfway full, I sink in, groaning at the scalding hot water. Then I turn on my vibrator and imagine Mylan's lips, his fingers, his cock.

I come within seconds.

I sip on my third cup of coffee, savoring the sweet taste while staring at the paperwork covering the bar. We made a killing last night. Triple what we usually do on a Friday. I'm sifting through the tabs when I come across one worth $50 with a $5,000 tip.

I find the signature. Mylan Andrews.

Are you kidding me?

Of course, he would flex like the rich bastard he is.

A rich bastard who has no idea what this money means to my employees.

Justine, one of my day shift servers, is in need of a new car after hers broke down. She was walking to and from work for weeks before we found out, and I've been giving her rides, or Ginger and anyone else who's available ever since. Mylan's generous $5,000 tip will be going directly to her.

Once finished, I gather up the papers, stuff them into a folder, and check the time on my phone. Ten a.m. I still have an hour before opening. I try to rub the exhaustion off my face and consider heading to Daisy's for a donut and a fourth cup of coffee. Like most nights, I only got a few hours of sleep. It's been that way ever since Tyler passed. By now, my body relies on caffeine or energy drinks to survive.

I start taking chairs off tables when the bell at the entrance jingles. Saturday is our busiest day, so Ginger and I typically work doubles. She's never here this early, though. Unless she has gossip and is eager to talk to me.

Oh, right.

She probably wants to grill me about last night. She's been texting me nonstop, checking in on me. I'm a horrible friend.

"Hey Ging, sorry I haven't responded to your texts. Yes, I'm fine and ready to talk about the movie filming here, and no, I do not find Mylan Andrews 'just dreamy.'"

"Not even a little?"

I'm holding a chair, seconds from putting it on the ground but pause before lowering it the rest of the way.

"We're closed," I say, not turning to face *him*.

"I know."

"How the hell did you get in?" Only my staff have a key to the place.

"Ginger."

How convenient of her to let him in then disappear. I'm going to kick her ass.

I still refuse to look his way, knowing that the moment I lay eyes on him, my body will betray me. I'm too tired to fight my hormones right now.

"So, uh, yeah. I asked Ginger for your number, but she told me you'd give it to me if I showed up here this morning."

Yep. She's going down, Battle Royale.

"We also need to decide which day to start going over Tyler stuff."

"Tyler stuff?" I say, my voice low—a warning that he better tread lightly with his next words.

"To go over . . . the role of Tyler?" he revises.

I grab the pen resting on my ear and search my pockets for a discarded receipt to write my number down. I hold it out to him, my eyes looking straight ahead at the wall full of old street signs. The Silo Springs police chief gifted them to me. He'd gotten them from an old buddy of his who works at the state's Department of Transportation. Apparently, they toss outdated or damaged signs in a landfill, but the chief knew I was looking for ways to decorate my bar and collected every single discarded sign for me. Now my walls are decorated with battered stop signs, faded one-way signs, and even a bullet hole-ridden mile marker when a hunter tracked a deer to the edge of the forest and missed his mark.

"You're not going to look at me?"

I grind my teeth and will myself to face him. He smiles in victory, and I silently curse my heart for beating a bit faster.

I shove the receipt out to him. "I'm off tomorrow. My place is above the bar. Come around back and the stairs are on the left side behind a tree and bushes. Ten a.m."

He takes the paper, unnecessarily brushing his fingers against mine.

"What about tonight?"

"Can't."

"Because you'll be here?"

I shrug, and he grits his teeth.

"Fine, I'll see you tonight, then."

He runs out of here before his words register.

Chapter 5 - Lana

Tonight is a madhouse. People are waiting in line to get inside. To make matters worse, the vultures are swarming—the paparazzi. I had to call Chief Hallows and he sent officers to keep them off my private property.

After an hour of enduring the chaos, I escaped to the bathroom where I hid for twenty minutes, trying to take control of the anxiety spreading throughout my body. I only emerged because Ginger pulled me out by the arm, telling me Mylan, Bruno, and a beautiful, blonde, white woman were here, sitting at the bar. I managed to hold in my jealousy at the mention of another woman at Mylan's side and asked Ginger how the hell they got in so quickly despite us being at full capacity and long lines out front.

Turns out, three regulars willingly gave up their seats to let the movie star, his date, and his bodyguard inside.

Is everyone plotting against me?

I approach the taps, where *he's* sitting and spot a glass of water in front of him. Hmm. No booze.

That's encouraging.

"I can't believe you were going to turn me away," Mylan says through a smile.

Damn that smile. I turn away fast as a blush spreads across my cheeks and chest, and start busting my ass, filling beers, mixing cocktails, and cashing out tabs. I try to ignore this beautiful man, the beyond beautiful blonde sitting too close to him, and Bruno, who stands guard behind them.

Except, ignoring Mylan Andrews is impossible. "I wasn't turning you away. I was going to make you wait in line like everyone else. You shouldn't get special treatment because you're a celebrity."

The mystery woman next to Mylan lets out a sharp laugh and my eyes dart to her.

"People are here because of him, Lana Banana," Ginger says while making drinks beside me. "If you wouldn't have let him inside, everyone would have left when he left."

"Lana Banana?" Mylan repeats, watching me over the rim of his water.

"Don't you dare," I warn him then flip off Ginger.

My eyes wander back to blondie. She's typing away at her smartphone, head bobbing to the music. Her hair is slicked back and braided with the long strand hanging over her shoulder. She's wearing a power suit with a light purple silk dress shirt underneath showcasing her cleavage.

"This is my assistant, Eloise," Mylan says, obviously seeing me ogling her.

Ohhh. Assistant. Not his date.

Eloise reaches out a tiny hand that I take it in a gentle shake. We both say 'nice to meet you' before she blushes and focuses her attention back on her phone.

"You want another drink, hon?" I point at the empty glass in front of her.

She glances up and gives me a shy smile. "Gin and cran, please."

The moment I turn away to make her drink, I hear Mylan say, "I could listen to her talk all night long in that sexy southern accent."

He didn't even try to lower his voice. He must know I can hear him. Of course, he knows. He's doing it on purpose. He's flirting with me behind my back because I told him to stop doing it to my face.

"She seems awesome," Eloise says. At least she's lowering her voice.

I can still hear them though. Over the years working in this bar, my hearing adapted to the noise. I hear everything like conversations not meant for me. I try to remain on high alert, ready to jump in when women drink too much and creepy men hover.

"She is awesome. Beyond awesome."

"You're totally going to fuck this up."

"Probably."

"She's too good for you."

"I'm aware."

"But maybe she's exactly what you need."

Mylan doesn't respond. Instead, he changes the subject.

"See any women you want to fuck?"

Ugh, why is he so crude? Why do I like it? I silently curse my heart for going wild every time he speaks. Not to mention how his voice and his presence are literally destroying my panties right now.

"Don't be an asshole, asshole," Eloise sighs but reluctantly answers his original question. "The waitress is fine as hell, but she keeps eyeing Bruno's ugly ass."

"That's Lana's friend, Ginger," Mylan says the same time Bruno says, "She is?" with a sparkle of hope in his voice.

Okay, so Mylan's assistant is a lesbian? Who has a crush on Ginger? And Ginger keeps checking out Bruno? I've been such a bad friend. She texted me nonstop to check on me, and I've yet to ask her about how she's dealing with all this. She was Tyler's friend too. It was the three of us in high school and college. People would rarely see us apart.

When Rebecca wrote the book, she'd reduced Ginger's role in my and Tyler's life, barely mentioning her throughout the story. Rebecca claimed she did that so it wouldn't take away from our story of love and inspiration. Still, having a movie filming in our town about our dead best friend must be having an impact on her. How is she handling it?

"I recognize that look," Ginger chuckles, bumping her hip against mine. "Why are you feeling guilty?"

I notice Mylan watching us like a hawk, listening, so I tug Ginger's arm to pull us into the kitchen.

"Are you okay? With all this? The movie about Tyler? Freaking celebrities here in our small town?"

The concern in her face eases. "That's what you're worrying about? Honey, trust me. I'm okay. I have been for a while. Are *you* okay?"

My eyes burn with the grief I'm struggling to hold in. I've wasted too many tears on this part of my life, and I'm so, so tired.

"No. But I will be."

Ginger pulls me into a hug. "Oh, Banana. I love you, and I'm here for you. You know that right?"

I let out a laugh and sob combination and pull away from my best friend. She sweeps her thumb over my cheek, wiping away an escaped tear.

"I can't believe you said my nickname in front of Mylan Andrews."

She grins, mischievously.

"You bitch. You did that on purpose, didn't you?"

She tosses up five fingers.

"Hell no! You are not pleading the fifth on this."

She zips her lips and tosses the key away and rushes out of the kitchen, me fast on her heels.

In the minutes we were away, the demand for booze and food grew. I rush in to help the bartenders on duty while Ginger assists the servers.

"What's wrong?" Mylan asks the moment he spots me, a hint of panic in his voice.

"Nothing," I say way too fast and turn to the wall of mirrors behind the bar. Shit. My eyes and nose are all red. Anytime I cry, or I'm on the verge of crying, my nose is the first thing to light up. I swing back around and shrug. "Allergies."

He doesn't buy it, and he might have pushed me further if it wasn't for the ear-piercing squeal of a microphone.

"All right guys, gals, and non-binary pals," the band's lead singer announces. The chatter dies down and heads turn to the back where the stage is located. "My name is Harkin, and we're Silo's Symphony. It's seven o'clock. Time for?"

"Rock Star Karaoke!" the crowd answers in unison, followed by cheers. Harkin swishes his long, greasy brown hair back and strums the chords on his electric guitar.

"What's Rock Star Karaoke?" Mylan asks.

Gary, a white bearded ZZ Top-looking regular sitting next to Eloise, leans forward to answer. "Karaoke with a band instead of the track."

"Oh cool. Like a rock star."

"Ain't you a bright one." Gary snorts.

I burst out a laugh the same time Eloise does, and we lock eyes. Okay, she's pretty great. I could see myself being friends with her now that I know she has no interest in Mylan.

What the hell? Why do I keep having jealous thoughts about who Mylan Andrews is or isn't dating?

Mylan frowns at Gary then turns his head back to me. "Are you going to sing, Lana?"

"She always does," Ginger answers, grabbing the round of drinks I poured for her to take.

"All right, folks," Harkin says, his voice cutting through the excitement filling the air. "We usually have our queen, Lana, kick off the night, but I was hoping that honor could go to someone else tonight."

The crowd goes wild in anticipation of the famous name Harkin is about to say.

"Mylan Andrews, what do you say?"

Mylan whispers something to Eloise then to Bruno, who nods. He stands and locks eyes with me.

"Let the king show you how it's done."

I roll my eyes, begrudgingly smiling, which pleases him to no end.

Such a brat!

With help from Bruno, and two of the officers Chief Hallows sent to deal with the paparazzi outside, now inside manning the crowd, Mylan makes his way through a sea of people, giving high-fives along the way. He jogs up the stairs like he's Mick freaking Jagger about to perform a sold-out show.

Damn it. That was hot as hell.

He sweeps his fingers through his messy dark locks, something he does a lot. Something I want to do a lot. He's wearing a similar outfit as last night—too tight jeans and a too tight t-shirt. So simple yet that outfit makes him look like the A-list celebrity he is.

My curiosity got the best of me, and I Googled him again this morning after his little visit. I wondered if I'd seen any of his movies. I don't watch many. When I'm not at the bar, I'm working on tasks for the Tyler's Team organization. In my free time, I visit my grandparents, or the cemetery for alone time with Tyler and my parents. Sometimes I read to escape my reality for a world of fairies or vampires or hot mob bosses falling in love with the women they kidnap. The only time I do watch movies is when Ginger drags me to one. Same with television. I don't even own a TV. The only show I watch is *Law & Order* at Ginger's place. It became a tradition and sparked our obsession with pleading the fifth anytime we wanted to avoid talking about something.

Mylan's been in dozens upon dozens of television shows and movies, including a popular science fiction trilogy about space that I never saw. The only film of his I recognized was a historic romance released two years ago called *Love Lost*. Apparently, it won several Oscars. Mylan was nominated, but he didn't take home the statue. I saw the movie with Ginger when it came out and loved it.

And I remember thinking the lead actor was cute but far too young.

Reading his Wikipedia page, I skipped over the section about his dating life, not caring to read about the sexy, thin models he's fucked. I also scrolled past the parts detailing his drug and alcohol problems. I couldn't bear to read it. To be honest, I wanted *him* to tell me. To make matters worse, I found myself wanting to know *everything* about him, things Wikipedia wouldn't have.

Harkin and his three other bandmates begin playing a classic. *Don't Stop Believin'* by Journey. Of course, Mylan would choose something so cliché to sing. The crowd roars to life and here I am smiling again. That cheeky bastard knows exactly what he's doing.

Mylan stares straight at me as he belts out the lyrics about a small-town girl. For his information, I do not live in a lonely world. At this point, I can barely hear him singing over the cheers. I only know he's at certain parts of the song because he's acting out each word.

Like right now. He points at me then draws a smile on his face. No sir, we will not share the night for a smile.

"Girl, he's singing this song to you," Ginger says, appearing by my side.

"That's what he thinks."

She snorts, and I tear my eyes away from Mylan to look at her, which was extremely hard to do. Despite being an absolutely horrible singer, he's magic up there on that stage. This is why he's an actor. The way he commands attention. He's making eye contact with every person in this bar. He's winking and smiling and pointing and being charming as fuck.

Ugh.

With all the phones pointed his way, this little performance will surely be all over the internet by tonight.

"You better let that boy fuck you."

"Ginger," I gasp.

She puts her hands on her hip and bobs her head at me.

Bitch.

"How long has it been?"

Double bitch.

"That's what I thought."

Triple bitch.

"He's too young, case closed."

"Permission to revisit evidence?"

"Denied."

"Lanaaaaaa," Ginger whines. "I'm not talking about a relationship. Just have a little fun for once."

I sigh and focus on pouring a beer so Ginger can't see the fear in my eyes.

"I can't. Not when I'm about to reopen my healed wounds. Not when I'm about to grieve Tyler again."

After Mylan got my phone number and left this morning, Ginger barged in and demanded I spill. So, I told her everything. I told her I agreed to help Mylan with the role, and she was thrilled. She thinks this will be the closure I need to move on with my life. Now I'm wondering if she's trying to play matchmaker with the two of us.

"I get it. I do, but I'm telling you, the way that boy looks at you just . . . go into this with an open heart. You deserve love again, even if that love comes in the form of a summer fling with a Hollywood hottie." She pauses and takes a deep breath, her voice shaky when she speaks again. "You're my best friend and you deserve the world and beyond. I hope you know that."

"Don't you dare make me cry again Ginger Ann Cartwright."

She pulls me into a hug, only releasing me because I squeeze her side, making her squeal. Payback for getting emotional with me in public.

Mylan's song ends and the crowd goes wild. I swear the constant cheers for this man are driving me crazy.

"Okay, that was badass," Harkin says and gives Mylan a bro-worthy handshake. He turns back to the swooning bar-goers. "Mylan Andrews everyone!"

Mylan opts to hop off the stage instead of taking the stairs this time, and he's escorted through the mass of people by Bruno and the two officers.

"Now that the king has performed," Harkin purrs into the mic. "Time for our queen to take the throne and show us how it's done. Lana?"

I don't receive celebrity-level applause, and I couldn't care less. I have no need to feed off attention like this cocky fool sitting back in his seat in front of the taps.

"Your majesty." Mylan raises an eyebrow at me. A challenge, daring me to do it better.

Oh. Two can play this game.

Brat, brat, brat.

Chapter 6 - Mylan

What a rush. I wasn't sure if it was the crowd pulsing with excitement and feeding me the adrenaline to sing and dance on stage as if I'm headlining a sold-out concert, or maybe it was the way Lana's cheeks reddened as I sang directly to her. She tried to fight a smile, but I saw it spread beautifully across that stubborn little face of hers.

I watch her like a predator, ready to attack and consume her, as she weaves through the packed house. I hope it's intimidating, but if I've learned anything in the past twenty-four hours of knowing this woman, not much scares her off.

Except the past and her grief.

How I wish I could fix that for her.

After telling the band her song, Lana takes center stage and tenses. Her body is rigid as if she's never done this before. Still, she holds her head high, takes in a deep breath and closes her eyes as the band starts playing.

I laugh out loud the moment I recognize the song.

You're So Vain by Carly Simon.

Oh, this song is most definitely about me.

Lana belts out the lyrics, her smooth and melodic voice weaving through me like I'm being possessed.

"Holy shit," I mutter underneath my breath.

Ginger nudges my arm. "She's amazing, isn't she?"

I nod but refuse to take my eyes away from the siren on the stage. She sounds exactly like Carly. No, better.

"How is she not a star by now? She could sing professionally."

Ginger chuckles like it was the dumbest statement I could ever make. "You see, Mylan Andrews—"

"You know you can just call me, Mylan, right?"

"—Lana has stage fright. She hates singing in front of strangers. It's usually not a problem here but," Ginger surveys the crowd, "yeah lots of strangers here tonight. She's got to be a wreck up there."

One of the bartenders I briefly met last night, Zack—a lanky emo dude with swooshing brown hair—sets down a tray of drinks. Ginger picks it up, winks at Bruno who blushes, then walks off to serve a group of fans who keep waving at me and taking pictures from afar.

"They are getting antsy boss. Should we let them over here now?" Bruno asks over his shoulder.

The moment we walked in, people crowded us asking me for selfies and autographs, but Bruno rushed Eloise and me to our seats at the bar. Then he stood behind us, arms crossed and looking intimidating enough that people backed off. Up until this point, and it's only been thirty minutes, they've kept their distance. However, I love my fans, and I don't want to snub anyone eager for a meet and greet.

Lana finishes her song, and everyone claps and cheers, possibly louder than what they did for me, rightfully so. She offers them a shy smile, cute as fuck, and I want to pull her to me and hug her and let her scent wash over me as I caress her hair while kissing the top of her head.

What the hell?

That's not who I am.

It's not, but it's what I've always wanted. I just never allowed it.

My *addiction* never allowed it.

Lana struggles to make her way back through the crowd, and I nudge Bruno for him to help. He does without questioning me and brings the two officers along with him. Of course, the moment Bruno walks away, the fans descend. They swarm me in a near suffocating way, attempting to take selfies with me or holding out pictures for me to sign. I spot a few of my headshots, photos of me modeling for magazines, and even paparazzi photos that people printed out.

Eloise is by my side, helping manage the queue, and one by one, I scribble my name, pose for pictures, listen to fans share their love for my movies or for me. I smile and laugh, genuinely, with every last person until, after what had to be an hour, the fans disperse.

I turn around in the stool, exhaling a long, deep breath and rub my hand over my face and hair. When I lift my eyes, I find Lana staring at me with something like . . . approval? Or respect?

I can't help the grin that spreads across my face. "Hi."

The corner of her mouth twitches. Not quite a smile, but I still claim it as a victory.

"You're good with your fans," she says while pouring a beer from the tap in front of me.

"They've always believed in me, even when I don't believe in myself. I'd be nothing without them."

Lana frowns in thought, maybe considering asking me what I mean by that. She doesn't, though, and instead gets back to work, setting the full glass of beer in front of Gary. She turns around and taps away at the cash register's digital screen. It gives me the perfect view of her plump ass. Tonight, she's wearing faux leather black pants that might as well have been painted on. Her entire back is exposed because of the shimmery purple halter top she's wearing. Besides the sleeve of tattoos along one arm that pours over the top of her left shoulder, tattoos also line her spine, from the nape of her neck to the small of her back. Before I can focus on each symbol—small minimalist designs—she whips around.

I avert my gaze but not quick enough.

"Mylan," she warns.

"What? You said not to flirt, but you didn't say anything about looking."

She rolls her eyes and this time she *truly* smiles.

Fuck.

That smile is as smooth as Tennessee whiskey and my dick is thirsty for those soft lips. Great. I'm hard again. I fucked my fist last night back at the hotel, then again, this morning in the shower, and once more after getting her number and returning to my sad little room.

This is only day two, and she's already consuming my thoughts day and night and wreaking havoc on my body. I desperately hope she lets me in. I hope that wall she built to keep me out cracks more every day.

I hope she lets it fall.

B efore heading to Lana's, I have my driver stop by a local donut shop—the only one in town. Eloise, being she's my assistant, was supposed to wake up and take care of this, but she declined all my calls and texts and refused to answer her hotel door. That means she's either sleeping off a hangover or she met someone and is still in bed with them.

Don't get me wrong, Eloise is an excellent assistant. I'm lucky she *stayed* my assistant after this last stint. So, I don't mind her blowing off steam to forget why I'm a horrible boss.

Despite not helping me with the donuts, Eloise still managed to wake long enough to send me links to all the articles about my past two nights at a bar, fresh out of rehab. I didn't read them. I'm sure there were plenty of pictures. I'm sure they painted me in the worst light imaginable.

Bruno goes inside Daisy's Donuts alone to avoid me getting bombarded by fans, and picks up a box, returning to the car with a confused look on his face.

"Ich glaub mein Schwein pfeift."

"Translation?"

"I think my pig is whistling."

"Try again."

"I . . . I cannot believe it. They had donuts I did not know existed. Donuts with cereal, Oreos, and bacon. There was an egg sandwich but with two donuts as buns." He blanches as he hands me the box with two black coffees in a tray on top.

I laugh at my European friend who, despite living in America for six years, still can't believe some of our overindulgent customs.

"Will Ginger be there?" he asks, hopefully.

"I don't think so, B."

He frowns.

"You like her?"

My massive, "tough guy" bodyguard blushes like the teddy bear that he is and the corner of his lip tilts up. "She makes my nerves sizzle like a frying pan. My stomach gets all twisty when she smiles and winks at me."

Bruno shrugs a broad shoulder.

"I know exactly how you feel, buddy."

I open the lid to the box of donuts and my mouth waters. Bruno got every single pastry he named off (minus the donut egg sandwich) and then some. Crème filled, glazed, cake donuts. I don't treat myself like this often, but as I was saying goodbye to Ginger and Lana last night, Ginger stood on her tiptoes and whispered in my ear to show up with donuts and coffee for our first meet-up about becoming Tyler Taylor.

Is Lana's best friend playing matchmaker?

We pull into the empty parking lot of Lilies, passing one of those huge backlit white signs near the road. Black letters spell out drink specials and promote Friday night bands and Saturday night Rock Star Karaoke. Paparazzi are camped on the sidewalk, hovering on the edge before it turns into Lana's private property. They yell my name as we drive past, clicking away. The sound of the shutter from the dozens of pictures they take can be heard through my closed window.

Lana's bar is rustic—two stories with a triangular roof and brown siding with darker trimmings. It looks like a luxurious cabin someone built in the woods to escape the world. Medium-sized bushes line the front with a few red and yellow flowers mixed in along the ground. The landscape is professionally kept, not only along the front, but in the back as well.

The patio area is a mini oasis with all the plants and flowers placed up against the back of the building and along the fence. The picnic tables on the massive concrete slab might be my favorite part—the perfect place to sit on a warm sunny day watching people throw axes at the tall blocks of wood or aim darts at a bullseye on boards hung along a fence on the opposite side.

It's impressive. Lana is impressive.

I find the stairs at the side of the building where she said they'd be, tucked behind trees and bushes and hidden enough not to be found unless you were drunk or lost and stumbled upon them.

I swallow the lump in my throat as I ascend the steps, trying to forget what Eloise told me about the conversation she overheard between Lana and Ginger at the bar while I was singing. About how Ginger urged her friend to fuck me. About how Lana deserves love again, even if in the form of a hot summer fling.

I'm prepared to give her that.

At this point, I'd give her whatever she asked for. Whatever she demanded of me. That should scare me. Instead, the idea of her ordering me around excites me to no end.

I adjust the box to one hand, coffee tray on top, and as I lift my hand to knock, the door swings open. Lana's beautiful hazel eyes find mine before moving down to the box.

I hold my breath at the sight of her. She's braless, wearing black sweatpants and a tight black tank top. It rides up slightly, enough I can see her belly button and stretch marks on her stomach. I have the sudden urge to drop the donuts and coffee and touch that stomach or trace those marks with my tongue. I want to worship her body, smooth my palms over her tattooed sleeve and admire the design—red, yellow, pink, and orange flowers, like the ones at the front of her bar, with dark green vines weaving throughout. I don't know what kind of flowers they are, but they're stunning.

"You brought breakfast?" Her question forces me to tear my eyes away from appreciating her body.

"Um, yeah. I hope that's okay. I didn't wake up in time to eat, so . . ." I lift the tray of coffees and hold the box out to her.

She opens the lid and the smile she was trying to hide breaks through.

"I fucking love donuts."

She takes the box and motions for me to come in.

"Great. Does that mean you'll take my strike away?"

I stand in the open kitchen combination dining area of Lana's loft, which stretches across the length of the bar and is decorated just as rustic—wood paneled walls and a chocolate cotton couch with a matching recliner. Underneath the couch and chair, a fake white fur rug covers mahogany wood floors. Beyond the living area is an alcove for sleeping where I can see the end of her bed.

"Not a chance. You earned that strike."

"I don't think I did."

Lana sets the box of donuts on a red-topped vintage table next to where I put down the coffees. She takes two paper plates from a stark white cabinet and grabs two sheets of paper towels.

"Want anything for your coffee?"

"No, I take it black."

She scrunches up her nose like a mean little bunny and bends over to fish creamer out of her fridge. It gives me the perfect view of her ass. My hands twitch to touch it, to fuck it, to spank it.

Lana pours way too much creamer in her mug then puts it back in the fridge before returning to the table.

"I gave you a strike because you didn't know what 'drunk as a skunk' meant, then I took it away because maybe it's not a common phrase, especially for your generation. Or maybe it's a southern saying. Then I gave the strike back when you kissed me without my permission. So ... yeah, strike stands."

"Okay, fine. I deserve the strike."

Lana wiggles her fingers as she inspects the box of donuts, trying to decide which one to take. She chooses a crème filled one. I grab a donut with bacon on top.

Lana bites into her pastry and lets out a moan so sexual, I nearly choke on my coffee and spill it down my front. She dances in her seat while chewing and washes the food down with her sweetened coffee. Watching her appreciate this meal is an entire sexual experience. One that I plan to revisit later when I'm alone.

"Jesus, woman," I say, a bit breathless. "Are you eating that donut or fucking it?"

She raises a brow then shoves more donut in her mouth, not breaking eye contact with me as she chews and swallows.

"Donuts are better than sex."

"What kind of sex are you having?"

She stands with her coffee in hand. "I don't believe that's any of your business, Mylan Andrews."

"I guarantee you that I'd be better than a donut."

"Inappropriate."

I ignore the warmth in my chest at the playfulness in her voice and stuff my own pastry in my mouth. While I don't moan, it's still a good fucking donut.

Lana moves into the living room as I'm swallowing my last bite. She opens her laptop, setting it on her thick thighs and clicks away at the mouse pad.

"My television stopped working last year and I never replaced it, so we'll have to watch everything on my laptop. I had all my videos and pictures uploaded on here a few years back."

I sit next to her, too close, and she shoots me a scowl. I hold up my hands and move over enough that we're no longer touching. Though, I can still feel her heat and smell her sweet scent.

It's hot as fuck inside this loft.

Right on cue, a drop of sweat trickles down her neck and into her cleavage. It takes everything in me not to climb over and lick it dry. Before I do, and ruin everything, she wipes her palm over the line of sweat and stands, handing me the computer to hold. She walks across the living area to the window and pushes some buttons on an air conditioning unit, sending a cool breeze blasting our way.

"The A/C for the bar doesn't work that well up here," she explains, taking back her laptop and sitting down. She starts scanning through the videos. "Have you seen the viral video yet?"

I shake my head, not sure if I'm capable of words sitting this close to her. Her vanilla and berry smell takes me back to Friday night when I held her in my arms and kissed her. The way her curves melded into my body. The way my lips begged to be consumed by her.

"Here it is," she says in a slightly shaky breath.

Shit. I *am* an inappropriate asshole. Here I am, lusting over this woman who's emotionally wrecked as she falls into another round of grief.

After a few more clicks of the laptop's mouse, she makes the video full screen, then hits play and sets the computer on the coffee table. She readjusts on the couch, tucking her legs underneath her and grabs a throw pillow to hug.

Tyler Taylor appears on the screen. He's in a wheelchair, bald, frail, and pale. Pictures decorate the pavilion where his twenty-second birthday is being held. Pictures of Lana and Tyler in high school and college—Tyler in his football gear with Lana posing beside him in her cheerleading uniform, them hanging out with friends at a lake, and them dancing while wearing crowns at prom or homecoming.

Lana was right. We look nothing alike. Tyler had light brown hair and brown eyes with hints of green. From what I can tell from the photos and before the cancer claimed him, he was huge, twice Lana's size. Makes sense since he was a football player. He had more muscles than me, which is impressive since I work out every day. Or try to when I'm not passed out on my living room floor.

I spot Lana in the video, eighteen years younger, standing next to Tyler and holding his bony hand. She looked like a different person: no tattoos, her natural hair dark brown, and she was thinner, but her curves were just as bountiful.

Lana takes a deep breath beside me, pulling my attention away from the screen. Her eyes are full of tears—full but not yet spilling over. She's trying to hold them back with all the strength remaining inside her. I reach out and rub her arm. She doesn't jerk away from my touch, but one tear manages to fall. She's quick to wipe it away.

"Hello everyone. My name is Tyler Taylor and today is March third, my twenty-second birthday," Tyler begins speaking. His words are slow as he struggles to breathe despite being on oxygen. "I have stage four Acute Lymphoblastic Leukemia. I was diagnosed about five months ago. The cancer spread fast to my other organs, faster than normal.

I've gone through chemotherapy and any and all treatments available. Nothing has worked. The doctors don't know why."

Lana's hand absentmindedly finds mine, and she holds it so tight it almost hurts. She's watched this video enough times, she's bracing herself for what comes next.

"My time on this earth is being cut short, but I would like my legacy to live on. I was going to school to become a social worker, because I wanted to help people in tough situations. Now I'm hoping you can help *me* in *this* tough situation. I don't need presents. What I'm asking is for you to donate. With help from my family and my beautiful fiancée, I have created an organization called Tyler's Team. Part of the money raised for this nonprofit will be used for A.L.L. research. The rest of the funds will support families whose loved ones are going through treatments."

I run my thumb across Lana's. I hope it's soothing for her. It is for me, because moments like this don't happen to me—when someone trusts me enough to show me their vulnerability.

"Anything you can give would help. I don't know how much longer I have left, but every minute of the rest of my life will be spent raising money for Tyler's Team. I'm not letting this disease win. I will fight on."

A picture montage scrolls across the screen with sad music playing. Once the video fades to black with text providing information on how to donate, Lana breathes. Her grip on my hand loosens, but she doesn't let go.

"When did he—"

"A week later."

Lana shakes her head, her eyes lowering. She notices our embrace and releases my hand.

"Sorry, I—"

"It's fine."

"It's not fine. None of this fine."

She stands and starts pacing.

"Argh! I hate this. I hate feeling this way again." She throws her arms up in defeat. "It's been eighteen years. *Eighteen*. I can't keep doing this to myself. I can't keep mourning him. I can't—"

She stops pacing and hides her face in her hands, sobbing.

I stand up to walk to her. "Can I hug you?"

Her tear-soaked face lifts, tilting way up since I'm that much taller than her.

"You're asking?"

"I am."

"To hug me?"

"That's what I'm asking."

She lets out a tear-laden laugh.

I open my arms wide. "Come on. I'm really good at giving hugs."

She hesitates, totally suspicious of me.

"Just a hug, I promise."

Her bottom lip shakes, her body shakes, her breath shakes as she collapses into my embrace.

We hug.

Just a hug.

Chapter 7 - Lana

The hug threw me off.

It was . . . nice.

Not only because I can't remember the last time a man hugged me like this—and the drunken embraces from regulars at Lilies or the hugs from my family and friends don't count—but also because I hadn't expected Mylan to be so compassionate.

He's just some beautiful Hollywood actor. He's only supposed to care about his fame, money, and good looks. But right now, as he eats his cake donut while scrolling through his phone, crumbs stuck in the hairs on his chin and around his mouth because he didn't shave this morning, he almost appears normal.

He must have felt my eyes on him because he glances up, then down, then back up.

He sets his phone down and smiles. "Were you staring at me?"

I clear my throat and hand him a paper towel. For some reason, I fail to form words, so I point around my mouth. He takes the paper towel, and with eyes locked on mine, he carefully, methodically, torturously wipes the crumbs away.

"I always make a mess when the donuts are this good."

I inhale a sharp breath as his earlier words repeat in my mind.

I guarantee you that I'd be better than a donut.

I stand up. "Okay, I think we've wasted enough time."

After watching the viral video, Mylan suggested we take a break for more donuts and coffee. I was surprised he offered. I was grateful he offered. And between this offer and the 'just a hug,' I almost took away his strike.

Almost.

I collapse onto the couch and pull my computer back into my lap, ignoring Mylan's infuriating grin as he sits next to me.

Exhaling like a deflating balloon, I pull up a photo gallery.

"Disney World. Our senior class trip in high school. I'd never been on a plane before this. I was so nervous. Tyler was too because even though he'd been on a plane before, he was scared of flying. Still, he comforted me. He held my hand and didn't let go until we were safely back on the ground. Because that was Tyler Taylor. He was selfless and compassionate. He was like that until the day he died."

I click through the pictures of us wearing mouse ears, eating all the amazingly bad-for-us foods, riding rides, and posing with the characters. I pause on the photo of Tyler embracing me in a kiss in front of Cinderella's Castle during the nightly fireworks show at Magic Kingdom, my leg flung up behind me.

I swallow hard, forcing the grief back down, refusing to let the tears consume me this time.

"You okay?" Mylan asks, his voice low.

I nod and scroll to a video.

My heart clenches.

"This is the night we found out something was wrong."

I click play.

"Arkansas State University, homecoming night, senior year. Tyler was the star quarterback. He was a great player, one of the best. He wanted to be a social worker but honestly, he could have gone on to play for the NFL if he hadn't . . . Anyway, coming to the end of the third quarter, we were up seven points. Tyler had the ball and found an opening to score a touchdown. He was running—" My throat tightens as the video of the night plays on. I struggle to continue, my voice merely a whisper now. "He was so close. He collapsed two yards short of the touchdown line."

Mylan suddenly stands and goes into my kitchen. He opens every cabinet until finding my cups. He takes one out and fills it with ice, which is probably covered in freezer burn since I never use my ice trays. After filling the glass with water, he brings it back to me and I take a sip, not caring that it tastes like disgusting freezer burned ice water.

I'll drink this entire damn cup.

The video is at the part where Tyler is on the ground, unresponsive. Mylan and I watch in silence.

The crowd is hushed, the air dead. So quiet, cars could be heard from the nearby highway. The ambulance rushes out onto the field and instead of kneeling to pray with the rest of the cheerleaders and football players, I run to Tyler's side, meeting his sister there at the same time.

I fall to my knees, tears drenching my face, my neck, my cheerleading uniform. My screams pierce the silence.

"Please, Tyler, get up! Get up! Please, you have to get up."

Tyler's coach and a couple referees pull Rebecca and me away so the paramedics can do whatever it is they have to do. After a few minutes, Tyler is breathing again, but he's still not awake and has to be taken to the hospital. Rebecca jumps in the back, but they don't let me in. The video cuts off as the ambulance drives away.

I take another drink of the horrible tasting water, draining half of it down.

"Ginger drove me to the hospital. We were one of the first to arrive, but the waiting room quickly packed full of people. I remember hugging Tyler's parents and his sister. I curled up in the chair in Ginger's embrace, waiting for the doctor to give us an update. After what had to be hours, a man with salt and pepper hair wearing a stark white coat came in."

I stop talking because it's too painful to recollect. My words stop, but my memories play on.

"Tyler Taylor's family?" the doctor announces upon entering.

Tyler's parents and sister stand up. I want to stand too, but I'm not lawfully part of the family yet. Tyler had only proposed to me a few weeks before.

"Could you please follow me?"

Rebecca trails behind her parents, but before exiting, she turns around. "Lana, come on."

I dart up to the door and grab her offered hand. The four of us follow the man down a quiet hallway. The sour smell of disinfectant makes my stomach cramp. The only sounds heard are the thuds of our footsteps. It takes us at least a minute to walk from the waiting room to the doctor's office, though it felt more like hours.

"I'm a little concerned with Tyler's white blood cell count," Doctor Brennan says once we're settled in. "It's high, too high.

I don't want to give a premature diagnosis, but I'd like to run some tests for cancer."

We gape at the silver-haired man.

"Excuse me?" Rebecca asks, not wanting to believe what he had just said.

Tyler's mother clutches her chest, her face giving way to fear. Tyler's father reaches over to her and grasps her arm.

"It's possible he could have an infection and the white blood cells are working overtime to fight it. But we couldn't find any injuries on his body that would indicate an open wound infection. Has he been sick recently?"

We all shake our heads in thought, but I'm the one who speaks up. "Tyler is the healthiest person I know. I can't remember him ever taking a sick day off from classes. He works out every day, eats all the right foods. He doesn't drink, he doesn't smoke." My voice rises as my anxiety mounts. Then something occurs to me, and I let out a sob. "He . . . he mentioned feeling tired lately, drained of energy. And he had a nosebleed last week too. We thought it was weird but not cancer. He also mentioned not having an appetite, but he has a lot on his plate with classes and his football games. I thought he was stressed. I mean, we're all stressed. It's college. I didn't think anything of it. Should I have? Oh God. Is this my fault? Are you sure the tests are accurate? We've only been here for a couple hours!"

"It's not your fault, Lana," Rebecca reassures me, squeezing my hand.

Doctor Brennan clears his throat. Cautiously he goes on. "We have labs here at the hospital. They ran a complete blood panel and based on the preliminary results showing Tyler's white blood cells higher than normal, and especially after the additional symptoms mentioned, I'd like to send him to the West Clinic in Memphis. An oncologist there will do a bone marrow test among others to be sure."

Mylan's hand on my arm pulls me from my thoughts. I exhale, my breath shaken. "Sorry, um, he was diagnosed a week later."

"Why don't we stop for today?" Mylan offers, still caressing my arm.

I stare at the way his hand moves over my skin, not at all sexual. His touch is calming. I crave it because I haven't had a man touch me like this in a long time. Like he wants to be there for me, care for me, love me.

"Okay, let's stop."

At that, Mylan pulls his hand away. I strangely miss the warmth of his palm.

"I'll email you the link to the site where I uploaded all the photos and videos. That way you can start working on the accent."

He nods and gives me his email address. After sending the link, I close the laptop and stand up.

Mylan does the same, tucking one hand in his jeans pocket and rubbing the other hand over his hair. It flops back chaotically, strands every which way, and I smile through my sadness.

"So, when should we meet next?" he asks, acting shy all of a sudden.

"Well, tomorrow's not good. I have to go to my grandparents to help clean out their garage for the annual city-wide yard sale next weekend. That'll be a job in itself, and I really want to pop into the bar to relieve the manager who will be filling in for me these next few weeks. We can do Tuesday."

"Or," Mylan begins with the most mischievous grin on his face, "I can help you at your grandparents."

I widen my eyes and straighten my back. "I don't think that's a good idea."

"Why not? We can talk while cleaning. You'll be done faster with my help."

I want to argue and list all the reasons why he can't go. I could say I don't need the help. *Lie.* I could say my grandparents don't like uninvited guests. *Lie.* I could also say I don't want him there. *Lie.*

I'm not going to say any of that because I do need the help and my grandparents have been pestering me to bring him over since Betty Mea called Gram, blabbering about the handsome celebrity who showed up at my bar.

And I *do* want him there.

I drop my tense shoulders and shake my head.

"Okay," I laugh. "But don't say I didn't warn you."

"What's that supposed to mean?"

Chapter 8 - Mylan

Silo Springs, Arkansas. Population 2,200ish. I can't remember.

So small that Lana tells me the drive from the hotel where she picked me up, to her grandparents' home, will take all of five minutes. Which I'm thankful for because Lana's car is an old, beat-up Volkswagen bug from the 70s with no working air conditioning and the window on my side doesn't roll down. Her radio also doesn't work but the cassette deck does. Except, fifteen years ago, a tape got stuck in there and only plays the same Spice Girls album over and over again.

The horrified look on Bruno's face as we approached the tiny car was enough for me to suggest he ride separately in the chauffeured SUV. It would have been easier for us all to ride together, in the bigger air-conditioned vehicle, but Lana was adamant about driving.

She's so damn stubborn.

"Do you know what this is?" Lana points at the console as soon as I jump into her car.

"Of course," I scoff. "It's a cassette player."

She shrugs a shoulder. "You're young, so I wasn't sure."

"You're obsessed with my age," I say, trying not to let my disdain seep through. I don't give a fuck how old she is. My body wants all of her. Her body wants mine just as badly. The way she breathes harder when I'm close or how her nipples push through the thin fabric of the shirts and dresses she wears. I want to take those peaks into my mouth and suck and nip and hope she'll forget about my goddamn age. "I worked on a TV series that was set in the 80s. So, yeah, I know what a cassette player is."

"Okay, fine. And I'm not obsessed."

She scowls at my snort.

"I'm not, Mylan."

I ignore the way my chest warms, as it always does, when she says my name.

"I'm pointing out how different we are. I'm trying to be real."

"You know what else is real? Hot summer flings."

Her hands grip the steering wheel tighter.

"Did you hear my conversation with Ginger?" she asks through her teeth.

"You had a conversation about me?"

"You are infuriating!"

"I've been told."

Her face shades red, annoyed with me. She's so easily riled up, and I can't help pushing her buttons.

The stifling heat in the VW bug weighs down on us. I'm sweating, Lana's sweating. I watch a line of sweat creep down her neck, and this time, I can't hold back. I reach out, using the tip of my finger to wipe it away from behind her ear, down to her collarbone.

She shivers and tiny goosebumps dot her skin.

"Mylan." This time, it's not my heart that comes to life. This time, the breathy way my name comes out of her mouth causes my dick to twitch against my jeans.

In a flash, she lashes out like a viper. Her tiny hand wraps around my finger and squeezes tight.

"You're distracting me."

She tosses my finger at me, flashing me a smile. A chuckle ripples through my chest. I swear I've never laughed so much around another human being.

"I for sure thought you were about to give me a second strike."

"Don't test me."

"I was never good at tests."

She huffs out a laugh. "Guess you had to rely on your good looks?"

"Oh, so you *do* think I'm good looking."

"You know you are."

"I know I am, but do *you* think I'm good looking?"

"Did I not just say it?"

"You said I had good looks, not good looking. And the way you said it was more of an insult than a compliment."

She rolls her eyes at me, still gripping that wheel so tight, her knuckles are turning white.

After a stretch of silence, I say, "Lana."

"What?"

I wince at the biting tone. Despite my need to push her buttons, I worry I'm going too far. She's tense, maybe even uncomfortable. Though, I feel she's only uncomfortable because she's attracted to me. She's not, however, attracted to my age.

"I'm sorry. I'll stop."

"Stop what?"

"Flirting with you."

A flash of . . . something . . . crosses her face. Disappointment? That would mean she doesn't want me to stop. Perhaps she can't admit that to herself quite yet. She puts that stern mask right back on and gives me a curt nod.

We don't speak the rest of the short drive.

The home we pull up to is chaotic, to say the least. The front yard is encased in a literal white picket fence full of metal ornaments: a frog, a rabbit, a turtle, a wind spinner with a rooster on top and two-sided arrows—one for north and south, another for east and west.

I spot a large tree, oak I believe, off to the side, and a tire swing hangs from one of the sturdy limbs. I'd give anything to climb that tree right now. I've skydived in Dubai and hiked trails along Mount Fuji in Japan, but I've never climbed something as simple as a tree.

Bushes adorn the elongated porch that wraps around each side. Beds of colorful flowers, including the ones at Lana's bar, are in front of each bush. The same ones tattooed on her skin. On the white wooden porch sit four Adirondack chairs, also white. In between the chairs is a medium-sized wooden table. I imagine that table is stained with ring marks from sweating cups of iced sweet teas during hot summer months.

The house itself is a light blue with white trimmings. I expect us to walk down the cement pathway through the dark wooden front door, but Lana leads us past the porch and to the back of the house. My eyes widen at the piles of junk back here. Rows of hollowed out cars and trucks with hoods propped open. Worn-out tires are piled next to one of the beat-up vehicles.

Another massive tree sits in the corner of the fenced off area with a treehouse built in. I want to go up there so badly. I've never been inside a treehouse, either. Not even for one of my films. It's sad that most of the things I should have naturally experienced through my childhood were done only on the big screen or in a television show. It was all forced, with strangers surrounding me, cameras pointed in my face, and hot lights over my head.

Before rounding the corner to the back of the house, Lana looks over her shoulder where we parked.

"Bruno's more than welcome to come inside."

"He would, but then he'd be obligated to help with the garage clean-up. He's a big guy, and his body isn't made for this heat. He said he'd rather wait in the air-conditioned car and listen to the chainsaw snores of my driver than die of heatstroke. I don't blame him, since I was the one to volunteer to help, not him."

She gives me a soft laugh at that, and we continue down a path of round stepping-stones. The back of the home has an enclosed porch and a creaky screen door that we walk through before opening another door to get inside.

Ancient appliances pack the decent-sized kitchen. Shelves line one wall, full of old cookbooks and porcelain animals like pigs, roosters, and cows. Another wall holds a row of white weathered cupboards with glass doors where I spot mismatched dishes: plates, bowls, cups. Below the cabinets is a red topped counter with more white weathered cupboards, but no glass doors.

An elderly woman with stringy white hair pulled back into a low bun, wearing a muumuu, stands at a vintage stove, cooking and humming to an old song playing on the equally old radio sitting on top the counter. She taps her foot on the white tiled floor, not hearing us come in.

"Hi, Gram," Lana sings.

The woman yelps and brings her hand to her chest.

"Heavens to Betsy, Lana Banana. You can't go around scaring old ladies like me," Gram says in the thickest twang I've ever heard. If I were watching a movie, I'd activate the subtitles to better understand a word she's saying.

"Old? You're a young eighty-five."

Gram waves Lana off with a disgusted snarl that makes Lana smile from ear to ear. It makes my chest hurt with . . . something.

Lana's grandmother spots me. Her thinning white eyebrows jerk up, and she plants a hand on her hip.

"Now, what do we have here? Is this the movie star everyone's been going on about?"

I stand behind Lana, suddenly feeling shy. I'm never shy. Ever. Lana drags me out by the arm to her side.

"Gram, this is Mylan Andrews. Mylan, my grandma, Lila."

Lana elbows me, and I hold out my hand. Gram wipes her palms on a kitchen towel and tosses it over the side of the deep tub sink to accept my greeting.

"Does he speak?" she asks Lana, who snickers.

"Sometimes too much."

Gram lets out a hearty laugh and releases my hand.

"You two look hungrier than a hog. Have you eaten today?"

"I'm starving," Lana groans with excitement. "What are you cooking?"

Gram walks back to the stove with Lana following.

"We have biscuits, gravy, bacon, and sausage. But it might be a little cold. I was expecting you over an hour ago."

"Yeah, sorry about that. I had to stop by and pick this one up." She points her thumb at me over her shoulder. "He was still asleep when I arrived, so I had to wait for him to get ready."

I'm standing in the corner of the kitchen, hands behind my back, listening as the two women talk about me as if I'm not here. Gram grabs two plates and hands one to Lana and one to me, which garners a funny look on her face when she notices me hiding.

"Oh, honey. What is the matter? Come on over here and grab you some grub. Don't be shy. This is the South. We like to eat around here. I know calories and fatty foods are a foreign concept to you Hollywood type."

Gram cackles at her joke and my shoulders relax. I crack a smile at the hospitality and welcoming air surrounding this woman. She also radiates that same 'I don't give a shit attitude' that Lana must have adopted from her.

"I like to eat." I take the offered plate and walk over to the counter next to the antique stove where a buffet of breakfast food is piled high on plates. I take two biscuits, top them with gravy, and complete the meal with a couple pieces of bacon and sausage.

Lana prepares her plate, then pours me coffee, remembering I like it black, and we sit at a small table against the wall, Gram in between Lana and me.

Gram rubs Lana's arm. "How you doing, honey?"

"Stressed. Anxious. Frustrated," she answers between bites. "I can't believe they're finally making a movie out of Rebecca's book."

"So much good has come out of the book. It helped boost fundraising for Tyler's foundation. I bet a movie will do the same."

"Of course, and donations have already started pouring in from the announcement of the movie. It's just, I'm being thrown into all the attention again and it's exhausting."

I take my time eating, too engrossed with Lana and Gram speaking—a granddaughter seeking advice and comfort from a grandparent. I never got to experience this. Once again, my heart clenches and my stomach flips, as I yearn for this type of relationship.

"It will be worth it in the end," Gram offers.

"Yeah," Lana says quietly. She swallows a bite of biscuit then points her chin at me. "Now this guy has me consulting him to become Tyler.

Gram pats me on the forearm.

"Ain't that a great idea," she says in a voice as sweet as honey, then to Lana, "you were right. He is handsome. You two would make a mighty fine couple."

Lana freezes, and I choke on my food. *You were right. He is handsome.* She talked to her grandmother about me?

"He's twenty-five."

"And?"

"I'm forty."

"Honey, what does that matter? Your father was older than my daughter."

"Yeah, by like, seven years. Look, do you want your garage cleaned, or not? Because I'll leave now if you keep on."

A man wearing baggy tattered blue jean suspenders over a dirty white tank top enters the kitchen at that moment. He smiles at Lana, flashing a near toothless grin, stretching his leathery tanned skin.

"What are y'all carrying on about, now?" he grumbles in a rough southern accent.

Lana gets up and hugs, who I assume must be her grandfather, and kisses him on the cheek. When she moves away, his wrinkled dark brown eyes land on me.

"Who in hell is this?"

"Pa, don't be rude! This is Mylan. He's here to film the *Tyler's Team* movie."

"The what?"

"The movie version of the book Rebecca wrote."

"Now they're doing a movie? I can't keep up with all that horseshit!"

Lana playfully slaps Pa on the shoulder and sits back down.

"How ya feeling?" she asks, scooping some eggs onto her fork.

"Finer than frog hair split four ways," he says, chin raised.

"And you're following Doctor Lowry's meal plan?"

"Hell, what does he know?"

"Maybe that you had a stroke earlier this year and you should be eating healthier, so it doesn't happen again. Gram?"

"Yes, he's eating the foods on the plan."

Pa sits at the table next to me, grumbling something about a big city doctor with a fancy degree. He judgingly stares me down. At this point, I'm so unsure how to act, I've stopped eating and hold my hands in my lap.

"What's your story, Martin?"

I dart my eyes to Lana.

"Pa, his name is Mylan. You better behave."

"If you're wanting to date my Lana Banana, think again! Don't make me bring out ole Betsy."

"Pa, you sure are a lot of talk when it comes to that shotgun. Truth is you'd never hurt a fly."

He locks eyes with me.

"Try me, Matthew."

Lana stands up, tugging on my arm. "Okay, we're going outside to start on the garage."

She pulls me out of my seat and out the same door we entered. Pa's evil laugh, and Gram's complaining, follows.

The garage isn't too cluttered, but dust coats the surfaces and cobwebs hang from the ceiling and corners. I shudder. I hate spiders. Taking up half the space is a car buried underneath a sheet that was white at one point but is now a dull brown. Next to the covered car, I count three rusty bicycles, a green push lawnmower, and a matching green riding lawnmower. On the other side of the garage are tall floor to ceiling metal shelves that you'd see in a warehouse with stacks of boxes labeled by black marker. Along the wall in the middle at the back is a long tool bench with every tool I could ever imagine and then some.

Lana's hand rests on her forehead as she observes the mess. She drops her arms dramatically and walks over to a tower of boxes.

"Are you sure you still want to help with this?"

She pulls a box from the metal shelf and coughs when dust flies in her face.

"If it means spending time with you . . ."

She drops the box on the ground and puts her hands on her hips. "Now, Mylan Andrews, I do believe you are flirting with me."

Why must everyone use my full name? It happens all the time. Mostly with fans. I just want to be Mylan.

"Let's make a deal. Stop saying my full name, and I'll stop flirting."

She raises a brow. "Maybe I'll call you Brat instead."

I close the distance between us and lean down into her personal space. She freezes, struggling with the decision to either step back or hold my heated stare.

"Do it. See what happens."

She narrows her eyes, not even affected by my threat. Her defiance is suffocating, and I crave more.

"Fine . . . *Mylan.*"

"Good girl."

The way her pupils dance tells me she liked my praise. She'd never admit that so instead, she rolls her eyes and attempts to hide a smile, but I caught it before she turned away from me.

Lana finds a paint bucket and turns it over to sit. She opens her box and cringes at the creepy dolls inside, quickly closing it and pushing it to the side. She points at it with disgust.

"That'll be the 'for sale' pile."

Lana stands up and selects two more boxes, one for me and one for her. She kicks another paint bucket over to me, and I place it right next to hers. Sitting, I open my box's flaps and find it full of old shoe boxes with loose pictures inside.

I pick up a stack and begin shuffling through them, as if I know any of the people in them. It's still fascinating. Nowadays, photos are mainly digital. Growing up, my parents had few physical pictures of me—only ones that were professionally taken like headshots or photos from set.

I don't even have pictures of my parents. Not that I'd want to see my abusive father's face. But my mother . . . I hate to admit that sometimes I forget what she looks like. Entirely my fault since my visits with her are becoming few and far between.

The quality of the shoebox pictures isn't the best, but it makes it all that more interesting. Every smiling face is genuine. These candid moments frozen in time. Real moments—a man and a woman posing beside a now-classic car, children wearing bathing suits, dripping head to toe as they run out of a lake, a family huddled together at a campsite.

A family.

Something I don't have. Both of my parents were only children and their parents died before I was born.

"My grandparents like you."

Lana's voice pulls my attention away from the captured memories, and I set the stack of pictures down to grab another. I have to clear my throat to chase away that tightening feeling that comes when I let my depressing life rattle me.

"Didn't your grandfather threaten to shoot me?"

Lana laughs. Her beautiful laugh—loud and melodic. Almost as if she never laughs and forgets the sound of it, only to be surprised when something amuses her.

"That's how we greet people here in the south."

"It's definitely not but okay."

She pulls a book from her box and opens it, pretending to read but I see her peeking over the top at me. "What was your deal back there, anyway? It was like you grew a whole 'nother personality around them."

I shrug while flipping through pictures. "I'm not used to being around grandparents. Or parents. Or family. I was out of my element. I wasn't sure how to act or behave around them."

"Isn't the whole point of you being an actor is to ... I don't know, pretend?"

I tilt my head. "You do realize actors have lives separate from movie sets, right? I may play pretend on the big screen but I'm a real human being with real human emotions and real human trauma."

Lana scrunches her nose, regretting her words. "You're right. Sorry. That was a bitchy thing to say."

She goes back to sorting through the books and magazines in her box.

I should be used to talking about myself. I do it all the time with interviews on television and the red carpet, but this is different. Personal. I only give the public a glimpse into my personal life, but with Lana, I *want* her to know everything.

"I didn't have much of a family growing up. I was basically left to fend for myself. My manager was more of a parent to me than my own father, and my mother, she ..." I shake my head. "Yeah, so, it's strange to see a family happy together, interacting, offering love and support ... to see what it could have been like for me. I don't know. I'm messed up."

Lana frowns. "I'm so sorry, Mylan. I had no idea."

"I don't share that part of my life with a lot of people, and my PR team manages to keep that, and a lot more, out of the press."

She pauses, perhaps wondering about the mysteries of my past. She opens her mouth to say something before shaking her head. "Well," she begins. "What about friends? I've learned over the years that family can be more than blood."

"My friends like me because I'm rich and famous," I begin, still scanning through the shoebox pictures. I found some from when Lana was younger (I only knew it was her because someone wrote her name and age on the back). One of her holding two fluffy kittens against her cheeks and grinning ear to ear. Another of her in the treehouse out back. Several of Lana and Tyler when they were in middle and high school. "I get them into exclusive clubs or take them on expensive vacations with me because I don't want to do those things alone. Though, it always backfires on me. I've been burned by so-called friends too many times. They'll learn a secret of mine and leak it to the tabloids for money. Or steal from me—my valuables, my clothes—to sell to my stalker fans."

"Jesus, Mylan. That's fucked up," she says, flipping through the pages of a magazine. "I'm starting to understand—"

She slaps a palm over her mouth.

"Why I'm an addict?" I finish the thought and peel her hand away from her mouth.

She winces. "I'm going to stop talking now."

I'm still holding her hand and squeeze it once. "Please, don't. Most of the time, people walk on eggshells around me, or tell me what I want to hear, or just plain out lie to me. I like that you don't do any of that."

Her eyes fall to our hands, and I immediately release my hold. I shuffle to the next photo in the stack—a young man and woman, embracing each other and smiling. I flip it over, but there are no names. I hold it up for Lana to see.

"Who are they?"

She squints at the picture. Her face drops and she looks away.

"My parents. They died when I was nine."

"I'm sorry," I say, placing the pictures back in the box. I close the flaps and stand to put it back on the shelf.

"Guess I've had a lot of people who were close to me die," Lana whispers.

I find another box full of old clothes and bring it over to my bucket to sort through.

"My dad died when I was ten. He was an alcoholic. Maybe that's where my addiction comes from."

Lana pushes her box of books and magazines to the 'for sale' pile and joins me to go through the clothes.

"Maybe, but I think our childhood, and how we're brought up, help shape who we become as a person. But willingness to change and to learn from our mistakes ultimately defines us."

I consider Lana's words, turning a black cowboy hat I found over and over in my hands. Instead of responding and saying something stupid, I put the hat on and stand, posing how I think a cowboy would pose.

I muster my best southern accent. "What a mighty deep thing to say, ma'am."

Lana cringes. "Aren't actors supposed to be good with, like, accents and stuff?"

"It wasn't that bad."

"It was atrocious."

"Want to hear my British accent? Aussie? I'm good at those."

I spot a pair of cowboy boots in the box and pick them up. I'm about to put them on too when Lana stops me.

"Oh, I'd shake them for spiders first. This is Arkansas. We've got Brown Recluses and Black Widows here."

I throw the boots across the garage, and sure enough, a spider runs out of one of the boots. I yelp while jumping over said spider, which causes Lana to burst into a fit of laughs.

The sound fills me with life. It jump-starts my heart, giving me hope.

I'm desperate for that hope to stay.

Chapter 9 - Lana

Sorting through my grandparents' garage took about three hours, and by the time we finished, Mylan and I were sweaty, stinky, and starving. Gram sent me off with leftovers, and she even had a container ready for Mylan. He smiled and thanked her for her hospitality. He was putty in Gram's hands, and it was the most out of character I'd seen him since meeting him a few days ago. With that on top of helping me with the garage, Mylan managed to redeem himself enough, so I officially took his strike away.

I'm not going to tell him. Not yet.

Learning about Mylan's life, his family and friends, or lack thereof, broke my heart. Strangely, it made him normal. Real. More than a celebrity. People put movie stars on a pedestal. When they're knocked down a peg, when they have real problems like everyone else, people no longer see the bright lights and fame. They see *them*. The real them.

The real Mylan is someone searching for a connection. He's lonely and desperate for affection. Could I offer that to him?

I think about Ginger's words. She's urging me to have a hot summer fling, but the more time I spend with him, the more I realize it's a horrible idea. I wouldn't be able to stop. Like donuts. There's a reason why I don't treat myself to them often. I'd become addicted. I'd gain one hundred pounds and never look back.

What would I gain with Mylan?

A life in the spotlight.

A life with extravagant things that I don't need or deserve.

A life with a man fifteen years younger than me.

On the other hand, having Mylan in my life could be good for the Tyler's Team organization. It could mean more celebrity endorsements, more money, more exposure. After the book was released, funding spiked, but then it died down. Now that the movie is being made, money has started coming in again. But how long will that last?

Being with Mylan could also make me happy.

The thought makes me shiver. I haven't allowed myself to be happy with another man since Tyler. I've had far too many relationships that started out great, but I'd always find a reason to end it. Small reasons. Stupid reasons. No one could ever live up to the sense of calm, security, and love that I had with Tyler.

But Mylan? He's different. I can't explain how, but I just know he is. Is it because he's young and new and exciting? Is it because he's frustrating and challenging and clearly attracted to me? Not that men aren't attracted to me; they are, but they've never looked at me the way Mylan does. With a fire, with intention, with an uncontrollable need.

When Mylan told me he'd stop flirting, my heart lurched. I don't want him to stop, which isn't fair because I was surely giving off mixed signals. I keep saying no, but the word is meaningless, because keeping him at a distance is not what I truly want.

This is stupid. It's only been a few days. My thoughts are going crazy, letting my vagina take the wheel.

Yes. This is my vagina talking. She's been neglected and every time Mylan is near, my desire awakens from the dungeons where I've imprisoned it. It begs to be claimed. My will to keep my hands to myself cracks with every heated look he gives me. It webs like broken glass with every filthy thing he says to me.

It's Tuesday morning and I'm getting ready to meet Mylan. I'm taking him up to the high school where some of Tyler's former teammates, now teachers, agreed to talk with us.

I'm anxious.

I hadn't seen Mylan since I dropped him off at his hotel yesterday afternoon. He needed to start working on the accent, and I decided to go to the bar despite Monday being my normal day off. Ginger worked out a schedule with my staff to allow me time off while helping Mylan, and I told her I'd be around most nights as long as day shifts were covered.

I'd expected Mylan to walk into the bar last night, even though I told him not to come. I said I was tired of seeing his face after spending an entire day with him, which was a total lie that he absolutely did not believe. But Mylan stayed away and gave me, and my lust for him, a night of peace. I told myself I was relieved despite the hint of disappointment that I quickly batted away.

It hasn't even been twenty-four hours since I've seen him, so why am I *excited*?

I choose a light blue Cami dress and flip-flops to wear today, knowing it will be hot as Hades in the school. During the summer, they turn off the air conditioning and open all the windows to save money.

Staring at myself in the full-length mirror next to my bed, I try to see what Mylan sees. Don't get me wrong. I know I'm beautiful. It took me years to love myself and my body. In college, I weighed 140 pounds and most of that was muscle from cheerleading. Now, I'm well over two hundred.

I tortured myself with exercising and limited calories because I had a role to play. I was the hot fiancée of the star college football player. In high school, we were the homecoming king and queen, the popular girl with the popular boy. We ruled the school. And for what?

Our popularity and so-called society acceptable bodies didn't stop Tyler from dying.

Now, as my eyes travel across all my curves, the stretch marks, the fat folds, I smile. This is my body now. This is the body my mind and soul belong to. This is the body I love and deserve.

I'm adjusting the spaghetti straps and admiring how amazing my tits look in this dress thanks to the built-in bra, when there's a knock at my door.

"Come in," I yell, knowing it's Mylan. He offered to drive today. Well, not him driving since he has a driver.

The door opens and out of the corner of my eye, I see him walk in.

"I'm almost ready," I say, flattening the fabric of the dress along my stomach. I angle my head to check out my ass.

No answer. The silence and lack of response from Mylan pulls my sight away from my reflection.

He stands frozen, staring at me with his mouth parted and breathing shallow.

He's *devouring* me with those wild blue eyes of his, leaving phantom burns on every inch of skin his gaze touches.

"Lana," he says in a low and husky voice.

"Yes?" I respond in a whisper.

He walks toward the bedroom area where I'm standing in front of the mirror, his steps slow and calculated. The energy in the room shifts and becomes *electrified.*

"Lana," he repeats, but this time, the way he says my name makes me whimper. It's full of want, full of demand, full of heat.

He heard the whimper.

He sees my puckered nipples through the thin fabric of the dress, as if rising in search of him.

He sees my fast breathing and heaving chest.

He's in front of me, looking down because he's so damn tall. "Do you have any idea what you're doing to me wearing that dress?" He whispers. I stare up at him, fluttering my eyelashes.

I swallow hard and lick my lips, which makes him groan.

"Do you have any idea how hard it is to not touch you right now?"

He reaches up as if he's about to cup my face, but he stops. He hovers his palms close enough that my skin tingles in response to his nearness. He moves his hands down, skimming my neck, my arms. Never touching.

"I said I'd stop flirting . . ."

His words trail off and the anticipation is killing me. I squeeze my thighs together, trying to contain the ache he's causing.

"But?"

"But I don't want to."

My will officially shatters, falling to pieces on the floor. It only took four days.

"So, what are you going to do about it?" I prompt, which makes his pupils dilate, leaving a thin ring of dark blue edges.

"Will you let me flirt with you, Lana?"

I nod.

"Will you let me *touch* you?"

I let out a shaky breath. "Yes."

"Yes, what?"

"Mylan," I warn.

"Say it."

A whine escapes my lips. "Please touch me."

He responds with a hum that almost sounds like a purr. Still, he doesn't make a move.

"Tell me how bad you want me to touch you, Lana."

I groan and refuse to play these games with him. I tug on his t-shirt and he wraps an arm around me. Our bodies collide roughly in an explosion of heat between us. Mylan nuzzles his nose in my neck, breathing in deeply and exhaling slowly, letting his hot breath fan across my skin.

I moan. Damn it, I moan.

He chuckles, that bastard, and pulls back enough to cup my neck and tilt my chin up with his thumb.

"I'm going to kiss you now, Lana. Can I kiss you?"

I manage to control my whimper this time, but I nod once more.

"Tell me, Lana."

"Just fucking kiss me, asshole."

And he does.

His lips are soft, almost hesitant, as if he can't believe I gave him permission this time. So, I open my mouth to let him in. To assure him this is what I want.

I do want this. More than anything.

His tongue sweeps over mine and moves like a dance: graceful, choreographed, beautiful. He tastes like coffee and toothpaste, and I never thought I'd enjoy the combination, but I salivate, begging for more.

I clutch the nape of his neck, tugging him down. I want him closer. I want more. I need more. He smiles against my lips.

"Greedy?"

"Mhm."

His hard body grinds against me, contradicting the soft, passionate kisses he's offering. I can feel everything. His hard chest, his abs constricting, his dick straining in his jeans. I move both my hands to roam his strong backside while Mylan takes advantage of my permission to touch. He drags his palms up and down my back, then down to my ass and squeezes hard enough that I grunt and arch into him.

"You like that?" he whispers.

I can't form words, so I push back into his grip, silently asking him for more. He squeezes again, then moves his fingertips to brush against the back of my legs, making me shiver. He lifts my dress and this time when he palms my ass, only the sheer fabric of my panties separates my skin from his. Panties I *almost* didn't wear today.

"Fuck, you feel so good," he groans.

It took me years to love and accept my big fat ass. It's too wide and too covered in cellulite. But Mylan seems to love it too by the way his cock gets harder against my stomach.

He hooks two fingers inside the band of my underwear, one on each side at my hips.

"What will happen if I take these off, Lana?" He traces one finger back and forth along the elastic. "How *wet* will I find you? Will it be dripping down your leg?"

I close my eyes and lean my forehead against his chest, trying to contain myself.

"Tell me what you need." He walks us until the back of my legs hit my bed. Like I did to him that first night, crushing him against the picnic table.

I can't answer. He's barely touched me, and I'm about to lose it.

"Do you need my fingers inside you?"

Yes, I want his fingers inside me. So goddamn bad. "Please."

"Please, what, Lana?"

"Mylan," I warn, lifting my head and finding his smirking face.

Brat.

"You have to tell me," he breathes against my mouth. His lips tickle mine, taunting me.

I let out a shuddering sigh. "Please fuck me with your fingers."

Mylan's pulling my panties down before I can utter the last word. He crouches before me, and I step out of the fabric. Mylan balls it up and tucks it in his pocket.

He stares up at me, fluttering his long, dark lashes at me. "Lift your dress, baby."

I squeeze my thighs together at his command—and him calling me baby. Something I should hate being called but don't. I do what he says and lift the hem of my dress.

His hand moves up the inside of my legs, leaving goose-bumps in its wake. "I need you to open these," he demands, and my heart beats faster.

When I spread my legs, Mylan sucks in a sharp breath. "So beautiful."

His palm skims higher, all the way up my thigh until he's cupping my cunt. I shiver violently and this pleases Mylan as a deep rumble vibrates from his throat. He traces my slick opening with his fingertip, teasing me.

"Soaked and ready. All for me?"

"Mhm."

Mylan stands, still cupping me, and threads the fingers of his other hand through my hair at the nape of my neck. He tugs roughly to force my head back, so I only see him. My pussy clenches and my arousal thickens.

Holy shit that was hot.

"Show me what my touch does to you."

He plunges a finger inside me without warning. I gasp and drop the hem of my dress to hold on to him. One hand wraps around Mylan's upper arm, and I feel the muscles moving like waves as his fingers work miracles. My other hand fists the fabric of his shirt at his side.

He draws his finger out then pushes back in, slow and tormenting. Once he's a knuckle deep, he curls the tip up to reach a spot I thought no man would ever find.

He responds to my moan with something similar to a growl. "I love the way your cunt latches on to my finger. So goddamn greedy, like your kisses."

He picks up speed, adding another finger and rubbing my walls perfectly. When he presses his thumb on my clit and massages, I scream, a guttural fucking scream and lean into his thrusting. I need more.

"Yes. Keep screaming, baby. I want to *hear* what my touch does to you."

"Mylan," I wheeze, gripping his arm so hard, I'm certain there will be bruises later. I'm *certain* I'll leave my mark as my nails dig in.

He grinds his palm on my clit while his fingers fuck me frantically, and it's too much; his rough thrusting, the pressure against those sensitive nerves that went untouched by a man far too long, his words of appreciation.

I close my eyes.

"Open them. I want you to see *my* face when I make you come undone."

That puts me over the edge. I somehow manage to keep my eyes open as my orgasm explodes. Mylan bites his lower lip, nostrils flaring while he keeps working me, even as my pussy latches onto his fingers. I scream so fucking loud while tugging on his t-shirt hard enough it could tear at any moment. My fingernails dig deeper into Mylan's arm. If it hurts, he doesn't say a word.

He lets my shaking body calm before removing his fingers. I watch as he raises them to his mouth, sucking my release off each one.

"You taste as delicious as a donut." He grins ear to ear. "*My* donut."

"Asshole." I push him away, which makes him smile louder. That damn unbearably sexy smile. I curse the fluttering in my stomach. "Give me my underwear back."

"Not a chance."

"Don't be a creep."

"But I'm your creep."

I step to him, and I cup the bulge of his straining erection. He hisses, not expecting me to grope him, and without breaking eye contact, I fish my panties out of the pocket he stuffed them in.

This time, I give him a shit-eating grin. "We're late. Let's go."

Chapter 10 - Lana

I lock up my apartment and walk down the stairs, waving to Bruno standing next to the waiting ride. Once inside and buckled up, we head down Main Street toward the school. I avoid Mylan's burning stare. I don't want to see his smug smile. I don't want to see that flawless face full of victory because I finally let myself give in to that undeniable attraction between the two of us.

I don't regret it.

The opposite. I needed the release. I've *been* needing the release. It was inevitable from the moment we met that Mylan was going to be the one to give it to me. It was better than I imagined and all he did was use his fingers.

Imagine what his cock could do?

Orgasms don't come easy for me. Not from a man's finger or tongue and especially not from a dick. Usually, I fake it to get sex over with. Men have tried to stimulate me, and while it feels good, it's never enough. They never seem to hit the right spot.

Mylan knows what he's doing, and I'm not sure if I hate it or love it.

"You're mad?" Mylan asks, though it wasn't a question.

"I'm not mad."

"You look mad."

I suppose I do. I have my arms crossed, staring out the window as we drive to the school, which is on the other side of town. Not a long drive, but enough that we're forced to have a conversation after I let him . . .

I sigh but don't answer.

"Are you mad because I made you come or because you let me?

I dart my eyes to the front where Bruno and the driver are speaking. They don't pause indicating they heard Mylan blurt out something so private.

Finally, I allow myself to look at him. "I'm not mad, My-lan." I force a smile, but he doesn't buy it. He purses his lips. "I'm just . . . I'm trying not to feel guilty."

"For what we did?"

"For giving in to you after four days."

"You think that's a bad thing?"

"I don't know."

He doesn't say anything, waiting for me to continue.

"Tyler . . ."

He closes his eyes, letting a long stream of air flow through his nose. He's not angry, he's . . . understanding.

"Do you think what we did is disrespectful to Tyler?"

I disappear into my shoulders. "Maybe?"

"And what about all the other men you've been with since Tyler? Before me? Did you feel like you were disrespecting Tyler then?"

I open my mouth, but no words come out. I have no answer for him. I snap my mouth shut.

"It's because we're working together on me becoming him."

I grimace.

Mylan reaches out and takes my hand, squeezing once. "Then we won't do that again. Not until you're ready."

"No, Mylan, that's not what I meant. I . . . I liked what we did. I really don't regret it. I just . . ." I remember Tyler's final words to me. Would he be disappointed? He never wanted this life for me—a life where I've been selfish with my love and my body, where I've held back from experiencing the pleasures of a new relationship. "I *needed* it. Trust me."

Mylan's tense shoulders relax and that vulnerability trying to push through fades. I attempt to release my hand, but he tightens his grip. So, we hold hands for the rest of the drive, only separating as we pull into the long horseshoe driveway to Silo Springs High School.

The single-story building is made of boring gray cement blocks, a red roof, and red siding housing grades nine through twelve; a decent-sized school despite Silo being a small town.

We step through the front doors and pass by the office on the right, entering a long hallway full of red lockers and a bluish gray carpet. Bruno follows, not too close, but near enough that if a problem arises, he'll be able to intervene.

The lights are low, the sun that's filtering in brightens the halls. Halfway down, we come to a crossroad where one direction takes us to the cafeteria. I stop us at a floor to ceiling glass case with trophies, ribbons, and pictures placed throughout. I point to the one front and center: a picture of Tyler and me at Senior night.

"The night he secured his spot at Arkansas State on a full-ride," I explain and notice Mylan pulling a rolled-up script out of his back jeans pocket. He retrieves a pencil from somewhere and starts writing. *He's taking notes?* Why does that make my heart clench with . . . something. Shock? Pride? I shake my head and continue. "Recruiters from all across the country, some from prestigious schools, had been coming all that week, watching Tyler kick ass. This was a tough game too. We were playing our rivals and at one point, we were down double digits. But Tyler was such an optimistic person. As team captain, he never let anyone feel bad about how they played. He'd always inspire through words, no yelling, no insults. He had this way of pulling you in. Like he was the sun, and everyone thrived off his golden rays."

I stare at the picture. Tyler's light brown hair was drenched from sweat, clinging to his forehead. His arm is thrown over my shoulder and I'm staring up at him, smiling.

I force myself to look away and see Mylan scribbling fast. Wow, his handwriting is atrocious.

"Why Arkansas State?"

"What do you mean?"

Mylan stops writing and looks at me. "If he had the chance to go to a prestigious college on a full-ride and play football, why did he choose Arkansas State?"

My heart drops to my stomach. I was wondering when this would come up. I'm not ready to share that part of my life with him yet.

"His dream wasn't to play. He wanted to be a social worker. And he wanted to be close to me." It's still true. Just not the whole truth.

"Still . . ."

I scoff. "Still what? Am I not enough?"

Mylan rolls his beautiful blue eyes at me. "Of course, you are. That's not what I'm trying to say, and you know it."

I sigh with my entire body and turn away from Mylan, lifting my hand to the glass. I should tell him. He should know everything about Tyler, right? But this? I . . .

"Lana," he whispers, seeing my struggle. "Tell me when you're ready. Okay?" He reaches up to wipe tears off my cheek. Damn it, I didn't mean to cry. Not in front of him, which I happen to do a lot. "I'm not going anywhere."

I'm not going anywhere.

A promise. A declaration. Words in the here and now with a subtext of forever.

I clear my throat, nod, and turn on my heel to walk down the hallway, past the cafeteria, until we reach the end where I veer right. All the way at the end of this hallway are double red doors with the words 'locker room' over the entrance.

The stifling air inside reeks of dirty men. We pass the benches and rows of lockers until finding Coach Harold's office in the back left corner.

"Well look at what the cat dragged in. The homecoming queen and the movie star," Coach says in his thick Arkansas twang. He stands up from his seat behind a metal desk, wearing a red t-shirt with the school's name and mascot etched on the upper left, a matching red hat, black shorts, and sneakers.

"You don't have to call me that every time you see me, you know," I say, amused. I flick my eyes to Mylan. "Mylan, Coach Harold. Coach Harold, Mylan."

The two greet as I keep speaking. "Harold was a grade below me."

"And I had the biggest crush on you, like every other guy in the school. *Still* have a crush on you." Mylan tenses at my side, his hands in fists. *He's jealous.* I brush my fingertips over the back of his arm, and he relaxes, almost immediately.

"Harold, you better stop, or I'll tell your wife," I tease.

"Please, Sheila knows about my crush. Hell, she has a crush on you too."

"Oh my god, stop!" I laugh, embarrassed by the flattery.

Harold shakes his head, hands on his hips, before focusing his attention to Mylan. "So, you're the big-time actor causing a tizzy around town?"

"A tizzy?" Mylan's brows furrow.

Harold waves his hand around. "The media, the fans. We usually have a good number of visitors trickling in during the summer because of the lake in the town over, but never this many. It's exciting, like the fair has come to town."

"Oh," Mylan utters. I expected him to shrink into his shoulders like he did at my grandparents, but he stands tall. "Let me know if there are any problems. I can control the media, to an extent, and my fans usually back off if I ask."

Coach Harold bobs his head in thought then slaps a palm on Mylan's shoulder. "I appreciate that, Mister Andrews."

I snort, and Mylan lifts a brow at me as we follow Coach out of the office.

"Mister Andrews," I mouth at him, and he shrugs.

Coach takes us deep into the locker room to the senior section. He points at locker twenty, Tyler's locker, which was transformed into a memorial for him shortly after his death.

Coach props a foot on the bench and leans over to rest his forearms on top his knee. "Tyler was the most selfless person I ever met."

Mylan unravels his rolled-up script again and begins writing.

"He'd always look out for us, his teammates. He'd know when we were struggling, either with schoolwork or maybe something going on at home. One kid, a freshman, couldn't afford new shoes and was wearing his brother's old torn ones. So, Tyler gathered donations and bought that kid three new pairs."

"I remember that," I say, smiling.

"Another time, a sophomore, Kyle, who would talk and joke around non-stop, showed up to practice one morning before school and sat on the bench, silent. Right away, Tyler knew something was wrong. When the rest of the team left for the field to begin warm-ups, Tyler stayed behind. He offered a safe space, he offered support, judgment free, and found out Kyle's father was physically abusing his mother and mentally abusing him."

Mylan's stiffens next to me. I glance at him and notice his tense face and clenched jaw.

Coach is still talking, so I can't ask Mylan if he's okay. Instead, I offer him my hand, which he takes after storing away his script and tucking his pencil behind his ear. His shoulder's drop, and he lets out the breath he was holding.

". . . the mother and father separated. She got a restraining order against him and Kyle was safe again. Tyler was always so observant. Might have saved that young man and his mother's life."

Coach waves at us to follow. If he noticed our embrace, he doesn't say a word about it. We walk through the gymnasium as Coach Harold points out plaques with awards or banners hung high listing division title wins that Tyler was a part of.

I'm still holding Mylan's hand and whatever dark memory appeared in the locker room is long gone. His ability to dismiss an emotion as quick as it arrives is incredible. Is he able to do that because he's an actor? Is he trained to do that?

Coach Harold rambles on for the next thirty minutes, going way off topic and not even telling stories about Tyler anymore. Every so often, I'd catch Mylan lifting his right hand and sniffing his index and middle fingers.

Sniffing me.

I curse my nipples for hardening in response and squeeze my thighs to ease the pulse in my cunt that comes to life around him.

Damn him.

He's doing it on purpose, teasing me, irritating me.

Turning me on.

By the time we've walked around most of the school, and we're back at the front, next to the office, it's been an hour. I manage to peel my fingers free from Mylan's tight hold seconds before Coach whips around to face us.

"Now, you've got some big shoes to fill," he says, waving a finger. "I've read some stuff about you, and I'm trusting you won't be doing any of that here?"

"No, sir," Mylan answers, and I actually believe him.

"Good. This movie may just be a job for you, but it's our life. Our history. It's our future. Tyler's legacy is our legacy. We work very hard, Lana works very hard, to make sure his final wish never dies."

Coach holds out a hand and Mylan takes it. The two men shake.

"Don't worry, Coach," Mylan begins. "I won't let everyone down." He turns his head to me. "I won't let you down."

My stomach fills with fluttering butterflies, and I look away from Mylan's searing gaze.

"You better not," Coach warns, as threatening as a kitten.

Once Coach leaves, I lead us down the hallway to meet with the school counselor, who was one of Tyler's mentors. He'd often visit with Mrs. Shinely to discuss his future as a social worker.

Mylan takes in the surroundings as we walk—the red lockers, the white painted walls with motivational posters or banners sporting the school's mascot of a black panther hung high. He's been acting since childhood, so I assume he never attended school. I bet he was taught on movie or TV sets. He's regarding this place with a bit of wonder and longing, perhaps imagining what it would have been like to live a normal life. I also see he's focused, determined, as if he's building a new world in his head. He's transforming his mind to become Tyler. It's a fascinating process that I'm excited to be a part of.

A spark of hope ignites within me. Could this be what I need to heal? This movie, this actor, this . . . whatever is happening between us. I think it's time I stop fighting my feelings for Mylan.

I think I'm ready to let myself live. Because up until this point, I've let my grief lock me inside the past. Perhaps Mylan holds the key to set me free.

Chapter 11 - Mylan

Addiction comes in many forms. People become addicted to substances, like I am. People become addicted to food, to exercise, to social media. People even get addicted to other people.

I'm starting to believe I'm addicted to Lana.

Ridiculous, right? It's Friday morning, and I've only been in Silo Springs for a week. One week for her vanilla and berry smell, her heartfelt laugh, her contagious smile to draw me in. One week for her taste, her lips, the way she's so wonderfully soft, to taunt my craving for her.

A craving not sated for three days.

There hasn't been time. When we're not meeting with people who knew Tyler, Lana is at the bar she owns. I've shown up to Lilies every night, sat on my self-designated stool near the taps, and read my script and the notes I've taken. However, concentrating on my lines when in Lana's presence was near impossible.

My eyes kept wandering, appreciating her thickness—her curves in tight fabrics, her tits begging to be held in my hands, her ass needing to be squeezed and worshiped. I'd hoped to tug her into the bathroom or a dark corner to steal kisses, but the problem with being me is always having a phone pointed in my direction, ready to snap pictures or record video. Lana wouldn't allow me to sneak her away. She avoided me like the plague.

We haven't been alone together since Tuesday when she allowed my fingers inside her.

Wednesday, with Eloise and Bruno in tow (Ginger had to work), Lana gave us a tour of her small, cozy town. We stopped in every shop along Main Street, speaking with the locals who knew Tyler. We visited some of Tyler's favorite spots, including an old-fashioned diner. The restaurant felt like something right out of a movie with miniature juke-boxes at each table, a bar lined with red vinyl seats, and a milkshake machine offering vanilla, chocolate, and straw-berry flavors.

My fans have been respectful, keeping their distance and only approaching me when I allowed it. The paparazzi, on the other hand, have been out of control. Not only have they been pestering me about the role, my latest stint in rehab, and the pictures of me at the bar (despite not a single alcoholic beverage spotted in my hand), but they've also been bombarding Lana with questions.

Lana, how do you feel about the movie being made about your dead fiancé?

Lana, what's your role in the movie? Will you be in it?

Lana, are you concerned about Mylan's problem?

Lana, are you and Mylan dating?

I was prepared to step in and carve those assholes a new one every time, but before I could say a word, Lana took control. She answered every question respectfully. She was honest, confident, and Lord was it sexy as hell.

I worried about the stories they would write, the pictures they would post of Lana and me, speculating that we were together. Lana surprised me once again by staying one step ahead.

She'd asked me for my publicist's contact information. Together, they came up with a plan and worked with the media to approve what pictures could be posted in exchange for exclusive content. Lana got final say in every single article published. Well, except for the content posted by sleazy tabloids and illegitimate fan-run sites.

Lana controlled the narrative the best she could. She followed my lead when it came to the fans. She could have let the attention that comes with this movie, with being seen with me, overwhelm her. Instead, she welcomed it with open arms.

I'm absolutely infatuated with her.

We spent the rest of the week away from crowds. Thursday morning, we hiked a mountain with Eloise and Bruno (again, Ginger had to work). We climbed a large rock face at the top of that mountain and sat with our legs hanging over the edge, taking in the spectacular view—miles of greenery with rivers weaving throughout.

Lana said Sugarloaf Mountain was Tyler's place of solace. The fresh and crisp breeze that high, untouched and new, calmed my damaged soul, even if it was for just a few minutes.

After climbing the mountain yesterday morning, Lana and I went to Tyler's parents' house, and we spent hours upon hours scouring through old photographs. We also watched home movies and listened to stories of his childhood.

Tyler was a remarkable man.

I will never be Tyler Taylor.

Lana could never love me like she loved Tyler.

Love. I shake the word from my head. It's only been a week. I'm not thinking straight. I'm letting my cock manipulate my heart into thinking this is love. It's not love.

One week.

Shit. It's been six days since I've had a single drop of booze. It could have been longer if I hadn't messed up and drank my first night in Silo. I don't even know *why* I drank—why I threw away those thirty days in rehab. I could start listing excuses.

I wanted to take off the edge.

I wanted the booze to cloud my social anxieties like it's done in the past.

I wanted to impress the pretty bar owner by buying booze at her bar.

Whatever the excuse, I still did it. It was only three drinks. That's nothing. I shouldn't even count it. But I will and now I'm only six days alcohol free. I am, however, thirty-seven days drug-free. That has to be a record for me.

Could this be it? Was this stint my last?

The thing about rock bottom, once you're down, there's only one way to go. I'm on my way up, but how long before I start falling again?

"What's with the scowl?" Lana asks, stepping out of bathroom looking like a freaking goddess.

She's wearing a translucent floral caftan over a black two-piece swimsuit. The halter top hugs her tits gloriously, making me jealous of the fabric. The high-waist bottoms begin below her belly button. My eyes travel across her pale skin, from the ink near her shoulder, to the beautiful designs of her stretch marks, and the curves of her stomach and hips. I desperately want to run my hands up and down her sides and around to cup that glorious ass of hers. I want to lick—

"Wow. That was fast."

My eyes snap up to hers. "What?"

"You went from scowl to lust like that." She snaps her fingers to prove a point.

I stand up from the edge of the bed where I sat waiting for her to change for our day at the lake. Bruno, Eloise, and Ginger are waiting in the SUV. Right now, here in Lana's apartment, is the first time I've been alone with her since Tuesday.

Finally.

"Because I can't stop thinking about the other day." I reach her in two long strides. "When you let me fuck you with my fingers."

Lana blushes and it's stunning; blotches of red paint the white canvas of her skin like an invaluable piece of artwork. I brush her long, dark red hair off her right shoulder, and I gently press my lips on her skin, a graze of a kiss that makes her shudder. My palm slides up the left side of her neck to the nape.

"No longer asking for permission?" she teases.

I weave my fingers within the strands of her hair and fist my hand, tugging her head back. She was so responsive the first time I did that. This time, I'm rewarded with a sigh-whimper combination.

I lean in, hovering my mouth over hers. "I think we're past asking for permission."

"Are we?"

Lana licks her lips, her tongue brushing my mouth and making me shudder. She gives me a vindictive smile and my cock responds with a jerk.

"Do I need to beg, Lana?"

She shrugs. "Maybe you do."

Her eyes dart down to my lips, silently demanding I kiss her. I don't. I move away, loving the faint whine she lets out, and without touching an inch of her skin, I trail my breath along her jaw and down to her neck.

"Mylan," she moans.

I tighten my hold on her hair. "Who's begging now?"

I don't give her time to respond as I bite down on her neck. Not hard enough to break the skin but it will leave my mark. It was well worth the desire that exploded from Lana's throat. I lick and kiss the spot I bit then suck hard, leaving it good and red.

"Tell me what you want, baby," I say against her skin.

She gently pushes me away. "No."

I arch a brow. "No?"

She places her palm on my chest. It's searing despite the fabric of my t-shirt between our skin.

"What do *you* want, Mylan?"

I choke on my words, struggling to respond. I didn't expect her to ask me that. No one ever asks me what I want. I'm always the one who gives—my money, my fame, my mind, and my body. Sometimes I give when I shouldn't. When I don't want to. When I'm forced.

I'm not the type of person people take care of.

Tell me what you *want, Mylan?*

Such a simple question. Why does it have my heart thumping wildly in my chest? It could be because I haven't fucked sober in a very long time. Even in my last relationship, I was either high or drunk during sex.

What if I'm not good?

When I lost myself to my addiction this last time, I no longer cared if I was good. Now, it's all I can think about. Now, I have my control back, and I'm obsessing over how I can be good for *her*.

Not that I expect Lana to fuck me at this moment.

She pushes at my chest, and we walk backwards, oddly mimicking what I did to her just days ago—what she did to me at the bar. The backs of my legs hit her bed.

"Tell me," Lana says, demanding, stern. It's hot as fuck.

"I want to taste you," I say, my voice unsteady. I'm . . . nervous.

She hums with a mischievous smirk.

She slides her palm down the front of my shirt, over my abs to cup my painfully hard dick through my swim shorts. It lurches at her touch. "You don't want me to suck your cock?"

"Jesus, woman. Yes, I will always want that, but right now I *need* to taste you."

I take hold of her arms and twist us around to shove her onto the bed. She yelps then giggles, and that sound almost has me coming right then.

I tug at Lana's nylon bottoms and relish at the way she fists the comforter and arches her back. Inch by anticipating inch, I peel the fabric down, making her squirm as I take my time. After tossing the bottoms aside, I smooth my palms over her freshly shaved legs.

Soft like silk.

My lips replace my palms, kissing along her inner thigh, tonguing her dimpled skin, and nipping it with my teeth. She attempts to close her legs on my head, but I push them wide open.

Full access.

Lana's hands find my hair, and she grabs hold of the strands hard enough that it pleasantly hurts. She pushes my head to her cunt, and I let out a laugh, my hot breath fanning across her glistening sex. She moans in response.

"So fucking greedy."

"Shut up and put your mouth on me."

I cluck my tongue at her, which only makes her groan in frustration. "I love when you tell me what to do."

I bury my nose in her cunt and inhale, and Lana tries to close her legs on my head again. My palms press down hard, keeping them spread.

"Be a good girl, Lana."

She whimpers on my words as my tongue lashes out and laps up her arousal from the bottom of her slit up to her swollen clit. I suck on it lavishly, and she arches her back again. I remove a hand from her thigh to splay my fingers over her quivering stomach and push her back down.

I start feasting like a starving man, thrusting my tongue in and out of her sweet pussy while massaging her clit with my thumb.

"More," she wheezes.

I oblige, adding a finger to her soaked warmth and moving my mouth back to that bundle of sensitive nerves. I hum against it and the vibration makes her moan. It's such a beautiful sound. By the time I'm adding a second finger, while tonguing and sucking, her pussy walls are clamping down.

She's close.

I speed up my thrusts and graze my teeth over her clit. Her legs trap my head and her grip on my hair tightens, attempting to push me closer. I hum once more and with the triple combination of the vibration, my pumping fingers, and hungry tongue, she bucks and explodes into orgasm.

I savor the taste of her arousal, consuming every last drop.

She relaxes her legs and releases my hair, the roots burning from how hard she gripped the strands. I surface, pulling my fingers out once her cunt stops pulsing. After licking my fingers clean, I crawl up her body. The urge to bury my cock inside her is getting harder and harder to resist.

Not yet.

As if reading my thoughts, her eyes travel down to my dick. She sweeps her tongue over her lips and opens them to say something, perhaps to offer that blow job again, but I cut her off with a kiss.

She groans, clearly tasting herself on my mouth. Her hands roam over my back and down to my ass. She pulls me to her, allowing me to grind my contained erection into her damp, bare pussy.

I'm too close to coming. Realizing I have my swim shorts on and not wanting to soil them anymore than I have, I lean back and sit on my heels. I pull my dick out of the bottoms and start stroking. Lana's eyes widen, either in shock at my size or because I'm jerking off right in front of her.

The lust in her eyes, the fire that sparks to life, fuels my movement. While holding Lana's heated stare, I fist my cock harder, faster until I'm spurting webs of cum all over her stomach a minute later.

I shake out the last drop and tuck myself in my shorts. I crawl back up Lana's body, making sure to avoid my release, and hover my mouth over hers.

"Next time, I won't be strong enough." I give her a quick, light kiss. "Next time I come, it will be inside you."

She whimpers, and I quiet her with a soul-catching kiss. A deep and passionate kiss as our tongues battle for dominance. We make-out for minutes, only breaking apart when both of our phones start chirping with text messages from our friends. When I pull away, I grin with satisfaction and hop off the bed to grab a wad of paper towels. I clean her stomach and my heart flutters with how intimate it is. How trusting she is to allow me to take care of her.

I needed this. Whatever this is. There's no way I'm giving this up once filming is over.

Chapter 12 - Lana

What the hell am I doing?

Mylan has rocked my world with only his fingers and mouth twice now. That's never happened to me. No man has ever been able to make me orgasm like that.

In the SUV to the lake, which is a thirty-minute drive, I don't talk, letting our friends fill the silence with excited conversation. I'm too deep in thought about this . . . relationship forming between me and a man fifteen years younger than me.

No. Not a relationship. A fling. A hot summer fling.

Mylan's not saying much either. Is he thinking the same thing? He's on my left, holding my hand between our bodies, out of Ginger's view, who is sitting on my right. Not that it matters. I've told her everything, and she *sees* everything. My phone vibrated with a text the moment I got in the car.

Ginger

> **Is that a hickey on your neck?**

I send a hand emoji and she responds with an eye-roll emoji.

Ginger

> **You can plead the 5th all you want but I see the evidence!**

I ended the text chain with a smirking face emoji.

Mylan's thumb sweeps over mine and those traitorous butterflies in my stomach flutter to life, tugging on the string controlling my equally traitorous cunt.

Bruno peeks back at us from the front passenger seat several times, noticing our embrace—the bite mark—but doesn't say a word about either. Mylan gave Bruno today off, wanting him to join us at the lake as a friend, not an employee. Same for Eloise, who's sitting in the very back with two other bodyguards Mylan hired to escort us any time we venture out in public. I told him we wouldn't need the extra security since the place we're going to today is secluded, only known to locals, and hidden to tourists. However, there's always the chance one of the locals shows up or a tourist happens to stumble upon the secret spot. And with Bruno off-duty today, I suppose bringing the extra protection was smart.

Once we arrive at Bluffs Lake, I direct the driver to follow the twisting road through the towering deciduous and pine trees. The branches with its dark green leaves sway in a gentle breeze. It'll be a welcome relief to the hot and humid day and the bright sun with few clouds to hide behind today.

We pass campsites, half of which are full of tourists with campers or tents. They fire up grills, cooking burgers, hot dogs, and steaks. Their coolers are stocked with sodas, beers, wines, and hard liquor. Music blasts and people dance wearing nothing more than swim trunks or slinky bikinis, leaving little to the imagination.

The lake, the cliffs, the hiking trails, and the mountain we climbed the other day are far enough away from Silo Springs, and tourists rarely venture into our small town. It's closer to find hotels in Beverly Springs, a five-minute drive from the campgrounds. Though, June and July tend to be busier months and Silo gets the overflow when all the campsites are full and every last room at hotels in Beverly are booked.

We're a hidden gem.

Hidden until Rebecca's book put us on a map. Then forgotten until Mylan's ridiculously handsome face showed up.

"You okay?" Mylan whispers. His breath sweeps across my ear, and I shiver, causing Mylan to chuckle.

Before I can answer, the turn to the secluded cliffs nears. I inform the driver, and he pulls onto a bumpy dirt road. The road ends a short minute drive later.

We're here.

We grab our bags, Mylan taking mine and the picnic basket I packed, and I swallow the nostalgia creeping up my throat as I lead our group down a half-mile-long trail.

I haven't been here in years.

The trees encasing the trail begin to thin and slivers of light blue sky emerge. The dirt ground fades away, revealing jagged rocks. I hold my breath with my next steps.

The forest opens and a vast canvas appears, painted with nature's best artwork. The sun sparkles in the dark blue waters of Bluffs Lake. We walk across the sedimentary rocks that make up the bluffs the lake was named after. Some cliffs around the massive, sixty-mile-long lake are forty feet tall. The ones we're visiting today are only about ten feet high.

The lake is too wide to see the land directly across from us, only shades of green to indicate lines of trees. Speed boats—pulling people on skis, or people in a tube, holding a beer in one hand while throwing up a fist of joy with the other—skid across the water top, creating small waves over the calm waters that lap up along the sides of the rocks.

"Wow," Mylan exhales next to me.

He tries to grab my hand, but I quickly pull it away on instinct. We haven't reached the holding-hands-in-public stage of our . . . whatever it is we're doing. Mylan clenches his jaw but doesn't say a word.

We set our belongings down, spreading out towels so we don't burn our asses on the sun-soaked rock. Ginger is the first to peel off her t-shirt and shorts, biting her lip seductively when she spots Bruno appreciating her full figure. Eloise rolls her eyes at the two but smiles beautifully.

The two extra bodyguards stand at the tree line, guarding the trail's exit, ready to intercept a wayward fan or paparazzi. They remind me of secret service agents with their buzz cut hairstyles and aviator sunglasses. Surprisingly, they're not wearing suits. Instead, they're dressed for the hot day in white t-shirts and khaki cargo shorts.

"Who's going to jump first?" Eloise asks, taking off her sundress. Underneath, she's wearing a deep red bikini. My stomach jerks with jealousy. She has an amazing body. I looked like that once.

I curse my fatphobic thoughts because I never want to go back to the woman I once was.

I was miserable.

"I'm going first," Ginger says. Her excitement is addicting, and I've missed how familiar this feels. We used to come here all the time in high school. It was our spot. Mine. Ginger's.

Tyler's. "But sunscreen first. Y'all are too white, and this sun is unforgiving. I'm Black and even I put on sunscreen during lake days."

Ginger doesn't waste time, slathering on a good amount of the lotion. Once done, she squeezes more in her hand before tossing the bottle to Eloise.

Ginger beckons Bruno. "Come on, handsome."

Bruno's face lights up, and he removes his shirt at record speed, ruffling his shoulder-length blond hair and revealing a tanned and toned body underneath.

My cheeks already hurt from smiling. I will myself to look away as the two flirt like crazy and take my own sunscreen out of the bag I packed for today, which also holds my towel, a few bottled waters, and a romance book.

Who needs to read a book when you're living a real-life, blossoming romance?

My eyes drift to Mylan and what happens next can only be described as a movie moment. Time slows down and seductive music plays as Mylan peels off his shirt. It's the first time I've *seen* his body. When he fucked me with his mouth and fingers twice now, he was still clothed.

I hold my breath, watching his muscles ripple and flex as the fabric lifts over his tight stomach, his defined chest, his broad shoulders. The shirt catches on his hair, tousling it beautifully.

Fuck.

I must have said that out loud because Mylan's head whips to me and he offers the sexiest smile, spread viciously across his criminally handsome face.

I'm frozen in place, staring at him. Hypnotized by him. He walks to me, tossing the shirt to the ground. It lands on the picnic basket of snacks I packed for us today.

"Can I have some of that?" Mylan points at the bottle of sunscreen. I nod, swallowing to wet my suddenly dry throat.

What is wrong with me?

Mylan holds out his hand, and I squirt a good amount in the center. Then I watch as he spreads it across the very chest I wanted to lick and bite and touch seconds ago. His palms move over his shoulders and arms, then down his stomach. Ugh. That ripped stomach. Abs for days. Abs I need pressed against me. Abs I need to touch.

I lick my lips, hungrily, his eyes following the sweep of my tongue.

When he's done, he winks (jerk move—he's aware of the power he packs behind that wink) and turns around.

"Can you do my back?" he asks over his shoulder.

I clear my throat and glance around. This is not a good idea. Touching him in public is begging for a paparazzi photo to be snapped. I'm not dumb. I know they're here, hiding in the trees or maybe on the other side of the lake ready to zoom in with their fancy cameras. Not one day has passed where they haven't somehow managed to sneak in a photo of us out and about.

I can only imagine how these photos would turn out. The act of putting sunscreen on someone is *intimate*. At least, that's how it would translate in a photo or video.

To be honest, I'm getting to the point where I don't give a fuck. Let them snap away and write whatever they want.

Without saying a word, I squirt a blob of sunscreen into my hand and begin spreading it across Mylan's back. He sucks in a sharp breath.

"Cold," he whispers.

The sexual tension taking my body captive lessens and I smile, genuinely. "Don't be a baby," I tease.

"I'm *your* baby."

My smile drops, and I cringe. He is a baby, compared to me.

"Don't," he says through clenched teeth, demanding my attention while peering over his shoulder again. "I'm a grown man. You are a grown woman. There is nothing wrong with you wanting me."

I glance to our friends, worried they can hear our conversation.

"Let them hear," Mylan says, answering my silent concern.

He's right. I've told Ginger everything. Well, everything minus this morning's feast. Though, she got an idea after spotting his mark. What about Mylan's assistant and body-guard? I'm sure he's told them about us. Probably too much since he can't seem to stop talking.

"Tell me about the lake," Mylan says, quickly changing the subject. "Tell me why this was Tyler's favorite spot."

"I know you read about it in the script," I say quietly. His back is now well covered with sunscreen, but I struggle to stop myself from touching him.

"I did, but like I said that first night, I want to hear it from you."

I swallow again. I swear my damn throat is as dry as the Sahara.

"Me, Tyler, and Ginger used to come here every summer since we turned sixteen and could drive ourselves. Some weeks, we'd be here every day. Some days we wouldn't leave at all, sleeping underneath the cloudless night sky and the sparkling stars."

"Sounds like heaven."

"It was."

"You don't come here anymore?"

"No."

"Why?"

"Too many memories. Mostly sad ones."

"Tell me."

Ugh. So bossy.

"This is where Tyler proposed to me." I focus on my hands moving across Mylan's defined back. His skin is so soft and tanned. I don't think there's an ounce of fat on this man. "Senior year of college, a couple weeks before he collapsed on the football field—before we found out."

Mylan turns and reaches up his hand, ready to console me, but I step back.

"Lift your arms out, I missed some spots on your sides."

Mylan waits, searching my face before lifting his arms. I put more lotion in my hand and smooth it down his sides, from near his armpit to his hip where I stop myself from tracing my fingertips over that mouth-watering V-shape of his. I can't help but notice how his body reacts to me, flushing slightly at my nearness. Plus, every time I touch him, his cock moves against the fabric of his swim trunks.

I force myself to finish with the sunscreen and hand him the bottle, turning around, so he can do me.

"Are you going to jump off the cliff?" I ask, trying to distract myself from the heat radiating off him. It matches my own blazing skin the moment his hands are on me, spreading the sunscreen across my shoulders and back.

"Are you?" he counters.

"Lana doesn't jump off the cliffs," Ginger blurts out, shimmying off her flip-flops to prepare for her jump.

Mylan looks her way for an explanation but Ginger's not paying attention to us. She's still flirting with Bruno, laughing at God knows what and playfully swatting at his bare chest.

"Never?" Mylan asks me. "Why not?"

He turns me around, finished with my back, and he's about to start on my front, but I stop him and grab the bottle. I'm already too wound tight with lust from his hands being all over me. If I let him continue a second longer, I'm certain to let out a moan or throw him to the ground and ride him right in front of everyone.

Okay, fine, I wouldn't do that, but I'll be thinking it the entire time.

"I'm scared of heights."

"Bullshit. You climbed the mountain the other day."

Crap.

"This is different."

"Why?"

"It just is," I snap.

Mylan narrows his eyes at me. He waits for me to keep going. I can't. Not right now. He must realize that because his face softens at whatever emotion I was showing him.

He sighs. "Okay. So, something happened in the past?"

I nod.

"A long time ago?"

I nod again.

"And you haven't tried jumping since?"

I shake my head.

"Well, you're here now, in the present. This movie has been forcing you to face your past head-on. Why not let this be another hurdle you tackle?"

"I . . ."

"You can't let a little fear stop you from experiencing life. From forming core memories. From experiencing those once-in-a-lifetime, spectacular moments."

He was making some sense but at those last words, I roll my eyes. He may not have pushed me to explain why I fear jumping, but he's still *pushing* me.

Brat.

"I don't think jumping off a cliff would qualify as a once-in-a-lifetime, spectacular moment." I chuckle.

Once I'm done with the sunscreen, I tuck the bottle back in my bag and place my hands on my hips.

Mylan must see this as a challenge. "I dare you to jump."

"What?"

"I double dog dare you to jump off the cliff today."

"What do you know about double dog dares?"

"Don't try to change the subject."

"I'm not jumping, Mylan."

He snorts and takes off his sandals. He walks to the cliff's edge and smirks at me over his shoulder. "Coward."

Oh hell no.

I march over there, ready to push him over the side, but I freeze, inches from the edge.

Mylan holds out a hand.

"Let's do it together."

I shake my head fast, my eyes surely bugging. My stomach churns with fear.

"Lana," Mylan whispers. "I've got you."

Tyler is the reason I don't jump off these cliffs—because of what happened the day we met. After that day, he called my fear irrational, then proceeded to taunt me about it, dragging Ginger in on the joke. They were relentless, constantly daring me to jump every time we came to the lake. I never did.

When Tyler died, I'd come here to visit at night, sitting underneath the moonlight and stars, talking to him. I did that for two weeks before it became too painful, when coming to the lake brought me sadness instead of joy.

I haven't been back since.

Now, being here with Mylan, his assistant and bodyguard, and Ginger, I'm hit with an overwhelming sense of closure. A new beginning. As if jumping off this cliff will leave the past behind. As if soaring into the waters below is a way to wash myself of the grief that is tied to this location.

Here I am with this surprisingly caring man beside me, offering me his hand. Offering me . . . a future?

I hush my over-thinking brain. It's just a cliff with no hidden meaning behind the jump.

Racked with determination, I place my shaking hand in Mylan's.

"Are you kidding me?!" Ginger screeches behind me. "All those times we dared you to jump and you're going to do it now?"

I ignore my best friend as Mylan leads me away from the edge for a running start.

"Just breathe. It's not that far down. I won't let go. I promise. Okay?"

I nod and Mylan counts down.

"Three . . . Two . . . One."

We run and jump, and I scream and then I . . . laugh!

It's exhilarating. The wind envelopes us as we plunge ten feet into the cool water below. We sink deep before I kick my legs wildly until we break the lake's surface. Mylan kept his promise. He didn't let go.

I gasp for breath upon emerging. Water runs down my face, and I wipe soaked locks of hair off my cheeks and forehead.

Mylan snakes an arm around my waist and tugs me against his body. He's going to kiss me. He palms my neck, tilting up my chin with his thumb. It's something he's done before that I find so fucking hot.

Before his mouth can claim mine, my best friend is catapulting herself over the cliff's edge, yelling 'cannonball!' as her only warning for us to move out of the way. She lands a few feet away, but the impact sends waves of water over us.

We laugh and when Ginger appears, we splash her furiously as payback.

I've missed this.

I didn't realize how much I needed this.

But *this* is temporary.

It has to be, right?

Chapter 13 - Mylan

I wake, my stomach and face pleasantly sore from laughing and smiling too much at the lake yesterday. It's the best feeling. Better than my stomach aching because I drank too much. Better than the queasy unsteadiness wrecking my body from whatever drug I swallowed or inhaled.

More than a week since I left rehab and not once have my bad habits called to me—aside from my slip-up that first night. I haven't craved the burn of whiskey pouring down my throat or the frantic high from snorting lines of crushed opioids.

I'm *happy,* and it's because of her.

Redness singes my skin, despite putting on sunscreen. The mild sunburn should fade enough before filming begins a week from Monday. If not, the talented make-up team will be able to fix it. I hope.

We spent hours at the lake yesterday, jumping off the cliffs and swimming, eating sandwiches and snacking on chips, and drinking the soda Lana packed in a cute picnic basket.

Afterwards, we stopped for ice cream then dropped Lana and Ginger off at Lilies, so they could work the Friday night shift.

I wanted to go inside with them, but if I did, Lana's presence would have distracted me, and I still had a few lines I needed to work on. Not to mention, the accent needs polishing. I'm so nervous about doing it in front of her. She keeps asking me but I tell her it's not ready every time. Then she rolls her beautiful hazel eyes at me, flashing me her bright smile. Her smile always makes my heart flutter like I'm some teenager with a crush.

Lana is letting her guard down. She's letting me in. She's finally letting herself live.

I can't push her. I need to give her her space.

I roll out of the horrible hotel bed and take a piss before heading to the kitchen to make equally horrible hotel coffee. As the coffee brews, I take out my phone about to scroll through whatever headlines have been posted about me when there's a knock at the door connecting my room with Bruno's.

"Breakfast," Bruno announces as he shoves his way into my room. He ignores my sleep rustled hair and naked torso—still in my boxer briefs since I've yet to shower and dress for the day—and sets down a recyclable takeout container on the small table. "I got you some bacon, muffins, and a yogurt from the continental breakfast downstairs."

"Thank you," I say through a yawn, returning to the kitchen.

I hand Bruno the coffee I made for myself, and he heads to the couch, turning on a morning news show. I make another cup and check the time on my phone while waiting. Barely ten a.m.

Once my cup is poured, I sit and eat, scrolling back through all the flirty text messages Lana sent me last night while she was working. I reread the last one from her before we wished each other a good night.

Donut

> Thank you for making the jump with me.

"You letting Miss Lana grab you by the balls of your feet?" Bruno asks, clearly noticing me smiling like a fool at my damn phone.

"The saying is she's got me by the balls."

Bruno's thick eyebrows pinch in confusion.

"She has me at her mercy," I clarify.

His face lights up with amusement. "Does she?"

"Yes. Very much so."

Eloise barges in, uninvited, and plops down in the only other chair at the table. She steals a piece of bacon then frowns because it's probably cold bacon by now.

"What the hell? You have a key to my room?"

She ignores my question, while ignoring my tangled sleep hair. She also doesn't react to my bare chest. She's seen me far worse, naked on the floor, next to my own puke. Still, I'd have at least thrown on pants if I knew she had a key to my room and was going to show up whenever she wanted.

"What are you two talking about?"

I roll my eyes and Eloise beams at my annoyance. She likes to push my buttons. Like a sister. *She's the closest thing to a sibling I've ever had.* 'Just keeping you humble, asshole,' she says to me every chance she gets.

"Mylan is getting his balls manhandled by Miss Lana."

I choke on my coffee, and it spills on the table. Eloise fake gags.

"Bruno, that's not . . ." I shake my head and wipe up my mess with the pile of napkins Bruno brought with my breakfast. I sigh. "He means: Lana has me by the balls."

Eloise fake gags again, which has Bruno laughing like a maniac. Eloise joins in and suddenly we're all giggling like high school girls at a sleepover.

Not that I've ever been to a sleepover.

Our laughter dies down and Eloise winces.

"You okay?"

She rubs her side. "Yeah, I'm just sore from jumping, and swimming, and laughing yesterday. I'm sunburned too."

My heart lurches because I can't remember the last time Eloise looked so . . . happy. Being my assistant hasn't been the easiest job. Eloise is such a private person to begin with and I'm honored to be one of the few people she's opened up to. She told me she'd once been hurt by someone she greatly cared about. I'm sure that's why the moment I began falling back into my addiction, she rebuilt her walls and slowed down any attachment she may have been forming with me.

She stopped caring about me when I stopped caring about myself. That's my theory, at least.

Then there's Bruno. In public, he's the intimidating bodyguard. When it's just me and him and Eloise, he's funny, always smiling, always positive. Then I messed it all up. After this last stint, there's a shade of sadness that threatens his sunny demeanor.

Eloise cursing pulls me from my thoughts. "Don't freak out."

I straighten my back, my stomach dropping. "If you're telling me not to freak out then I'm probably going to freak out."

She grimaces at her phone. "The paparazzi found us at the lake. There are . . . pictures."

"How bad is it?" I ask quietly.

"Lana putting lotion on you. You and her in the water, nearly kissing. The two of you laughing and flirting."

"The headlines?"

Eloise gulps. "Is romance blossoming between Mylan Andrews and the real Lana Young?"

"That's not too bad."

"No, but the comments . . . the things people are saying about Lana . . ."

I bury my head in my hands, combing my fingers through my hair.

"Shit." I sit there for a minute, thinking—panicking. Eloise doesn't have to elaborate on what those social media comments say. Humans are vile, and they'll criticize anyone who doesn't fit the world's unrealistic body and beauty standards.

Lana told me she hasn't been reading comments on the articles posted about us. I don't read them either. This is different, though, because before, we were working together professionally. Now people see that we've become more, and, like every celebrity, I have crazed fans. Fans who will send her death threats just for being in a personal relationship with me.

What will Lana think? We've been so careful up until now. Lana and my publicist have worked hard to control the photos and articles posted online. I knew it wouldn't last. If the media smells a big story brewing, all bets are off.

I stand up. "I need to talk to Lana."

It's ten thirty in the morning and Lilies doesn't open for another half hour. The article with the pictures went live hours ago and word spread fast because the vultures are already hovering. A crowd of paparazzi is waiting on the sidewalk in front of the bar. It's as close as they can get since the sidewalk is considered public property. They've been threatened with jail time the moment they step off the sidewalk and into the parking lot, which is private property.

The parking lot, which winds from the front of Lilies around the left side of the building and to the back, is empty except for Lana's beat-up, light blue Volkswagen. My driver pulls around to the back to let me out, out of sight of the paparazzi. I'm sure they're hiding in the field behind the bar (despite that also being private property). It's the only part not contained by a fence.

Up until now, we've explained that I'm visiting Lana to work on Tyler's character. Now? Now they know it's more than that. I hop out of the car, leaving Bruno behind. Eloise stayed at the hotel, waiting on my call about how to move forward.

I knock frantically and within seconds, Lana answers. My words catch in my throat as my eyes travel up and down her body. She's wearing a black, silk nightie, with a matching silk robe. She tugs it tight around her curves, but not before I saw her glorious tits pouring out of the top.

"Mylan? What's wrong?"

She didn't see my ogling. Maybe the panic on my face masked my never-ending desire for her.

"We need to talk." I push my way in, and she scoffs.

"The hell, Mylan? You're making me nervous." She heads to the freshly brewed pot of coffee. She pours two mugs full and hands me the one without cream or sugar.

I set the mug down on the table and stand before her.

"There are pictures," I begin, and Lana pauses before taking a sip of her coffee. "From the lake. Of us. Together. Looking . . ."

She sets her mug on the table next to mine and holds up a hand to stop me from talking. She crosses her arms and looks up, locking eyes with me.

"I don't care, Mylan."

"What?"

"I'm so tired." She sighs with her entire body.

"We can fix this."

"Fix what, Mylan?" She rubs her temples. "When the book was released, I let the media dictate my life. I let them scare me into hiding. I moved out of the house my parents left me when they died and sold it. I told myself this time would be different because this time, it isn't about me. It's about Tyler and making sure this movie gets made right, making sure Hollywood doesn't tarnish his legacy. So, yeah, I don't care. At the end of the day, I'm confident in who I am, and I know my truth. They can print, post, report whatever the fuck they want."

I let out a long breath and comb both my hands through my hair. "I can have my publicist release a statement."

"And what would it say?" she laughs. The sound eases the tightening in my stomach. "That we're in a relationship? That we're fucking? We're not."

"Not yet," I smirk, attempting to mask my nerves. She huffs another laugh and gives me a sad smile.

"The paparazzi and the attention will only get worse. I understand that. I'm ready for that. We've been careful together out in public so far, but I knew it wouldn't last. And maybe this is a good thing."

I step closer to her and before I can say more, before I can offer her assurances, she holds up her hand again.

"Mylan," she begins and by the tone in her voice, I anticipate she's about to crush my soul. "It's okay. I'm okay."

She places both of her palms flat against my chest and I cover them with mine, closing my eyes because her touch is warm, invigorating.

"You're shaking," she whispers.

I am. I'm rattled. My entire body is overwhelmed after I let my thoughts run wild with how Lana would react to the paparazzi thing. Scenarios played over and over in my head the entire ride over here of her yelling at me, pushing me away, never wanting to see me again.

Irrational thoughts because that's not who Lana is.

I take a deep breath, trying to push down the over-exaggerated emotions. This is what she does to me. She heightens every part of my life. All I want to do right now is grab her and pull her to my body or toss her on the bed and fuck her into a blissful orgasmic coma.

Lana smooths her hands down my chest to my stomach, making me tense.

"Your body," she whispers, not so much to me but herself.

I can't stop the groan in my throat when her fingertips slip underneath the t-shirt I hastily threw on at the hotel. My skin inflames as she skims those warm palms over my abs, up and down as if she's memorizing every inch. They stroke my pecks, my shoulders before she slides them back down, spreading out her fingers as if to make sure no part goes untouched.

She stops at my pants; her hazel eyes dart up to mine.

"You're still shaking. How do I make you forget?"

My shaking no longer has anything to do with those fucking paparazzi pricks. Now I'm shaking because Lana is touching me.

"I am yours, Lana," I whisper, barely able to form words. My voice and body belong to her now. "Do what you want."

She pauses and focuses on my face while considering my words. Maybe she sees my desperation. Maybe she understands what I need is *her*.

"Take this off." She tugs on the hem of my t-shirt, and I'm pulling the piece of clothing off faster than she can blink.

The sound of her breath inhaling sharply as she scans her eyes up and down my body, as if she didn't see me half-naked yesterday at the lake, makes my cock twitch. It comes alive when she's around, and I want nothing more than to bury it inside her this very moment.

She stands on her tiptoes and leans forward to place a gentle kiss on my lips. Then her kisses travel down my neck, to my chest, to my stomach until she's squatting down and undoing my pants.

I choke on my breath; not entirely sure this is real.

I must be dreaming.

Her fingers grazing the skin of my lower stomach as she slowly unlatches the buttons is all too real. I'm so fucking hard right now it hurts.

She pulls down my pants and briefs. A light gasp escapes her swollen lips as my erection springs out. She doesn't hesitate and takes it in her grip, wrapping her fingers around, the tips almost touching. I shudder at the contact of her soft and smooth skin.

Beads of pearly pre-cum start dripping, and Lana licks her lips at the sight of it. Her eyes find mine again, and I'm pleading with her. I'm begging her to take me.

I jerk forward the moment her warm mouth closes over just the head but it's more than enough. She flails her tongue against the sensitive skin as she laps up the pre-cum. Then she takes more. It's greedy and my stomach tightens as she slides me deep. My dick touches the back of her throat briefly before she's sucking back up the length. The way her tongue wraps around my shaft . . .

"Fuck."

She starts bobbing while squeezing the base of my shaft and it feels so fucking good. My hands grip her hair, and she releases her hold, giving me permission to fuck her mouth. I thrust once, to the hilt, and when she doesn't gag, I start pumping harder, faster. She welcomes me by relaxing her jaw and throat, allowing me to go deeper.

I'm not going to last long.

She moans around my length and the vibration sends shocks all the way to my spine. The moment she cups my balls with one hand, those shocks expand and ripple through my abs. I fuck her mouth harder, causing her to dig her nails into my hips. The massaging of my balls, the pain and pleasure of her nails, mixed with the way those wide hazel eyes stare up at me—

Fuck. I'm coming.

My release pours down her throat, and she takes it all. Her eyes water, her leftover mascara from the night before smears with tears. When I'm finished spurting, Lana makes sure to lick up every last drop.

She removes her lips from my cock with a pop and proudly smiles. Hell, I'm fucking proud. I've had more blow jobs than I can count, and they've never been that good.

This woman.

I refuse to let her go.

After leaving Lana's, following a quick make-out session post blowjob, I'm walking through the hotel lobby in a good fucking mood when a familiar voice calls out my name.

Jensen Boliver. The director of *Tyler's Team*.

Good mood officially killed.

I knew this day would come. I dreaded seeing my former best friend after he dropped out of my life.

Jensen is your stereotypical Hollywood director. I swear to God. He's got the black-rimmed glasses, the beanie with brown curly hair feathering underneath, framing his round face. He wears dark jeans (rolled up at the bottom) and a long-sleeved, flannel shirt despite it being near ninety degrees outside.

He's tall, though a few inches shorter than me, and thick. Jensen confessed to me one drunken night that he struggles with body dysmorphia. He said he hated his tree trunk thighs and flabby stomach. I wonder if that's why he covers it up with this hipster lumberjack persona. Jensen may hate his body, but women love it.

"Never thought I'd be working with you again," he says, and I was sure he meant it in jest, but disdain weaves through his words.

I don't respond as he attempts to greet me with our secret handshake—three palm slaps, two fist bumps, a fist to the chest over the heart. It's a stupid handshake, and maybe not even original, but we made it up as teens and have been doing it ever since.

Well, we did when we were friends, up until my downfall. Before he abandoned me like all my other so-called friends.

Jensen must have realized what he was doing and quickly drops his hand.

What a tool.

Jensen and I grew up together. He's a year older than me, and he was an actor before a director. We'd audition for the same movies and television shows, and I'd get cast as the hot lead while Jensen played the fat funny friend (not my wording, Hollywood's. Like, it legit said that in the casting calls).

That 80s series I told Lana about was one of the shows we worked on together. We were teenagers at the time of filming, me sixteen, him seventeen. We were on set together for hours upon hours a day, six days a week, every week, eight months out of the year for three years before the series was canceled. During that time, Jensen became interested in directing. He bought a camera, and we'd film stuff between scenes. I'd write a short script, and it'd make no sense, but then I'd act it out and Jensen would direct it. We even got some of the other cast members to take part.

Jensen released those short films on YouTube after our careers took off. Then, when I got my first Oscar nomination, the short films received more attention. Enough that Jensen booked a directing job on an indie film that won all sorts of awards.

In the two years since my career began to tank, Jensen has directed two Oscar-nominated movies. He didn't win for either one, but it was enough to garner him top picks on whatever project he wanted.

That used to be me.

Now here we are. Two Oscar-nominated pricks. One asshole director who drops friends when their addiction becomes an inconvenience and thinks he's better than everyone because he was once on Forbes list of thirty under thirty. The other, an asshole actor who had it all and fucked it up because of his disease.

I don't know what to say to Jensen. This is the first time we've spoken since he abandoned me at some New York City club while I was downing bottle after bottle, sniffing line after line. I'd just gotten fired as the lead for an unnamed Ron Howard science-fiction action flick. I'd gone out to drown my sorrows, dragging Jensen with me. He left when I began singing and dancing on furniture, making an absolute fool out of myself.

He stuck with me for two years while I tanked my career but, in the end, he wanted no part of my downward spiral.

Still, he could have at least dropped me a rope, so I could pull myself out.

That was months ago.

Jensen's brows pinch together at my silence. Did he expect us to pick up where we left off?

He asks me about the script and learning my lines.

"Great," I say. "I'll be ready a week from Monday."

Jensen latches a hand on my shoulder and shakes it. I grit my teeth and restrain from doing what flashed across my mind (tearing Jensen's hand off my shoulder and breaking his wrist).

"You're here early," I manage to say.

"Yeah, gotta finalize the shot list and other pre-production bullshit. The production coordinator is flying in tonight and the first assistant director will be here tomorrow along with the production manager. You know how it goes."

I do. The crew will start setting up this week and by next weekend, the rest of cast should arrive. Then after a month, we'll pack up and do it all again in Jonesboro, the town where Lana and Tyler went to college.

"Oh, I want to do a final table read the Sunday before filming starts since you missed out on the original one."

Jensen releases my shoulder, and I force a smile. "Sounds good, man."

My ex-friend glances to my right and frowns. I follow his line of sight and notice Bruno is standing next to me, massive arms crossed, sneering at the man. He has murder in his eyes and it's terrifying.

Jensen quickly ducks his sights away from Bruno's scrutiny and gives me a nervous smile. He points over his shoulder at a group of men and women, some with familiar faces. "You're welcome to come over there with me and meet some of the crew."

"Thanks man, but I want to run through the script a few more times. Gotta make sure the accent is perfect too."

Jensen nods, and I don't miss the flash of surprise across his face. As if he's stunned that I actually care about this project. "You've been working with that Lana chick, right? The real one?"

That Lana chick? I swallow the anger building in my throat. I must not have been holding it back enough because Bruno's hand wraps around my elbow, pulling me back slightly.

"Yeah," I bite out. "She's great. I've learned quite a bit from her about the character."

"Good," Jensen says and turns around, only to pivot on his heel, holding up a finger. "I saw the pictures. At the lake?"

Is that a question? Where is he going with this? He pauses, waiting for me to respond. When I don't say anything, because I'm not sure what he's trying to ask, he shakes his head, disappointment pouring off him.

"Can I give you some advice?"

I absolutely do not want his advice, but that doesn't stop him from offering it.

"Just . . . don't. Not with her."

What the fuck does he mean by that?

Before I can demand he clarifies, Eloise exits the door to the staircase, calling my name.

"Did you get my texts? Tony is pissed and wants to talk to you. So does your publicist."

I'm breathing hard, teeth clenched so hard, it almost hurts.

Jensen gives me a shit-eating grin, and I swear if Bruno wasn't holding on to me, I'd be punching this asshole.

The moment I put a hand on him, I'm done. My career over. And I'd have failed Lana.

I make myself turn away.

How the hell am I going to survive the next three months working with this prick? And while sober?

I know the answer. I hope she's willing to be my solution.

Chapter 14 - Lana

The bar is chaos.

The line to get inside is longer than it was last Saturday night. Last night, even though I announced that Mylan wasn't going to show, people still stayed. They drank, they bought food, they danced.

They were respectful, for the most part, aside from a handful of people who kept demanding I call Mylan and force him to come to the bar. Those are the ones I kicked out.

When the book came out, I was so agitated with the sudden fame that I hid. I wanted no part of this life. I couldn't understand the obsession, why people so-called "stanned" mine and Tyler's story. I couldn't understand it until I spoke to some fans last night.

Two women, one who had to be closer to my age and size, with light brown hair and matching brown eyes, and the other woman a near carbon-copy but a few decades older, sat down in front of the taps where Mylan usually sits. The mother and daughter told me their connection to the Tyler's Team organization. The mother, Brenda, had a son who died of cancer seven years after Tyler died. He wasn't a college football star, or popular, or had a story that would inspire the world. He was an average student with average good looks who made average good grades.

His name was Victor.

Brenda said when Victor died, she went into a deep depression. She stopped going to work, stopped taking care of herself. She neglected her daughter Lydia, who was only a teenager at the time.

Then Rebecca's book came out. Brenda spotted it at Walmart when she managed to peel herself out of bed to grab some boxed wine and junk food. She stayed up all night reading it. It helped her grieve, it helped her heal.

Reading mine and Tyler's story inspired her to start living her life again. She wanted to help others in similar situations who struggled to move on. She began volunteering with the Tyler's Team organization.

Speaking with Brenda and Lydia changed my attitude towards the fans, the ones who wait for hours upon hours outside in the hot humid night for the chance to be in the same room as someone who made such an impact on their life.

Everyone's story is different. Everyone's reason for loving the things they do is different. These fans, who I looked down on because I couldn't understand their obsession, are just like me—with trauma like me, looking to escape, like me.

That was last night. Now, tonight, instead of Brenda and Lydia staring back at me across the taps, I see a wide smile stretched over sparkling white teeth. I see wild blue eyes squinting from laughter. I see a man with messy raven curls, swooshed across a forehead.

I see Mylan.

I see him and he sees me. He *really* sees me. All of me, including this body that I deprived of pleasure for close to two decades. A part of me convinced myself I didn't deserve it. I didn't deserve a happy life or someone to love because I already met my soulmate. I met him, and he died, so why should I get a second chance at love when some don't even get one?

Tyler was the one meant to go on and inspire the world. Not me. I was just the girl who loved him. I was nobody, not compared to him.

Mylan is the first person since Tyler to look at me like I'm important. He looks at me like I'm his future. It's different from the way my grandparents or Ginger or all the other people in this godforsaken town look at me. They see my past, they see my pain, they see a woman lost.

"I thought I'd find you here." A smooth voice pulls me from my thoughts.

Mylan's warm smile turns cold. A handsome man walks up to the counter. He's wearing black-rimmed glasses, a black beanie with brown curls poking out, and a red flannel shirt. He squeezes his thick body in between Mylan and Gary. The regular gives him a scowl before scooting his stool over to make room.

"Jensen," Mylan says through gritted teeth.

Jensen leans on the bar and locates the drink sitting in front of Mylan. He points at the glass. "Hope that's water."

"Can I help you?" I ask, feeding off Mylan's anger.

Jensen averts his green eyes my way, a perfectly groomed brow arching.

"Ah, you must be the one and only Lana Young." He holds out his hand. "Jensen Boliver, *Tyler's Team* director."

My breath hitches in surprise, almost as if I forgot the movie was still happening, despite spending every day with the leading man.

"Oh, hi. Yes, I'm Lana. Nice to meet you."

I take his cold and clammy hand. Sweat lines his forehead. Why is he dressed for winter when it's a furnace in here and even hotter outside?

After Jensen drops my greeting, he turns to scope out the place. I quickly wipe my palm on my skintight skirt before he pivots his big body back around to stare at Mylan, who refuses to look at him.

The tension between Mylan and Jensen is wound tight, like a rubber band pulled to its snapping point. Bruno stands at Mylan's back, arms crossed, scowling at the movie director. He's ready to move in at any moment. Eloise sits on Mylan's left, her blue eyes narrowed on the man, and I'm not sure who I'm more scared of, Bruno or Eloise.

"What can I get you tonight?" I ask, attempting to de-escalate whatever the hell this is.

Finally, *finally*, Jensen looks away from Mylan. "I'm not sticking around. Just came in to check on . . ." he waves his hand to Mylan before sweeping it around. ". . . to check *out* the local establishments."

Ginger stops to gawk at the scene while everyone else in the bar is oblivious to what's going on. I'll admit, I don't know what's going on either.

Mylan's going to say something. I'm worried that he'll regret whatever words come out of his mouth. Or it'll be caught on video and shared around the world.

"This *establishment*," I begin, my voice conveying the same authoritative tone I use when drunks complain about getting cut off, "is amazingly busy tonight, so I'd appreciate it if you would either order something or head on out so paying customers can take your place."

I'd never say that to a customer. Anyone can come to my bar and sit and not order a thing. But privileged assholes who come here just to agitate recovering alcoholics are not allowed to stay.

Jensen's eyes tighten with fury as if he's never been spoken to like that before. He's probably the one used to barking orders.

He points his thumb at Mylan. "You do realize that this man is an addict?"

I cross my arms. "Yes."

"He got out of rehab, like a week ago."

"I'm aware."

"Then you're aware he shouldn't be here . . . at a bar . . . with alcohol?"

Mylan stands at this point and gets in Jensen's face, nose to nose. Bruno takes hold of Mylan's elbow, tugging him back but not away.

"Do it," Jensen seethes. "Hit me. Hit me, so I can fire your sorry ass."

I've never moved so fast in my life. I'm around the bar in between the two by the time Jensen is saying the word, 'ass.'

"Mylan," I whisper and place my palm on his chest. My touch brings him down from the anger fueling his actions. His eyes flutter before finding my concerned stare.

Immediate regret stares back at me.

"It's okay. You're okay," I say, moving my palm up to his cheek.

"Jesus Christ," Jensen scoffs. "It's worse than I thought."

Before I can turn around to kick Jensen out of my bar, Bruno is on the move. He takes the man by the arm and drags him out.

"I'm sorry," Mylan says, his voice wavering. "I . . . Jensen and I have history and . . ."

"Hey," I interrupt. "If you weren't going to punch him, I would have. So please, don't feel bad at all."

At that, Mylan's tense shoulders relax, and he lets out a long breath. His hands comb through his hair and I can't help myself, I run my fingers through the dark locks as well.

Shit. What am I doing?

You know what? Fuck it. I want to run my fingers through his hair, and I don't care who sees. Our relationship has been outed, so all bets are off.

After making sure Mylan is calm, I return behind the taps to serve the busy crowd.

I watch him to see how he's handling the aftermath of the encounter. He sits back on the stool, rolls his neck, his shoulders, and cracks his knuckles before inhaling half of his water. He needs an outlet. I assume he'd turn to drugs and alcohol in situations like this. Despite me wanting to stab Jensen, he might be right. My bar is the last place Mylan should be.

And maybe I shouldn't be with a recovering addict.

"All right guys, gals, and non-binary pals." Heads turn to the back of the bar to the stage and the hum of chatter transforms with excitement. "My name is Harkin, and we're Silo's Symphony. It's seven o'clock. Time for?"

"Rock Star Karaoke!" the entire bar screams and cheers.

Mylan lifts his head, and his mood shifts to excitement. Once again, I'm amazed at how quickly he can shut off emotions, flipping to a new one as if he's changing the channel on the television.

"If you were here last weekend, you'll remember we started with a special guest. Well, he's back tonight, and he asked if he could kick things off. Mylan Andrews, will you do us the honor?"

The crowd goes crazy. Mylan nods his chin at Harkin, who nods back. Before heading up to sing, Mylan turns back to me.

"In case you have any doubts, this song is definitely about you."

He winks, and I roll my eyes but damn my mouth for smiling against my will. And damn Ginger for clawing at my arm and squealing like a banshee.

Bruno and the extra security Mylan hired, not only for himself but also for my bar to keep the crowds in line tonight, escort him up to the stage.

He doesn't tell Harkin the song, but the band starts playing anyway. My eyes narrow. Did they plan this? The beat is light, fun, easy to dance to. Wait. I recognize this. I haven't heard it in ages though.

"Come over here," Mylan whispers into the microphone, pointing at me.

What?

He's summoning me with that finger, and I'm shaking my head 'no' fast.

When an electric guitar starts strumming, the name of the song comes to me.

Need You Tonight by INXS.

My cheeks heat as I watch Mylan dance across the stage. He jerks his hips back and forth, in sync with the music. His dancing is atrocious, yet I can't keep my eyes off him. Everyone in the bar can't keep their eyes off him.

He's magic up there.

He starts belting out the lyrics. Man, he's such a bad singer. Why does that make him even more charming? When the song says slide, he slides, and he's rewarded with deafening cheers. When he sings the part about being one of his kind, he points at me again, curling his fingertip, begging me to join him on the stage.

A combination of feelings passes through me: embarrassment, excitement, awe, *lust*.

Then I'm being pulled through the crowd by Ginger, protected by Bruno and the extra bodyguards. My best friend, who I will certainly murder after tonight, shoves me onto the steps, and I walk up on stage. I hide in the corner, arms wrapped around my stomach as if that will protect me from what comes next.

The song talks about sliding again, at which Mylan slides his way over to me. He's so tall, it feels like he's smothering me as he sings at the top of my head. He gyrates on me, grinding his dick on my hip before leaning down and giving me a big, wet smack of his lips on my cheek.

I cover my face as if that will turn me invisible, as if to hide from Mylan and the fact that I'm super embarrassed right now.

And super turned on.

Mylan finishes the song to an explosion of applause, praising the amazing performance, despite the out-of-tune singing voice and the off-beat dancing. I don't give him time to bask in the accolades. Instead, I latch on to his arm and pull him off the stage to the hallway leading to the back exit. Bruno and two other bodyguards follow. We manage to sneak out without any fans stopping us.

Mylan doesn't question me as I walk us up the stairs to my apartment, leaving his small protection team at the bottom. They'll likely stay out there, keeping watch until the bar closes and the crowds disperse.

I close the door, my back against the warm wood. Mylan approaches, slow and predatory, until we're sharing the same electrified air. He leans down, his mouth inches from mine.

"You sang that song to me?" I breathe.

"I did."

"Do you need me tonight?"

"Desperately."

"Then I'm yours."

"Are you sure?" he whispers, his breathing shuddering against my skin.

"I was sure the first time you touched me."

The corner of his lip quirks up. "Liar."

I take the fabric of the black t-shirt he's wearing and fist it, tugging his body closer to me.

"Don't make me give you your strike back."

His face drops from amused to serious. "You took it away?"

"I did. After cleaning out Gram and Pa's garage."

Before I can say another word, he crushes his mouth over mine. His lips are soft, plump, delicious. He moves them rough and demanding. He can't get enough. Neither can I, so I part my lips, letting his tongue slip in. It clashes with my own in a battle I never want to end.

But it does end as I'm easing my hands underneath Mylan's shirt, prepared to take it off. He pulls back. I whine and grip the nape of his neck, trying to bring that talented mouth back to me.

"So greedy, Lana," Mylan growls and rests his forehead on mine. "Let me make one thing clear. This is going to happen, but we're not going to rush it, okay?"

Wait. Is he trying to back out of having sex?

"Because if we go fast, I won't be able to worship your body the way it deserves."

Oh.

"My lips and hands will cherish every curve, every dimple, every beautiful mark. I want to taste every inch of your skin."

He grinds his hips into my stomach, his hard dick straining in his jeans.

"Do you feel what you do to me?"

I nod and he kisses me, rougher this time. His teeth scrape on my lips then he bites down. Not hard enough to draw blood, but damn, does it make me moan. He tugs my lip before letting go, moving his love bites along my chin and down to my neck, where he nips harder this time. He sucks on the skin, making sure to leave his mark on me again.

Almost as if saying *mine.*

Then he steps back, the rush of air between us cruel yet a relief at the same time. Mylan takes my hand and drags us away from the door.

"Something you should know about me, Lana."

I lift my brow, intrigued.

"I'm not very good at control. Drugs, alcohol, my life . . . I lose control a lot. But sex? When I have control in the bedroom, my addiction is no longer in charge."

We've reached my bed, and he positions me at the side, his hands on my shoulders.

"Don't get me wrong, I love when you boss me around, but tonight, you're going to listen to what I say." He slides his hand off my shoulder to palm my neck, tipping my chin up with his thumb. His favorite thing to do. *My* favorite thing he does. "You're going to *do* what I say. Understand?"

I swallow hard, only nodding my response because this man has me surrendering—my voice, my body, my will.

"Good. Slip off those sandals and then I'm going to undress you."

I suck in a breath and Mylan smiles. He gives me a brush of a kiss, and I squeeze my legs together because I'm so dang anxious at the idea of Mylan taking control. Because all my past sexual experiences have been beyond horrible that I've been the one to voice my needs and guide the men. Yet, they never satisfied me.

Mylan clucks his tongue. "Spread your legs, baby. I'll give you your relief. Don't you worry."

I do as he says and stifle a groan as my arousal leaks onto my thighs—because I didn't wear underwear tonight.

After I shimmy off the sandals, Mylan slips his fingers underneath the fabric of the black, short-sleeved crop top I wore.

"Arms over your head."

I lift my arms, and he peels the top off, sending my tits bouncing free.

Mylan's sharp whistling breath tells me he enjoyed that. "No bra," he whispers, cupping my breasts with his large hands. His skin is warm as he squeezes. He does this for a few seconds before his mouth finds my painfully tight nipple. I throw my head back at the wet and hot sensation of his breath. He sucks and flicks his tongue over the hard peak, and I arch into him.

"Yes," I moan.

He switches and gives the other breast the same wonderful attention. I'm so worked up, I'm panting. My knees will surely go out at any moment, so I dig my nails into his sides, holding myself up.

Mylan teases my nipple with a graze of teeth, and I jerk with a grunt that makes him chuckle.

"You're being so patient, Lana."

He rewards me by twisting my nipple between two fingers, making my stomach tighten and my cunt pulse. Then he moves his soft lips up my chest, across my shoulders, and to my neck all while he skims his palms over my sides and around my back, up and down before squeezing my ass.

Worshiping my body.

His fingers hook the band of my black high-waisted body-con skirt. The stretchy fabric allows him to tug it down over my wide hips and ass. He pauses. "No panties, either?"

He gets on his knees and leans in, inhaling my scent, then proceeds to huff hot air on the sensitive area. I nearly keel over at the sensation. Mylan hums, satisfied with how my body reacts to him as he continues to strip me. He rolls my skirt down with such deliberate, unhurried movements that the anticipation has me electrified with want, ready to explode at any moment. He taps my ankle and I lift one leg, then the other to step out of the skirt.

He peers up at me—his pupils blown out and darkening with . . . something. Not desire, because that was already there. No. This is . . . beyond carnal. The look he's giving me is as if he's been without water, food, and oxygen for months, struggling to breathe, struggling to survive, and my naked body is bringing him back to life.

His now scorching palms skim along the inside of my leg, from the ankle all the way up until reaching the wetness of my inner thigh.

"Fuck, Lana," he breathes.

"All yours," I pant.

I hold onto his shoulders, convinced my knees are about to give out, as the tip of his finger strokes my soaked entrance, teasing me.

He growls. Literally growls and stands.

"Get on the bed."

I do, falling onto my back. When Mylan starts getting undressed, I hoist myself up on my elbows, watching. He's going slow. Too slow. So, I start touching myself, twisting a nipple with one hand while moving the other hand down to my pussy, holding Mylan's stare the entire time.

"Don't you dare take what's mine."

My hand stops as my fingertips reach the top of my trimmed bush.

"I'm going to be the one to make you come. Understand?"

I nod and let out a slow, shaky breath.

"Good girl."

I toss my head back at his praise. Why is that so hot?

Mylan continues undressing until one final piece of clothing remains: dark gray boxer briefs. His dick is so hard, the thin fabric struggles to contain it.

"Mylan, please." I can't stand it anymore. I need him now. I'm begging him.

He smirks at me, that brat, and removes the underwear. His impressive dick pops up, bobbing until it points directly at me. I lick my lips, more than willing to take it in my mouth if he'd let me. But I have a feeling tonight isn't about his pleasure. Tonight is about me.

About worshiping my body.

This beautiful man is torturing me in the best possible way, and I both love and hate him for it. He approaches my feet, leaning down to place a kiss on top of one.

"Tell me what you need, Lana." He places more gentle kisses along my ankle and up my leg.

"I need you. Now."

Soft lips caress my knee and the inside of my thigh.

"Need me how?"

I whine and reach for him, but he intercepts by grabbing my wrists and pushing them into the bed at my sides.

"Tell me."

"I need you to fuck me."

He lets go of my wrists to spread my legs wide, palms flat on the dimpled skin as he lowers his head to my cunt. My fingers weave into his hair, gripping the long locks tight the moment his tongue licks my opening to the top of my clit, lapping up my wetness.

"My sweet little donut," Mylan whispers, more to my pussy than me. I start to laugh at him calling me donut, but when he slides his finger inside me, that laugh morphs into a moan.

I arch my back, and he splays his hand on my stomach to push me back down. Why does it feel so good when he does that?

"Is this cunt ready for my cock?"

"Yes," I breathe.

He sticks two fingers in and pumps slow, curling the tips once deep enough to hit that spot that has been neglected most of my life.

"Mylan, please."

"I love it when you beg."

He removes his fingers and crawls up the rest of my body. He lifts the fingers that were just inside me to his lips, ready to lick them clean, but I grab his wrist instead and pull his hand down to my mouth. I suck his fingers, coated with my arousal, holding his heated gaze the entire time.

"Lana," he whispers as my tongue swirls over the pad of his index finger. "That was mine."

I release the finger and grin.

"Tell me how good you taste."

"Not as good as you."

He groans and his cock jerks. Beads of precum pool at the meaty head.

My words must have broken his patience. He starts fisting himself, then scans the floor to find where he threw his pants. "I need a condom."

"Wait," I say, and he pauses in between my legs. "I can't get pregnant. And I'm clean. Are you clean?"

His brows furrow, perhaps weighing whether to question me about that.

"They tested me in rehab. I'm clean."

I sit up, my mouth grazing his. "I want you to come inside me."

I crush my lips to his, parting to let his tongue in. A ravenous tongue that consumes me, leaving me bare and starving for more. Mylan's arms wrap around me, and he lowers me onto my back. He pulls away from the kiss to focus on entering me.

He grabs hold of his cock and rubs the head up and down my opening.

"So wet, Lana. Wet for me."

He pushes in, just an inch, and fuck, he's huge. I spread my legs wider and lift my hips. He shoves in another inch, and I arch my back. Two more inches and I'm oh so full. Then he thrusts hard, all the way in.

I wail with pleasure and pain—pain because he's too big. A wonderful pain. My cunt stretches beautifully as it wraps around him.

My eyes roll back in my head as he draws out slowly only to slam into me again. He lifts one of my legs, tossing it over his shoulder and I see stars. This angle is bliss and allows him to go deeper. He pumps fast, grunting and panting in tune with the slaps of our bodies.

Without losing his rhythm, he reaches down to play with my clit.

Fuck.

"You like that, don't you baby?"

I nod. Yes. Fuck yes.

"Use your words, Lana."

"Yes, please."

My response has him pounding into me faster, gloriously rougher.

"Play with your nipples. Pinch them."

I do as he commands and the combination of him fucking me, flicking those sensitive nerves, and me twisting my aching nipples threatens to put me over the edge.

"You're close, aren't you?"

I bite my lip, nodding.

"Mhm. Your cunt is so tight right now." Mylan tilts his head back, savoring the feel of me.

He picks up speed, the satisfying smacking sound of our bodies drowns out our moans. He drops the leg he'd slung over his shoulder and leans over to wrap an arm underneath me. Another angle that allows him to fill me to the hilt.

I'm done for.

I come loud, long, and luxurious.

Mylan slows his thrusts but doesn't stop until my pulsing pussy calms. He places a gentle kiss on my lips.

"One orgasm down."

Chapter 15 – Mylan

The sight of Lana orgasming is one I never want to forget. The way her face tightens as she comes, her mouth parting to moan, her cheeks reddening with bliss.

Sweat coats our bodies, and we've only gotten started. I made sure she had her release first. Jesus, it felt so good. Her pussy sucking my dick like candy almost had me breaking my control and spilling inside her.

She's panting, still coming down from that earth-shattering orgasm.

"I want you on top," I say, reaching out my hand to help her up.

She narrows her eyes, and it almost makes me pull her across my lap to spank her. I'm not sure if she's ready for that.

She takes my hand and I maneuver us, so I'm now on my back. She's sitting on her knees next to my hips, staring between my hard dick and my smirking face. I rest my arms behind my head, waiting for the show to begin.

"Go on, donut."

"Donut? Seriously?"

"You told me donuts are better than sex. You're better than any donut I've ever had. Therefore, you're *my* donut. My sweet little donut," I explain with a shrug that only seems to piss her off more. Why is she getting so mad?

Wait, she's not mad. She's . . . nervous? About what? Getting on top?

I sit up and grab her jaw. "Whatever you're thinking, don't."

"I'm too big."

"Wrong."

"Mylan."

"You're perfect."

"Bullshit."

Still clutching her chin, I kiss her and nip her lips with my teeth, making her whimper. God, I love it when she whimpers. When I pull back, I lock eyes with her. "Get the fuck on my dick. Now."

She rolls her eyes and smiles, mumbling, "So freakin' bossy."

She mounts me, leaning on one leg and taking hold of my dick, which jerks in her hand. Shit, I nearly lost it at her touch. Then she's lining me up with her wet warmth. Once in position, she sinks down. My fingers bite into her hips as she reaches the hilt and I groan, arching my back.

She feels so good.

She starts moving on top of me, but I can tell she's holding back. She's trying not to put her weight on me.

"Lana, you're not going to hurt me. I promise." I rub my palms over her thighs and hips and around to her ass. I give her a hard squeeze. "Put your hands on my chest for leverage and *fuck* me."

She rolls her eyes again but does as I say. Her tits fly near my face the moment she leans in, and I grab one, pulling it to my mouth to suck her hardened nipple. My tongue twirls over the sensitive peak before I graze it with my teeth.

Her pussy clenches around my cock.

Fuck.

I repeat my worshiping with her other breast before releasing the beautiful mounds.

"I want you to ride me hard. Understand?"

"Yes sir."

Yes sir? I groan and thrust up into her. She cries out and digs her nails into my skin.

"Oh, you like that."

"Yes, Mylan, please keep doing that."

"No, baby, I need *you* to ride me." I thrust again and that gets her going. She starts bouncing on my dick, slow but oh so good. Then she finds a rhythm, a wonderful rhythm that has her picking up speed.

She's getting more confident.

The way her cunt slips and slides up and down my cock is like nothing I've ever felt before.

It's so fucking satisfying.

"Wow," she breathes, and I'm not sure if she realizes she said it out loud.

Has she never been on top before?

Her pussy walls clamp down, massaging me wonderfully. She's about to come again. I sit up, our chests crashing together.

"Plant your feet on the bed," I demand, and she does. I wrap one arm around her waist, the other gripping the nape of her neck tight to anchor myself to fuck her.

It only takes a couple more thrusts before she orgasms. This time, I don't slow down, and her scream is twice as loud, if possible. I take a nipple in my mouth again, relishing in the way her body responds anytime I play with her breasts (which is why I do it so much). I lap and flick and graze my teeth across the hard peaks, making Lana throw her head back and cry out.

"Fuck, Mylan," she hisses.

Now I'm the one getting close. I've held off as long as I could. I squeeze a hand between our slick bodies, finding her clit and playing with it. The bundle of nerves is swollen, tender. Lana leans her forehead on my shoulder, her fingernails digging into my back. Hard enough that I'll have scratches for sure.

"I can't," she cries. "I can't come again."

"You can and you will. Be a good girl and do it for me."

Her cunt tightens around me. Third time's a charm. Lana explodes with another orgasm, coaxing my release. I bury my head into her neck and grunt as her walls milk me. Then I let go, pumping cum into her endlessly. More cum than all the times I've jerked off since meeting Lana. Even more than the time she took me in her mouth.

"Three orgasms down," I say, my breath fanning against her throat. She lets out a wonderful laugh full of humor and satisfaction.

Wrapped in each other's arms and still inside her, our breathing begins to subside. After another minute, she carefully lifts off me. My cum, her cum, drips down her thighs. She goes into the kitchen and grabs a wad of paper towels, running them under water first. She wipes herself clean, then grabs fresh ones to hand to me.

"I need coffee," she says, taking the paper towels from me once I'm done. "Do you want coffee?"

"Isn't it a little late for coffee?" I ask, knowing exactly where she's going with this.

"Not if we don't plan on sleeping tonight."

The sun is rising when we finish our fifth round of sex. After Lana rode me like a queen on a prized horse, we decided to cuddle. Then we cooked something to eat (for energy). Once our stomachs were full, Lana sucked me off, and I thanked her by eating her out. We showered and fucked in the shower. Then we blasted music and had a dance party in the middle of her living area. She laughed until she cried at my attempts to twerk, and I dared her to do it better, briefly forgetting that she was a cheerleader in high school and college. The cocky smile on my face dropped fast the moment she began moving, remembering every routine as if she performed it yesterday.

She was so sexy in that moment, seducing me with her gyrating hips and shaking tits. Enough that I scooped her in my arms and threw her on the bed.

Our last round of sex wasn't so much sex as it was making love. It wasn't frantic or hard or rough. It was slow, sensual, both of us wanting to savor the moment. It was the most intimate sex I'd ever had.

Now the day is fully awake and neither of us have fallen asleep. Golden rays of sun peek through the closed red curtains. The loft is quiet, peaceful, except for the birds chirping outside and our shallow breaths inside.

"Can I ask you about what you said earlier tonight? About not being able to get pregnant."

She doesn't answer for the longest time, and if it weren't for her body tensing beside me, I would have thought sleep finally claimed her. She let out a deep breath that she must have been holding from the instant I asked such a personal question.

"When you questioned me about Tyler not accepting an offer from a bigger, better school," her words are slow, cautious, "he stayed because I got pregnant."

Wait, what? That wasn't in the script.

"I lost the baby. Tyler had already accepted the full-ride to Arkansas State. We talked about him changing schools, but he said he couldn't leave me, not when we both just lost our child. I told him I would have followed him to any school, but that was unrealistic because I didn't have a scholarship to those other schools like he did. I had grants to pay for my tuition at Arkansas State. I couldn't afford to go to any other school. Therefore, I stayed, and he stayed too. For me."

"How did losing the baby affect—"

"They had to do an emergency hysterectomy."

"Oh, Lana—"

"It's a lot of uncomfortable, graphic details that I don't want to share, and you don't want to hear."

But I *do* want to hear. I want to know everything, but I won't push her to tell me anything she's not ready to disclose.

"Ask me something else," she whispers.

I think about the other interesting thing that happened tonight. "Have you never been on top before?"

She snorts and sighs. "Yes, but it's been a while."

I wait for her to keep talking because she has more to say. She's working up the courage to explain.

"Not since Tyler . . . when I was skinny."

"Lana," I warn.

"Don't." She tugs on the sheets, not to cover herself but more to keep her hands busy while her mind gathers her thoughts. "I love myself and my body. I do, but that doesn't mean I don't have insecurities. After Tyler, I thought I was broken, because every man I'd been with since . . . well . . . they weren't good. I don't know if that's because I didn't allow them to be or if I was holding back. And was I holding back because of my grief or because my body was changing, and I hadn't learned to love it like I do now? I basically gave up. I stopped trying to discover what I liked. Sex became unenjoyable."

"Sounded like you enjoyed it with me."

She laughs and slaps my chest and I pretend it hurt.

"You're only good because you're a sex addict."

"Self-diagnosed."

She snorts and turns on her side to look at me. I do the same.

"When's the last time you had sex?" she asks.

"Three months ago."

Her eyebrows shoot up, not expecting that answer.

"Three months is the last time I remember, at least. It's possible I slept with someone since while high or drunk, which is why I got tested in rehab."

"You said you like to have control when it comes to sex. That doesn't sound like you had control."

"Yeah," I whisper. "The downside of hitting rock bottom—you lose control over everything, including the things you take pride in. I can't tell you how many times I'd pass out, wasted in the middle of parties. Me being unconscious didn't stop people from stripping me down and taking advantage of my naked body, snapping pictures and selling it to those shitty tabloids. My lawyers were able to get them taken down pretty fast, but the damage was already done. The pictures were shared and re-shared and they were everywhere. So, yeah, I lost control over my body, and consequently sex, which is why it's important I have that control back."

She rests her palm on my cheek, and I close my eyes at the intimate touch—more intimate than what we just did five times.

"Oh, Mylan."

Her words are full of compassion. Not pity, like most. That's what I love about her.

Love.

I tuck the word away in the depths of my heart. "Why do you do the key thing at the bar?" I ask, changing the subject once again. I had to, afraid that her compassion for me, for my failures, will turn into the pity I hate and fear.

She scrunches up her nose, and I fight the urge to lean forward and give it a little kiss.

"I told you my parents died when I was nine?"

"You did."

"It was a drunk driver." Her words are so quiet, I barely heard. "My parents were coming home from their anniversary dinner. The driver swerved into their lane, hit them head-on, and sent their car rolling into the ditch and a pole. My father died instantly. My mom . . . she suffered. She was impaled by a piece of wood from that utility pole. She sat there, bleeding out until the ambulance arrived—"

Tears cut off her words and I pull Lana onto my chest, rubbing her back and kissing the top of her head.

"The driver left a bar, like the one I now own. He'd had too many drinks, but the place was too busy to notice." She wipes her tear-covered cheek on my bare chest, and I don't even care. She could cry a river onto my body and let me drown if it'd make her feel better.

"What happened to the driver?"

"A broken arm." She scoffs, letting a bit of anger infect her grief. "He was sentenced to twenty years on vehicular manslaughter charges and released ten years later on good behavior and overcrowding. *Ten years.* My parents lost their lives, and this man walks free. It's not fair."

"It's not. I'm so sorry, Lana."

She sighs against my body, and I wish I could stay here, like this, forever. She feels so good in my arms—like she belongs.

"Did you always want to become an actor?" she asks, quietly. She starts tracing a scar on my shoulder. A small diagonal line from the one and only time my father put his hands on me. I was eight. He'd pushed me against the wall, my shoulder hit the window, breaking the glass, causing a chunk to fall and slice my skin. It was the first time I ever got stitches.

"No, not at all. I was forced into it by my parents. They moved us from some small town near Sacramento down to L.A. They took me to endless auditions. I hated it. All I wanted to do was play video games, or watch cartoons, or go to the park and play like the other kids. I wanted a puppy. I've never had a puppy."

Lana smooths her palm over my chest, soothing the building anxiety.

"You don't hate it now though?"

"No."

"What do you love about it?"

"That it lets me escape. I can be anyone in the world."

"Anyone but yourself?"

"Yeah, well, sometimes being me is tough."

"Is it not exhausting? The fame, learning the lines, becoming a different person every time?"

I sigh because it *is* exhausting but being me is near debilitating.

"It's ... exciting. Challenging. I wasn't lying when we met. I research every role I take. I talk to people similar to the character, who knew the character, or to the actual person the character is based off. I came here early to meet the people of this town who knew Tyler. Then I found you. You helped me understand the importance of this role—how important Tyler was."

Lana lifts her head to look at me.

"Tyler was important to everyone."

"And to you?"

She lets out a long breath. "He was my soulmate. The love of my life. We met when we were kids."

She smiles to herself, the memory likely crossing her thoughts. I read about how they met in the script, and I'm eager to hear it through her words.

"He managed to turn the worst day of my life into my best. My parents had just died, and I decided to run away. I loved my grandparents, but I didn't want to move in with them. I didn't want them as my parents. How horrible is that? I wasn't thinking because I was just a kid. I was confused, shocked, in denial. So, I left, and I wasn't planning on returning home, either. I packed clothes, toys, and food—no money because I really thought I could sell my toys. Anyway, I got on my bike and rode it all the way to the cliffs, the same one we jumped off, the one where Tyler proposed to me. That cliff was also where my parents used to bring me a lot. I went there to say goodbye, because a part of me thought if I ran away from Silo Springs, the pain would also go away.

"The cliffs were miles and miles away. It took forever to get there and when I showed up, I was surprised to find Tyler. His light brown hair flopping all over his big head in the hot summer breeze. He smiled at me and waved. He was missing a tooth, his canine I believe. I thought he looked ridiculous, and I was pissed that he was there at my special place. I crossed my arms and stomped over there, demanding he leave. Instead, he laughed at me. He laughed and pushed me over the edge of the cliff, my packed bag of clothes, food, toys, and all."

"He pushed you?" That part wasn't in the script.

She laughs. "Yeah, can you believe it? I hated him so much in that moment. Then I started panicking, struggling to keep my head from going under. I started swallowing water, choking. I thought I was going to die. Then Tyler jumped in after me and pulled me to safety."

"That was the reason you never jumped off the cliffs?"

She nods.

"Anyway, he helped me climb up the rocks back to the top. He apologized and offered to share the lunch his mother made since the food I packed was ruined. We talked and talked. I told him my parents just died, and he told me his father got a job in Silo. How strange that we met there, miles away from both our homes. As if we were destined to be together."

"How *did* Tyler end up there that day?"

"They were new to town and Tyler's parents wanted to explore the area. They drove to nearby towns, including Beverly, and that's when they stumbled upon a nearby picnic area. They stopped to eat the lunch Tyler's mom packed. After they were done eating, Rebecca went swimming, but

Tyler wanted to hunt for snakes, so he wandered off and found the cliff. I found him minutes later."

I give her a hum of understanding and she keeps talking.

"We became friends first. All through elementary school we were the best of friends, plus Ginger. She was our third, the three musketeers some would call us. Then we grew up. In middle school, puberty hit. I stopped seeing Tyler as a friend and decided I wanted to kiss him. So, I did. I kissed him on a rainy day out on the playground after school. He froze. He didn't know what to do. I pulled away and said, 'don't be a wuss, kiss me back—'"

"You would say that," I snort.

"—and from then on, we were boyfriend and girlfriend."

At first, I don't say anything, letting the story soak into my own memories. A beautiful story of friendship and love that I won't ever want to forget.

"I understand," I eventually say.

"Understand what?"

"Your grief. Why it's difficult for you to let go."

Her brows pinch together.

"Grief is always harder when the love you have for a person is that deep, that pure." I shrug. "I didn't mourn my father when he passed because he didn't deserve it for what he did to my mother and me. I hated him. I still hate him. I didn't cry one single tear when he died because I was relieved. I thought my life was finally about to get better."

"Do you want to tell me about it?"

She's staring up at me, her chin still on my chest. I should tell her all my dirty, dark secrets now, but I'm enjoying my time with her too much. If I tell her about my demons, she'll run away.

I boop her on the nose and grin ear to ear. "Some other day?"

She answers with a mischievous smile, and then we're making love for a sixth time.

Chapter 16 - Lana

The next week flies by. Mylan and I spend as much time together as possible. Most nights, I'm at the bar with him sitting in front of the taps in his usual seat, going over his lines and reading the notes he wrote. Bruno keeps guard, but the excitement over Mylan being in town has died down enough that the crowds aren't as bad. Eloise tags along most days, tapping away at her smartphone.

I found out she helps run Mylan's social media accounts. She showed me a few recent pictures, and I have to say, they look professional—Mylan leaned over the script, pencil behind his ear, his black hair falling across his forehead as he concentrates. Another of him, shirtless, at the cliffs on the lake. One of him on stage singing, the lights sparkling behind him as he smiles brightly.

My favorite is one Mylan took himself—a selfie with me asleep on his chest. You can't see my face because my red hair covers most of it. Just the tip of my nose, a glimpse of my lips, and my eyelashes show. He posted it himself, so he could caption it DONUT with a ton of hashtags that I didn't try to decipher.

Even though Mylan told me not to, I scanned through some of the comments. The majority of them were positive—people loving that Mylan and the real Lana Young from the book are 'in a relationship.' However, there were plenty of negative comments about my weight and my age. Words that would have bothered me if I were young and naïve and still cared what people thought about me. I was also surprised to see a good amount of death threats to me. Mylan assured me that his PR team reports each threat to both police and the social media companies where said threats were posted.

I'd asked Mylan's publicist to release a statement about our relationship. I told her to say that we're enjoying our time together as two single adults. We're taking it day by day and will decide how to proceed once filming is done. I'm sure she wrote something way better, but that's the gist of it.

Going into this . . . hot summer fling with Mylan, I knew what was going to happen at the end of filming. Mylan would go back to L.A., and I would stay here in Arkansas.

Now I have doubts. Now I'm letting myself wonder.

My life is here. My grandparents and my friends are here. My parents and Tyler are buried here. I own a bar here.

But what would happen if I gave it all up?

I could focus more on the Tyler's Team organization.

The organization has kept me busy this past week. Donations are pouring in with the news of the movie, so I've been helping with paperwork and answering emails from fans and the press, scheduling interviews with our head of publicity (though everyone requests me). It's the busiest I've been since creating the non-profit with Tyler, up until I took a step back when Rebecca released the book.

Mylan and I made another visit to Gram and Pa's. This time, he was far more comfortable. We held hands in front of them, and the moment Pa spotted our embrace, he turned on his heel and returned with ole Betsy. Mylan freaked out, thinking my grandfather was really going to shoot him, which had Pa bursting into a fit of giggles. Pa offered a hand for Mylan to shake that he proudly accepted. Then Pa had to ruin the moment and offer Mylan a beer. Gram yelled at Pa, apologized to Mylan, then explained that Mylan is a recovering alcoholic.

My favorite part about visiting my grandparents this second time was spending time with Mylan at the massive oak tree in their front yard. We took turns pushing each other on the tire swing. Then he climbed the tree, onto the large limb, where he sat for several minutes smiling and swinging his legs. He looked so young and innocent up there. He looked happy. Content. He told me it was his first time climbing a tree.

My heart clenched at how much life Mylan must have missed out on because of his career—how fast he grew up because he was a child actor. Still, he's lived a life one could only dream of; the places he's traveled, the people's he's met, the once-in-a-lifetime spectacular moments he's experienced.

That's the thing about strangers. You can envy their life yet, in turn, they will envy you for different reasons.

Now it's Saturday. Rock Star Karaoke is underway, and Mylan is killing it on stage. I slip out during his third song of the night, taking a breather on the patio, which I only keep open during the day for ax throwing and darts. Years ago, someone sliced a finger after too many drinks one night that forced me to shut down the patio once the sun sets. Now anyone who wants to throw an ax must sign a form saying they haven't had a drop of alcohol.

I was lucky that person was a regular and decided not to sue me.

I'm sitting at one of the picnic tables, picking at the carved names, when Ginger finds me.

"Hey Beyotch," she quips.

"Hey Hoe," I counter.

She sets a glass of water in front of me, and I gulp half of it down.

"Everything okay in there?"

She nods and sits across from me. "Mylan frantically searched for you while on stage then bombarded me once he was done, asking where you were. I told him you were outside and needed a break from his clingy ass."

I gasp. "You did not."

She shrugs. "I did, and it's true. He's clingy as fuck."

I roll my eyes and smile.

"Seriously, though, why are you out here? You okay?"

We've talked some about me hooking up with Mylan, but most of the time, our conversations were interrupted, either by someone walking up to ask for a drink or by Mylan, Bruno, or Eloise being nearby and not wanting them to overhear. Talking over text isn't the same.

"I'm okay, but I've missed you these past couple weeks."

"Right? That Hollywood dude is taking up all my Lana Banana time."

I laugh and reach out, taking her hand. "I have no idea what I'm doing."

"You're—"

"Having a hot summer fling. I know, I know."

"Do you?"

I toss up five fingers.

"Oh hell no. You did not plead the fifth on me."

"Tell me about you and Bruno," I say, baiting her with the change of subject.

She bites. I'm a horrible friend and while we've talked plenty about me, I've barely offered an ear for her to talk about her budding relationship with Bruno.

My friend's dark brown face lights up underneath the bright moon. She blushes. "He's amazing. So sweet. I feel safe when I'm with him, which makes sense since his job is to protect people."

I squeeze her hand, urging her to keep talking.

"He makes me laugh at the dumbest things. He has these sayings; they sound so profound but make no sense whatsoever. I think it's because the translation from German to English doesn't make sense. The other day he told me I'm as beautiful as the ground when the rain falls. Like, what?"

I giggle, remembering one of those Brunoisms, as Mylan calls them. "I overheard him telling Mylan once to savor the moment like the last piece of pizza at a pizza party."

"He'll speak German to me, trying to be all sexy, and I don't have the heart to tell him how unsexy the German language is."

We burst into a fit of laughs that has my stomach hurting.

"So, you're saying, German language, not sexy. German accent super sexy?"

Ginger grins and blushes. "Oh yeah, the accent is hot."

"What about the sex?"

"Girl." She fans herself. "He's so big. Like, huge. I've never orgasmed so much in my entire life."

"Guess we're both having hot summer flings."

"Hell yeah." Ginger holds up her fist and I bump it with mine.

Ginger has had more long-term relationships than I have. She was even engaged once, seven years ago. The wedding was called off when she found out he was cheating. She vowed to only have hot summer flings from there on out, until finding the quote, 'right one.' Part of me wants Bruno to be that for her.

We sit there for a few seconds, listening to the booming music inside before Ginger sighs.

"Filming starts Monday," she states.

"I'm nervous. Rebecca will be there."

"Ugh. Not a fan of hers."

I snort. "Because she didn't include you in the book?"

She tosses her hands up. "I was downgraded from best friend to girl who had a couple classes with you!"

She laughs, I laugh, then we both frown because she didn't *really* want to be in the book about our best friend who passed away.

"Are you sure you and the rest of the staff are cool with covering the bar while I'm on set? I don't have to stay all day. I can come in later to help."

She taps my scrunched-up nose.

"Don't you dare feel guilty. We shifted everyone's schedules while you helped Mylan become Tyler, and it's worked out wonderfully." She reaches across the table and takes my hands in hers. "Banana, you're my best friend. Always have been, always will be. I will go to the ends of the earth and back for you. We all would. Especially if this movie is one step closer to the closure you've been needing."

The way her voice inflects on the last word, she has more to say.

"And?"

"And . . ." She grins, mischievously. "Maybe this movie is also your future."

Ah. She hopes my 'hot summer fling' with Mylan will turn out to be more.

Won't it?

"I'm just saying that you two together, it . . ." She sighs like she's dreading saying the next words. "It reminds me of you and Tyler."

"Because he's literally learning how to become Tyler."

She shakes her head. "No ma'am. He's Mylan Andrews around you. I've only seen him as Mylan Andrews with you. I'm telling you right now, you two look comfortable together. Like, two lost souls that finally found each other."

I stand up, not wanting to hear this.

Because maybe it's true.

"Don't be ridiculous. He's only been here two weeks."

"You think love gives a shit about a timeline?"

I start walking back to the bar. "Love can go fuck off."

"I'd like to revisit the evidence!" Ginger screams at my back.

"Request denied!"

With that, I go back into the bar, brooding for the rest of the night.

Monday. First day of filming. My stomach knots with worry. I'm scared to see Rebecca. It's been years since I last spoke to her, and more than a decade since I last *saw* her. What will she say when I confront her about not telling me the movie was filming here?

On top of stressing about seeing Rebecca, I'm also nervous about watching the actors perform the scenes. Can I handle the emotions that will surface? Will it be like I'm watching my memories?

Mylan knocks at my door, here to pick me up to head to set. He didn't stay over last night because he had a table read at the hotel. With today's early call time, we agreed spending the night apart would be best. He needed the rest and anytime we're alone together, sleep and rest are the last thing we're concerned about.

I tossed and turned for hours last night without him.

Mylan is due on set at six a.m., too damn early. Even the sun struggles to wake. I need at least five more cups of coffee to be able to stay upright.

"You ready?" he asks, walking in.

"No."

He laughs, leaning down to give me a quick kiss on the lips. "Too bad." Mylan smiles and holds out his hand.

I take it, and he starts for the door. "Wait!"

He stops, raising an eyebrow.

"The accent."

He lowers his head, smiling. "Right. The accent."

"Let's hear it buddy."

Mylan grates his hands over his face then shakes his shoulders and clears his throat.

"This is a line from the script. Is that okay?"

I pause for a second then give him a curt nod.

He takes my hands, his eyes locked with mine, and proceeds to bring my world crashing down.

"Let's skip classes today and drive to Beverly. Let's go to our cliff and lie in the sun. Let's stay there until the sun sets and the stars come to life. I want to forget about the world and get lost in each other. Do you want to get lost with me, Lana?"

The rest of his words fade away.

Those are the words Tyler said to me the day he proposed. The ones I told Rebecca and she wrote them in the book. I was stressed about senior year with the class load for my business management degree, the most I'd ever taken on. Tyler convinced me to escape our worries and we left campus, drove three hours to one of our favorite spots where he got down on one knee, pulled out a small diamond ring—that belonged to his grandmother—and asked me to spend the rest of my life with him.

Mylan must have watched the videos I sent him dozens of times, studying the way Tyler's country twang softened when he said my name. How it'd thicken the more serious he got. The way his mouth would tilt up on one side every time he was nervous.

Mylan stops talking the moment he notices my face, my shaking lip, my watering eyes.

"It's . . . it's perfect," I whisper through a cry. It *was* perfect. Not to mention the way Mylan manipulated his voice to mimic Tyler's . . . it's haunting.

Beautiful.

Tears fall down my cheeks. Mylan cups my face, soft and assuring. He leans in and cleans up the wet streaks with gentle kisses. Such a loving act that has me craving more. He pulls back once satisfied the tears are gone, and I thank him by claiming his mouth, raw and full of hunger, laced with a need that never seems to be satisfied. This kiss I demanded from him is hard and urgent, unlike the patient and caring ones he trailed along my cheeks.

He wraps an arm around me, pulling me close to his body. His other hand snakes up my back, until his fingers reach my braid. He grabs hold at the nape and tugs it slightly. I hum against his lips.

"I want nothing more than to throw you on your bed and fuck you right now," he growls, his breath tickling me.

Fingers still gripping my braid tight, he gently pulls my head back to expose my throat. Those magical lips of his trail down, offering nips of his teeth in the process. My nipples tighten and grate against his chest, prompting Mylan to move his mouth down to claim one viciously.

I gasp the moment his teeth bite through the fabric of my shirt. Mylan chuckles, satisfied with his torture.

Torture interrupted by a knock at my door. Mylan pauses, mouth still claiming a nipple.

"Mylan," I manage to say through the lust paralyzing my body. "I know you heard the knock."

We can't ignore the next one because it sounds like a SWAT team is on the other side getting ready to bust down my door.

"You two better not be fucking in there because we don't have time for that shit," Eloise says, her voice muffled.

Mylan growls at the same time I laugh.

"I'm going to fire her."

"You better not." I check my shirt to make sure Mylan's wet mark can't be seen. Thankfully, the blouse I chose to wear is dark enough. I offer my hand to Mylan. "Come on. We can finish this later."

Mylan begrudgingly takes my hand, and we leave.

Over the past week, Silo Springs High School had been transformed into a movie set. White box trucks line the horseshoe driveway at the front. Police and security teams are in place, ready to intercept any fan or media person who may try to sneak on set. There's already a decent crowd of them gathered when we arrive.

Mylan takes time to greet his fans, sign his autograph on a variety of items, and take pictures with every single one of them. They even wanted me to sign things and take selfies.

The pit stop with the fans made us slightly late to set.

Once inside the school, Mylan holds my hand tightly as we weave through busy crew members, some wearing headsets, others wearing gear that I couldn't begin to explain what it's used for. The hallways are also packed with equipment: carts, dollies, tall lights on tripods, a camera on a track so it can roll along with a moving target.

It's all too much to take in, both exciting and terrifying. Terrifying because this movie about my dead fiancé—about me—is really happening.

We reach a holding area located at the end of the hallway before the entrance to the locker room. I spot more of the crew standing and talking, pointing down at a small stack of white papers. Next to them is another group, clearly part of the cast. They're all too beautiful to be otherwise. Not that there aren't any handsome and gorgeous crew members. But the big-breasted woman standing beside Jensen Boliver, the asshole director of the movie, has an air about her that says model-turned actress.

The moment she spots us approaching, her face lights up.

"Mylan Andrews, alive and in the flesh. I can't believe it."

Mylan narrows his eyes at her before turning to me. "Lana, this is Michelle Miller. She's playing you."

Michelle's judging gaze flickers to me. "A way younger you," she clarifies and scans my body, up and down. She smirks, and it's not a nice smirk. "You certainly changed, haven't you?"

"What the fuck does that mean, Chelle?" Mylan asks through clenched teeth. His grip on my hand tightens.

Before Mylan can crush my hand, or blow a gasket based on how red his face is turning, I laugh. Mylan's tense shoulders relax but barely.

I laughed, but I'm not about to let this woman get away with her fatphobia and ageism.

"Time's a bitch and you'll realize that one day. Unless you fix your aging with a doctor and a vial of poison. Even then, no one but you can change the ugly you store inside that fit body. Take some advice, stop caring about what the world thinks about you and live how you want to live, eat what you want to eat. You'll be much happier, I promise."

It's wild how much Michelle Miller looks like college me. Typical cheerleader type, skinny but muscular.

"Oh, um, yeah, well . . ." Michelle struggles to compose a comeback, choking on her words. "I just meant you're all tattooed with red hair now."

"Sure, sweetie."

I turn to Mylan, who looks like he's about to die with how hard he's trying to hide his amusement. He squeezes my hand.

My eyes find Jensen next, who's been silent since we walked up.

"Lana." He acknowledges me, then glares at mine and Mylan's embraced hands. "So glad you could join us on set today."

His words are forced. He's not glad at all.

Mylan stares at his former friend with all the hatred the world could offer. Jensen must not see it, or maybe he doesn't care. He lifts his chin and wags his finger at Michelle and Mylan.

"You two should get to hair and makeup and wardrobe. We start filming in an hour."

Mylan's brows pinch with concern. He looks at Jensen, then back at me. He does not want to leave me.

"It's fine. I'll be fine."

"I'll take good care of her," Jensen adds, and I consider kicking him in the nuts for egging Mylan on.

Mylan searches my face and I nod. He reluctantly accepts that he has to go and kisses my forehead before stalking down the hall. Michelle Miller follows, scurrying her short legs to catch up.

Once they round a corner, guided by yellow signs that say 'Hair & Makeup,' Jensen lets out a loud sigh.

"I appreciate you helping him."

I turn away from the now empty hallway, as if expecting Mylan to reappear if I keep staring. Jensen adjusts his black framed glasses, his shoulders tight, face scrunched. He's worried, and I'm not sure if that worry is for his movie or his former friend.

"I'm sorry about my behavior at the bar."

I jolt because *that* I wasn't expecting.

"What happened between you two? I've asked Mylan, but he always changes the subject to avoid talking about it."

Jensen swallows hard and scratches the stubble along his round jaw. He looks around then waves his hand to indicate we walk away from the holding area and into the hallway where fewer people are gathered.

"Mylan and I were best friends. Then he let his addiction get between us."

I scoff. "You mean you let his addiction push you away?"

He narrows his eyes at me. "It's not that simple. I was there for him. I was *always* there for him. I cleaned up his messes, I covered for him far too many times. I offered him help, I *wanted* to help, and still, he never accepted it. What was I supposed to do?"

"Not give up?"

He shakes his head. "It was too hard. Have you ever seen someone you love willingly wilt away? Destroy their life with no regard to those around them?"

I bite my lip because it makes sense. I'm starting to understand. Did I judge Jensen too quickly? Maybe. He's still an asshole, though. "Mylan needed support. He needed friends."

We reach the end of the hallway and turn around, causally heading back down towards the cameras where several director chairs are placed up against the lockers. I assume this is where the first scene will be filmed.

"Mylan had support. He had friends: me, Bruno, Eloise. He had people who begged him to get help." Jensen sighs, his breath slightly shaky. "He reached a point where he was so far gone that I no longer recognized him as my best friend."

"Maybe this last stint worked. He's doing better now. He hasn't had one drop of alcohol or any drugs."

That I'm aware of. I'm not even going to mention that first night at the bar.

"Yeah, he does this. It's a vicious cycle. He'll stay clean for a few weeks, or a month, then something will happen, something will trigger him, and he'll start falling again. You should know while booze was an issue, it wasn't the root of his problems. Not until he started adding the drugs—opioids, coke, molly, whatever else he could get his hands on."

He's telling me this to scare me away. If I'd met Mylan yesterday, it might have worked. But it's been two weeks. Two weeks with a man who gives me more of himself than I deserve. Except, why do I still feel like he's nothing more than a familiar stranger?

"I should also warn you—"

"Lana?!" a shrill voice interrupts whatever warning Jensen was about to give me. Not that I would have taken that man too seriously. He seems to be on a mission to kick Mylan while he's down.

Chills run up my arms once recognition sets in. That shrill voice belongs to the woman responsible for all of this.

Rebecca Taylor.

Chapter 17 - Lana

Tyler's sister.

Rebecca started writing *Tyler's Team* five years after his death. It took her a year to finish and another year for someone to publish it. Seven years after Tyler's death and suddenly my life was thrown into the limelight: my life, my private love story, my grief.

Rebecca included all our stories, everything from how we met and Tyler pushing me off the cliff to the last words he said to me before he died. The only thing she did not include was the loss of our child and the hysterectomy that followed. When she told me she was writing the book, she promised that personal and heartbreaking moment in my life would be left out. It wasn't in the screenplay either, otherwise Mylan would have known.

I didn't read the screenplay. Mylan offered but I refused, knowing I would be here on set to relive those memories through the actors. I knew I could only put myself through that once. If I'm honest, I may not be able to handle it at all.

Besides my love story with Tyler, Rebecca also included the inspirational parts of starting the organization for cancer research and helping families of loved ones going through the same fight. She shined a light on how Tyler spent his final days, making sure others would have better futures.

Seven years after Tyler's death, the book became an instant hit.

Eight years after Tyler's death, Rebecca informed me a Hollywood producer contacted her, a big named one, who wanted to turn *Tyler's Team* into a movie.

Ten years after Tyler's death, once the legalities had all been worked out, the screenplay was being written.

Twelve years after Tyler's death, and I was done. I told Rebecca I couldn't be part of the process anymore. It was taking too long, and I was ready to move on, ready to heal.

Eighteen years after Tyler's death and filming begins. Healed wounds are reopening. My grief revisited once again.

"Lana," Rebecca's sweet as honey voice pours down the hallway as she walks to where I stand with Jensen. She opens her arms wide, swaying her curvy hips like she's a beauty queen contestant on stage showing off her gown. Her light brown hair falls over her shoulder in perfectly styled waves. She looks exactly the same. She's five years younger than me, yet she could pass for someone in their twenties. It's not a fake beauty either. Her skin is smooth and flawless. A plastic surgeon or Botox couldn't create such art.

And her body. She was never thin but not big either. She's midsize and as breathtaking as ever.

"Rebecca," I manage to say. I even manage to sound happy to see her.

She wraps me in her strong arms, her firm tits pressing against my soft body. Okay, maybe at least one part of her is fake. Did Rebecca get implants? She squeezes me hard enough that I wince before we part.

"I didn't know you'd be here," I lie.

"Of course, silly," she purrs in that thick Arkansas drawl that has to be as manufactured as her tits because she hasn't lived in Arkansas in a very long time. Certainly, long enough to water down her twang. "I wrote the book *and* the screenplay. This project has been my baby for nearly thirteen years. I plan to be here every day."

Jensen sighs heavily beside me.

Rebecca's sharp eyes cut to him. She purses her lips and raises her chin high. "Jensen."

Oh. This is interesting. Do they have beef?

"I need to finish prep." He turns to me. "We'll talk later?"

He doesn't give me time to answer, and it would have been 'no thanks.' If Jensen has more to say about Mylan, I'd rather hear it all from Mylan himself.

"Ugh," Rebecca says the moment Jensen is out of sight. "I can't stand that man."

She swallows her disgust fast before plastering on a forced smile for me. "How've you been, sweetie?"

Time to put on my battle gear.

Now it's my turn to narrow my eyes at her. "Could be better."

That fake smile of hers drops. "Oh please, Lana Banana. Don't be so dramatic."

"Do. Not. Call. Me. *That*," I seethe. Rebecca blanches. My words sting because she remembers how much that nickname means to me. Tyler was the first to use it and my grandparents and Ginger quickly adopted it. A nickname that Rebecca does not have the honor of repeating.

It's also why I won't let Mylan use it. It doesn't seem right.

"You should have called me." I cross my arms.

Rebecca sighs and rubs her temples. "Lana, you were very clear when you dropped out six years ago that you no longer wanted to be a part of the movie."

"I didn't want to be a part of it because I wasn't mentally strong enough. I had to put this grief to bed and that meant stepping back from everything, the book, my role with the organization, and especially the movie. A movie I thought would be shot on some Hollywood sound stage, far away from me. Not here in our town, at our school, at Tyler's favorite places—"

My words shake, and I hate myself for showing Rebecca my vulnerability. She's going to feed off it.

Except . . . she doesn't and pulls me into another hug that I don't hate this time. It actually cracks the emotional walls I'd built for this very moment.

"I'm sorry. I really am. When I emailed you earlier this year to tell you filming would begin this summer, you didn't respond. I didn't expect you to. Then when I found out we were shooting here on location, I knew if I told you, you would have felt obligated to get involved again. I knew you didn't want that. I was trying to respect your wishes."

I close my eyes, digesting her explanation. I suppose I can understand. I hadn't answered her emails, texts, or phone calls in years. I brought this upon myself. All I had to do was respond, to ask for more information.

"And I did not expect that actor to find you and ask for your help. He shouldn't have done that."

She holds me at arm's length, brushing a fallen piece of hair out of my face.

"You're much stronger than me, you realize that, right?"

I inhale sharply, not expecting her to say that. I study Rebecca's sincerity, my eyes scanning her face—a face too similar to Tyler's: eyes, mouth, a short stubby nose. Looking at Rebecca used to be disheartening, but now, seeing the shadow of Tyler, it's almost . . . comforting.

"You were able to move on. Me? I coped by writing the book. I'm healing through this movie. But honestly, I think it's making me miss him more than ever. How crazy is that? It's been—"

"Eighteen years," we say together.

"Yeah," she laughs.

"I haven't moved on though. Not really."

She tilts her head, releasing my arms. She takes a step back and smooths her outfit, a dark purple wrap dress that shows off all her curves—too fancy for a movie set.

"Haven't you?"

"What?"

"The actor. How's that been going?"

The sudden change in her demeanor tells me she knows the answer. She's seen the pictures and now she's demanding an explanation.

"Working with Mylan has been great."

She snorts. "I bet."

"I'm serious. I'm grateful I was able to guide him and make sure he doesn't mess this up, but you know what else I realized while helping Mylan? I still have a lot of healing left. This grief, it's endless and exhausting."

The defensive front she's showcasing eases slightly.

"Right. I . . . I'm sorry. The stories, the photos . . . it looked like . . ."

"Like I replaced Tyler with the man who's about to portray him in a movie?" I sigh on my words.

Rebecca grimaces. "Yes, but I don't really believe you replaced Tyler. It's just strange seeing you with someone else so publicly." She pauses and frowns. "My therapist tells me I get defensive to shield my own grief. I think that's what I just did to you with the accusations."

"It's fine. I understand." The Rebecca I used to know would never admit to being wrong. She'd never apologize for those wrongs either.

"I'm serious. I'm sorry I did that to you because I really do hope you've moved on. You deserve it. More than anyone."

My throat aches with tears waiting to fall the moment I think, or talk, about Tyler and the life we should have had together. Of course, Rebecca had to be the one to set them free with her kind words. Words I never expected from her.

I reach out and take Rebecca's hands in mine. "He would have been so proud of you. The book was a beautiful eulogy to him. And this movie . . ." I wave my hand around the set. ". . . you're bringing his legacy to life."

Rebecca's bottom lip shakes and now she's crying and I'm crying, and we're standing in the middle of the busy movie set, hugging. Crew members in motion, preparing to shoot the first scene of the day, dodge us left and right. Yet no one interrupts us. No one tells us to move out of the way. They know who we are. They must because they give us space.

"Tell me more about Mylan," Rebecca says as we part.

I don't want to talk about my relationship with the man who's about to play her dead brother on the big screen.

"Actually, tell me what's up with you and Jensen first."

She rolls her eyes, her earlier disgust reappearing. "Okay, so getting the movie made has been a legit nightmare. Every director who previously signed on bowed out because they wanted the script to go a certain way, and I wasn't budging. My one stipulation when selling the rights to the book was me having a final say in the screenplay. This isn't a piece of fiction they're messing with, it's real-life, my life. Right?"

I nod, looking around to see people staring at us as Rebecca speaks with her outside voice.

"Well, Jensen was hired, and this was it. If he dropped out like the others, the movie wasn't going to get made. It started out with the same ole bullshit. He came to the table with a list of changes. Unnecessary changes. It took two weeks of meetings and so, so many compromises, to finalize the script. I relented. I had to. Anyway, the point is,

Jensen is frustrating and freaking bossy. I want to rip my hair out when he's around. He's young, and he thinks he's some hot shit know-it-all, but he's not. He's a baby director, not Steven Spielberg."

"Steven Spielberg would have quit the moment you opened your mouth." Jensen says with boredom, walking up behind Rebecca. If I'd have seen him approaching, I would have warned her.

She points her hand at him. "See what I mean?"

Jensen ignores her mounting fury and continues his prep work, whatever that may be. He holds that same short stack of papers in his hands that I see everyone carrying around.

Rebecca must see my confusion. "Those are called sides, like mini versions of the script for the scenes being shot today."

I follow Rebecca to the row of director chairs. I spot one with my name placed next to hers.

"We have our own chairs?"

Rebecca smiles and sits. "Pretty cool, right?"

It takes me a lot longer than I want to admit to sit my ass in the flimsy chair. Now I'm worried it's going to collapse beneath me.

"Okay, spill," Rebecca says, referencing back to Mylan.

"He's going to be amazing. I brought him up here to talk to Harold, remember him? He was Tyler's teammate and now he's the football coach here. I think he was a senior when you were a freshman." Rebecca nods. "We also talked to people around town. Did your parents tell you we visited?"

"They did. They said Mylan was a nice young man. Very respectable. Said he took a lot of notes." She smiles but it doesn't reach her eyes. "They also said you looked happy."

My heart clenches at that because most people in this town know I'm a bit of a grump. A bitter bitch who can't move on.

"You're not worried about . . . his problem?"

I scrunch up my nose. "Yes, always, but he's been clean since I met him." Minus that first night.

She thinks about that and nods.

"Well, if you're happy then I'm happy."

I wave off her words. "It's . . . nothing serious."

Why do I have to keep convincing people of this? Or maybe I'm trying to convince myself. Four days, and I let him touch me. Eight days, and I let him inside me. Two weeks, and I find myself falling for him. Three months left, and I may never find my way back to the surface.

Chapter 18 - Mylan

I wring my hands, and worry my lip, and shake my knees as Mary, the hair stylist, sprays some blonde highlights into my hair. I refused to wear a wig, and I wouldn't let them permanently dye it to match Tyler Taylor's light brown locks so this was the alternative.

"Son, I'm going to need you to stop moving," Mary says, frustrated. She rests her hand on her round hip, blush tinting her pale face as she shakes her white bobbed head at me.

"Sorry, Mary," I mumble.

I can only imagine the filth Jensen is feeding Lana right now. What if he's telling her about my darkest days? He should know, he's seen most of them. What if he tells her about the last relationship I was in? How it broke me. How she let me love her and trust her and ruined everything all for her own personal gain.

What if he tells Lana I'm a poison that infects those close to me? I'm on edge every day, waiting for my toxic life to push

Bruno away, to force Eloise to quit, because eventually, they all do.

Like Jensen. After nearly nine years of friendship, he left me when I needed him the most.

You wouldn't let him help.

"What's your problem?" Michelle asks. She's in the chair beside me as the other stylist, Farlan, works on her hair. They style Michelle's hair into a high ponytail with a bow—like Lana used to wear in all those pictures I saw of her when she was younger.

Lana.

Fuck she's going to hate me after speaking to Jensen.

"Nothing. Mind your business."

Chelle snorts at me. "It's that woman, isn't it?"

That woman? I stifle a snarl and ignore her. My silence only infuriates her, and she keeps talking.

"What's so special about her anyway? She's old and fat."

"Shut the fuck up," I say, this time letting that snarl lash out at her. Jesus. What did I ever see in this vile human? I briefly dated Chelle about five years ago after we worked on a Netflix rom-com together—her first movie crossing over from model to actress. Our relationship lasted a month before I realized she's simple-minded and pathetic.

"All done," Mary announces. I jump up from the seat and exit the trailer without a word, leaving a stunned Chelle behind. If I stayed another minute, I would have said something worse to her.

I should tell Lana about my history with Michelle.

My head isn't where it needs to be, which is ironic since this is exactly what my manager warned me about. Tony was pissed after seeing the pictures from the lake and finding out our relationship had turned into more. He sees Lana as a distraction and advised me to end things immediately, but to me, she's my guide. She's keeping me on the straight and narrow. I even went as far as confessing my first night in Arkansas, at the bar ordering drinks, and how Lana was the one to convince me to stop. Tony eventually backed off. He can advise me all he wants but, in the end, I'm still his boss.

After a brief stop in makeup, I follow the signs to wardrobe. Bruno and Eloise trail behind. Eloise, who doesn't typically come to set, is only here to snap photos of my first day filming for social media. Bruno technically doesn't need to be here either. The production company hired enough security guards, but ever since a fan managed to sneak on the set of one of my films years ago and attacked me with adoring hugs and unwanted kisses, Bruno stays by my side.

By the time I return to set, we only have a few minutes until filming starts. I find Lana sitting in a director's chair placed along a row of red lockers, and a Barbie doll type woman sitting next to her.

Shit. That must be Rebecca Taylor.

As I approach, Lana laughs at whatever Rebecca had just said. She spots me and does a double take. Her face drops from smiling to gaping. Rebecca follows her stare and her demeanor changes, copying Lana's.

"Mylan?" Lana whispers. I stop in front of her, taking her cheek in my palm. She grabs my wrist and closes her eyes, forcing a tear to fall. I wipe it away with my thumb.

"Holy shit," Rebecca murmurs, pulling my gaze away from Lana. "You, uh, you look like Tyler."

I do? Lana said I looked nothing like him. Though, I suppose with my lighter hair, combed to how Tyler used to style it, and dressed in similar clothes he used to wear . . .

Lana clears her throat. "Yeah, but only at first glance." She manages to return that contagious smile of hers. She removes my hand from her cheek and kisses my palm. "So what scene are you filming today?"

"The day Tyler got his scholarship."

Lana flinches. It's brief. If I hadn't been staring at her, and I'm always staring at her because I'm obsessed, I wouldn't have caught it.

"This month, we're shooting all the high school scenes and scenes around town. There will also be a week of production on flashbacks from when you and Tyler were young, including when you two met."

Lana told me how she met Tyler at the cliffs but the part about him pushing her into the water wasn't included in the movie script.

"What happens after you're done filming all those scenes?"

"Then we'll film on location in Jonesboro at the college."

"You're going to be leaving Silo?"

Shit. I haven't talked to Lana about this yet. We'll be there for the last two months. I was planning to ask her to come with me.

"I assumed you knew."

"I guess I didn't think about it, but it makes sense." She shrugs but I can tell she's . . . not pissed but sad maybe? Disappointed? "It's for the best. I wasn't going to be able to come to set every day for three months anyway."

"Lana—"

"Okay, everyone," Jensen interrupts. "We're already behind schedule for the day. It's going to be a long one, so let's get started."

"Can we talk about this later?" I ask, palming Lana's cheek again.

"What's there to talk about?" she answers, shrugging once more. "It's fine."

Shit.

She's masking her true feelings. Her words are saying 'it's fine,' but by the way her body tenses, lips pursed, she's upset. *She cares.* She cares that I'll be leaving her. A flare of hope burns my chest, and I quickly douse the flames.

"Andrews," Jensen yells. "Take your mark."

I roll my eyes over my shoulder then turn back to Lana. "You're not fine about this at all." I clutch her chin and bring her mouth close to mine. "It's because you're greedy, and you want me all for yourself."

I don't give her time to deny my words and kiss her hard before releasing my grip.

As I'm walking away, Rebecca says, "wow," drawing out the word.

"Shut up," Lana responds through a laugh.

Michelle Miller stands at an open locker in the middle of the hallway, and I take my mark at the end. Background actors gather, waiting for their cue. The crew makes final preps.

"Camera ready?" Bri Downley, the first assistant director, a tall Black woman with a head full of braids, asks.

"Ready," the camera man, a large fella named Bob, responds.

"Quiet on set," Bri continues. She pauses to listen, her hand on the headset she wears. "Roll sound."

"Sound is speeding," the sound guy says, a scrawny man who resembles Shaggy from the Scooby Doo cartoons.

The camera assistant, a young petite woman with her brown hair in a low ponytail, steps in front of the camera, holding out the clapperboard. "*Tyler's Team*. Scene 1, Take 1." She slaps the arm down.

"Set," Bob barks.

"Background," Bri yells, and the young men and women playing high school students—most are drama students at Silo Springs High School—move around the hallway.

Jensen ends the chorus of commands with 'Action!'

I run up the hallway, weaving through the students until I reach Chelle at her locker.

"Lana!" I say, the name drawn out in the accent I've perfected. "I did it! I got the scholarship to Arkansas State. Full ride. Can you believe it?"

"Babe, that's amazing," Chelle answers, scooping me into a hug.

I cup her face. "I knew I would. Now we can be together." I kiss Chelle then continue my lines, talking about looking for places to stay and how we'll decorate.

When Jensen yells cut, my eyes go to where Lana sits, but she's not there.

I move, ready to go find her.

"Where are you going, Andrews?" Jensen yells, glancing around a monitor as they check the scene. "Back on your mark."

I fist my hands at my side and take deep breaths, stifling the scream I want to unleash on this douche. I need to find Lana and make sure she's okay. I know she's not. She'd still be here on set if she were okay.

We just started shooting. Getting a break to find her could take hours.

I hope it won't be too late.

I don't get a break from filming for at least an hour, and I only have about ten minutes before I'm due back. I find Lana in the school's greenhouse behind the building, where she's been since storming off set. Thankfully, Eloise followed her and texted me updates, which I read in between takes until Jensen took my phone away, since I'm not allowed to have it while filming scenes.

Lana sits on a concrete bench, tossing flower petals onto the ground. Colorful petals like the ones in front of her bar and tattooed on her arm.

"Hey," she says quietly, either sensing me behind her or hearing me walk in.

"You okay? You didn't come back."

She shrugs, and I swear if she keeps doing that, I'm going to follow through with that punishment I wanted to give her the first night we made love. Still, I don't think she's ready for that side of me yet.

"It was too weird."

I sit beside her and take her hand, kissing her knuckles and flipping it over to kiss her wrist.

She finally looks at me, her eyes faded. Tired. "I don't think I can go back. Not today, at least." She brushes off the petals gathering on her jeans before turning to me on the bench. "Since Rebecca didn't include my pregnancy in the book, watching the scholarship scene almost felt ingenuine. In reality, Tyler telling me he got the scholarship was more emotional, a relief, because it meant we were going to be together when the baby was born."

"Did you want the pregnancy included? In the book or the movie?"

"I . . ." She sighs with her entire body, and if I could leave set and take her home, so we could cuddle (or fuck if it meant making her happy) for the rest of the day, I would. "When she was writing the book, no. I felt it was too soon. Too personal to include, only because a part of me felt ashamed."

"For getting pregnant in high school?"

"Yes, but also for losing the baby."

She winces at whatever my face is showing.

"I know that's ridiculous, but back then, women who suffered miscarriages faced a stigma. It was a taboo subject. It still is. I realize now that sharing the story of our failed pregnancy could have helped other women, other couples, going through this trauma. I was selfish, and now I regret not asking Rebecca to include it."

Before I can respond, a frantic production assistant bursts through the greenhouse door. "Mister Andrews, um, the reset is finished, so they need you back on set now."

"I'll be there in five minutes."

"I—"

"Five minutes."

"Okay," the mousy woman says and backs out slowly.

"And what do you have planned for the next five minutes?" A smile spreads across Lana's face.

"Don't tempt me, donut."

"You're really going with the donut nickname, huh?"

"Yep."

"Don't you think it's cliché to name a fat girl after a pastry?"

"You know exactly why I call you donut."

She bites her lip and blushes, perhaps letting those sweet memories of me tasting her cunt replay.

"I hate it," she lies.

"Would you rather me call you Lana Banana?"

"I swear I will punch you in the dick."

"You like my dick. You'd never hurt it."

She laughs, a full belly laugh, and my chest tightens at the beautiful sound. "True."

"You were mad earlier. About me leaving Silo in a month to film at the college."

I palm her shoulders to keep her from shrugging. She tries, though. "I wasn't mad. I was surprised. I don't understand a thing about film making. I thought the whole movie would be shot here, which makes no sense now that I think about it. Why wouldn't the college scenes be shot at the actual college?"

"Are you not planning to come to Jonesboro?"

"With the bar . . . I don't think I can."

"From what Ginger told Bruno who told me, the bar will be fine. Your staff has it covered."

"They do, but I still feel guilty for making my employees work overtime just because their boss can't get over a death that happened eighteen years ago."

I hate that she keeps torturing herself over this. Grief has no timeline.

"What about coming to visit me once or twice a week?"

"I'll think about it."

"Yeah?" I lean in, my mouth inching close enough to hers that she licks her lips, begging for a kiss. My hand travels from her shoulder, down to the front of her jeans. I unsnap the top button and reach for the zipper. "You don't think you'll miss this?"

My fingertips slide behind the opened jeans, searching for her underwear.

I growl when I find none.

"You're killing me not wearing panties, donut."

She nips at my lips. "Easier access."

Lana opens her legs to allow my fingers to reach her warm cunt. So fucking wet.

"We only have a few minutes. So, I'm going to need you to come fast. Understand?"

She nods, her forehead resting against mine.

I plunge my fingers inside her and drown her moan with a kiss. I thrust, hard and fast, putting pressure on her clit with the heel of my palm.

She groans, a little too loud. "Quiet," I hiss.

She whines into my mouth and fuck, I'm so hard. Yeah, this wasn't the best idea. I'm going to go back to set with a boner.

Lana takes hold of my arm, gripping hard as she gets close to coming. I'm kissing her, refusing to take my mouth away to prevent any of her pleasurable cries from slipping.

Seconds before I'm due back, she's shaking on my fingers. As I finish licking up her arousal, the PA barges back through the door.

"Mister Andrews, please. They need you now."

I stand, adjusting my aching cock. "Coming," I say over my shoulder then give Lana a smirk. She rolls her eyes at me.

"Please say you'll come back to set."

"Let me think about it some more, okay?"

Before I leave, I lean down to give her a deep kiss, making sure she tastes herself on my tongue.

Lana doesn't come back to set.

Chapter 19 – Lana

I couldn't do it. I couldn't go back to set. It was too . . . painful. And I hate that. I hate that I'm still allowing my past to debilitate me.

Why does grief have to be so vicious and never-ending?

I promised myself I'd let the pain in. If I could just *feel* it, maybe I'd eventually become numb. Maybe the pain would eventually become bearable. I couldn't do it when the book came out. But now? I'm older, I'm stronger, I'm ready to move on. I thought I was ready before but now it's . . . different.

Is it because of Mylan?

He's certainly been the key to opening my closed doors. The grief I've kept locked away is ready to be freed. Time to place it in a part of my heart that I can easily revisit but not let it consume me.

Mylan is my stepping-stone to cross the deep waters I've let myself drown in.

Could he be more? I . . . that I cannot answer. It seems improbable. We come from two different worlds, from two different decades. We've lived two different lives. Though, have we? We both have our demons. His are more demanding than mine.

Loving someone means accepting their faults. Accepting that it won't be easy. There will be times of pain, suffering, and heartbreak. With Mylan, and his addiction, loving him would be the biggest challenge I'd ever face.

Two weeks, and I'm talking about love. I must be losing my mind. It's not love. It's not. It's . . . lust. Infatuation.

It's a hot summer fling.

Possibly the biggest lie I've ever told myself. It's more. It has been more the moment he walked into my bar. Still, if nothing serious comes out of this . . . summer with Mylan, maybe we can stay friends. We've certainly connected. Not just sexually either. I find myself missing him when he's not around. Or wanting to text him about a scene in the book I'm reading because, turns out, Mylan reads a lot of books.

We've spent hours upon hours talking about our favorite books, ones we hated, and ones we want to add to our ever growing 'to be read' piles. He mostly enjoys thrillers, science fiction, or fantasy books, but he said he reads all genres. He even wants to start reading the spicy romance books I enjoy (for research purposes).

It's the next morning. The day after the first day of filming. I'm still in bed, lost in my thoughts when my phone chirps with a text.

Brat

> Good morning donut

I roll my eyes at the nickname that I tell myself I hate but secretly love.

Me

> Good morning you annoying brat.

Brat

> Me? Annoying? Never

When Mylan and I first started texting, he'd make fun of me for ending texts with a period. Question marks and exclamation points are fine, but he told me nowadays no one ends texts with periods. Something about it being too aggressive and final. Seriously. I Googled it. Who knew? Whatever. One more thing to make me feel old around him.

Me

> I see how you didn't deny you're a brat.

Brat

> I'm *your* brat

I send him three eye-roll emojis and he responds with three winky-eye faces.

Brat

> **Are you coming to set today?**

I roll over and groan into my pillow. I knew he'd ask me again. He asked me last night when he called after they finished filming. It was late, near midnight. He must have been giving me space because he didn't ask to come over. I *wanted* him to come over. I wanted to cuddle, but that would have led to a sex-filled, sleepless night and an exhausted Mylan showing up for his eight a.m. call time.

Another text pops up after I don't answer right away.

Brat

> **We're filming a scene similar to the story Coach Harold told me about Tyler helping that kid and his mom**

My heart flutters with curiosity. Everyone in our school talked about Tyler helping his teammate for weeks. They called him a hero. The newspaper wanted to do a story about it, but Tyler refused. Rebecca included it in the book, but they obviously changed it for the movie. I want to see what they did.

I can do it. I can be strong this time.

Me

> **Yes. I want to go to set today.**

Brat

Good because I'm at your door

Walking into the school-turned-movie set for the second day isn't as overwhelming. People don't seem as frantic. First day jitters are out the door, replaced with determined mindsets.

Mylan leads the way to his trailer, located behind the school in a line with other trailers belonging to the stars of *Tyler's Team*. I'm on alert, eyeing everyone we pass, hoping we don't run into Jensen. Not only because Jensen stresses Mylan out, but because I don't want him to start talking shit to me the moment he gets me alone.

Mylan and I smile and wave at people who greet us as we walk by. I expect their judging stares as we hold hands, but they all seem to mind their business. I wonder if that's common in the entertainment industry. See something, don't you dare say something.

We make it inside Mylan's trailer with no interruptions. It's nicer than the small studio apartment I shared with Tyler in college. So clean with white everywhere, including a plush couch and chair, a large flat screen television and a small kitchen with two stove top burners (no oven, but there is a microwave).

Mylan shows me the bedroom, cramped with a full-sized bed. A shelf packed with books sits above the headboard. I crawl onto the mattress, tilting my head to read the spines. Mylan mentioned how he brought an entire suitcase of books with him for filming. This must be a fraction of them. I glance over my shoulder to ask him which one he's current-ly reading, and of course, Mylan sees me on the bed and his mind goes to the gutter. He wiggles his eyebrows at me, and I crawl back to him and playfully slap his chest.

He has to leave in a few minutes to get ready, otherwise, I might have taken him up on that silent offer.

Mylan wraps his arms around my waist and kisses me, sweet and long and desperate before pulling away. "Do you want to hang out in here while I'm in hair and makeup?"

Hiding in his trailer would be what old Lana would do, but I can't keep running from this past. "No, I'll go out to set. It'll be fine."

His forehead pinches. He didn't expect me to say that. Maybe after walking off set yesterday, he hoped I wouldn't want to go back without him. Tension ripples from him. He *wants* me to stay in the trailer.

"What are you not telling me?"

"I don't know what you mean."

"Mylan, you look like you'd rather eat nails than have me go out on set."

He drops his hands from my waist to rake them over his face and hair. It flops back in place, and I can't fight the urge. I comb my fingers through the soft strands, no longer dark because of the temporary highlights the stylist put in the day before.

My touch relaxes him. He closes his eyes, savoring my caress while gathering his words.

"Jensen is going to find you, and he's going to tell you things about me, and you're going to hate me afterwards. Or you'll run away. Far, far away."

I wonder if this has anything to do with that warning Jensen had for me.

"Don't let him hold that power over you. If there's something I should know, *you* be the one to tell me first."

Mylan hasn't shared too much about his past, especially about his family and addiction. He's given me glimpses, and at times, I feel like he's leaving out details either because they're too painful or because he doesn't want to me to pity him.

Mylan sits us down on the end of the bed, and he takes my hand. He's nervous, which makes me nervous.

"My last relationship . . ."

"With Michelle?"

He pauses and swallows hard. "You know about that?"

I bite my lip, embarrassed. Mylan tugs it free. "I Googled you."

After our day together at the lake, I caved. I read about his dating history, surprised that the majority of women he dated were not only older than him (by a few years, no one as old as me) but *bigger*. Fatter. He most certainly has a type.

Michelle Miller did *not* seem like his type.

"Yeah, well, dating Chelle was a mistake. She's a conniving bitch and only cares about her image. She's a bully, and being around her made me want to . . ."

Mylan shakes his head. He doesn't need to finish the sentence. She drove him to the bottle. Or whatever drug of choice he was partaking in during that time of his life.

"How are you able to work with her now?"

He smiles at me, palming my cheek and rubbing his thumb back and forth. "It helps having you here," he whispers.

His words make my stomach flip-flop. It also sends jolts of worry throughout my body because I still don't know if I'll be able to be there every day with him while he's off shooting at the college.

Will he fall back to old habits without me?

Mylan drops his hand from my face, and I stifle the whine, almost begging him to put it back where it belongs.

"If you Googled me, then you know I dated Michelle Miller five years ago. I'm talking about my most recent relationship with Olivia Hadford."

I *did* read about her. She's an up-and-coming plus-size model/actress. I have a feeling that what I read about their relationship and their breakup isn't as bad as what really happened.

"She was only dating me to cash in on my fuck-ups. She encouraged my drinking and drug use. Then we'd go out in public, and I'd be wasted, making a fool out of myself. She'd record the videos and sell them to the tabloids. Or sometimes she'd tip off the paparazzi, and they'd show up. I had no idea Olivia was making money doing this until one of the reporters at Entertainment Now got wind of it and told me. I was . . . devastated, to say the least."

Yep. *That* part was not reported.

"She also cheated on me with the director of the movie she was filming. I'm pretty sure she was cheating the entire six months we were together."

"Jensen?" I ask.

Mylan's jaw ripples with tension. "No."

He's quiet for a while that I think he's done talking.

"Jensen is the one who introduced me to Olivia, but how would he have known she was going to do that to me?"

"When was this?"

"We broke up six months ago." Mylan slouches slightly, easing some of the tension he's been holding in his shoulders. "I thought I loved her. I trusted her, which is hard for me to do. I should have known that she didn't feel the same. If she loved me, she would have urged me to stop, she would have helped me seek treatment. Instead, she encouraged my addiction. She was an enabler. It fucked me up and after she left, I started drinking more, pairing it with pills. I wanted to feel numb. I think Jensen felt guilty, so he'd go out with me and make sure I got home all right. He supported me and was there for me until he wasn't. When he gave up on me."

"There has to be a reason."

Mylan shrugs a shoulder. "I wouldn't let him help me."

"Mylan, you have to see it from his point—"

"I do . . . I did . . ." He falls back onto the bed, rubbing his face with his palms. I lay back with him, turning my head, so I can see his flawless profile. "I get it, I do, but it still hurt all the same."

"And what do you think Jensen is going to say to me to push me away?"

"He'll probably tell you I'm beyond saving. Or maybe he'll tell you that I'm so desperate for attention that when I find someone I'm attracted to, I fall fast. I became obsessed and dependent on them. That's what happened with Olivia. I was vulnerable when I met her. I too easily handed over my trust to her when I'm usually so careful with it."

Is that what Jensen meant that night in the bar when he said, 'it's worse than I thought?' Maybe Jensen still cares for Mylan. Maybe he worries I'll earn his trust and steal it away like Olivia did.

"He'll tell you to stay away from me because I'm a poison that needs to be contained."

"You're not a poison. You're an elixir with the wrong label. What matters is what's on the inside."

He barks out a laugh. "That sounds like something Bruno would say. It makes no sense, but in a weird way, it does."

We sit in silence for several seconds before he turns his head to me. "You make me a better person, Lana."

I suck in a sharp breath. "That's a lot of responsibility to put on someone."

"It is, and I'm sorry but it's true. When I'm with you, I want to do better. I have this overwhelming need to impress you, to make you proud. When I'm with you, nothing and no one else matters. Only you."

"How can you say that when we just met? We hardly know each other."

He doesn't respond. He knows 'we hardly know each other' is a lie. I've shared more about my life with this man than any other man I've dated since Tyler. And here he is, revealing his very private life to me, trusting me to protect it when others have failed to in the past.

He studies my face. "When filming is over—"

My heart lurches, and I jolt up. I lean over Mylan and cover his mouth with my palm. His eyebrows pinch together.

"Let's . . . not talk about that right now. Or tomorrow. Or next week."

"When?" he murmurs against my hand.

I wince because if it were up to me, I'd never have this conversation with him. If we talk about it, it becomes real. Perhaps I should follow Jensen's warning, whatever it may have been before Rebecca interrupted us. Mylan is still an addict. Is thirty days of rehab enough? There's a vulnerability in him that I worry once breached, it will make him fall back to those bad habits.

I can't allow myself to be the reason he slips. I won't.

I let myself indulge in this relationship. It was never going to be some hot summer fling. Now it's more, and that scares me. It scares me because I *need* him just as bad as he needs me.

Still, the decision to uproot my life, after decades of familiarity, isn't an easy one to make.

What I do know is that Mylan *will* be in my life in some way after this movie is done filming, but before I can talk to him about it, I have to find peace with my grief. I'm so close, I can sense it, almost touch it.

"Lana?" Mylan mumbles, making me realize I still have my palm over his mouth.

The moment I peel it away, Mylan takes hold of my wrists, flipping me onto my back. He straddles me, holding my arms over my head.

Shit. This is hot.

He smirks, like the brat that he is, and leans in. He's seconds from kissing me when someone knocks on the door of his trailer.

He growls against my lips and adjusts his hold on my arms above my head to one hand. All so he can twist my nipple with the other. I buck my hips in response, moaning so loudly my face heats because I was certain the person at the door heard it.

"Five minutes!" Mylan barks.

"Mister Andrews," the muffled voice calls, cautiously. "I already gave you five minutes. Now you're late to hair and makeup."

He rests his forehead against mine and I inhale his cedar and citrus musk.

"You're lucky, Lana," he says, quietly. His coffee and toothpaste breath fanning against my lips. My mouth waters, wanting his kiss more than ever at this moment.

"Oh?"

"I was going to punish you for refusing to talk to me about—"

"Punish . . . punish me how?" I interrupt in a shaky breath.

The interruption must have pissed him off by the way he tightens his grip around my wrists above my head—by the way his smile turns cruel. Neither of which I find threatening. It's . . . sexy as hell. Mylan is clearly a dominant. I've never been one to submit, but for him?

"How will I punish you? I'll start by throwing you over my lap and spanking you." He kisses me, soft and careful, unlike his damning words. "I'll spank you until your ass is red and your cunt is dripping. I'll spank you until you beg me for more. Are you going to let me spank you, my little donut?"

Fuck.

I've been spanked during sex before, but I have a feeling it's nothing like what Mylan wants to do to me.

The panicked production assistant bangs on Mylan's door again.

"Please, Mister Andrews."

"Mylan, the only person you're punishing is that poor PA by not getting your ass to set."

He groans and kisses me one last time. This kiss is harsh, hungry, consuming. When he comes up for air, my face is as hot as the day is humid. My nipples are so fucking hard, and Mylan sees it. He reaches down to twist one again, but I manage to peel my wrist out of his grip and slap his hand away.

"Go!"

"Oh yeah, I'm going to punish you."

"I look forward to it."

He groans again and crawls off me, adjusting his hard cock.

"Don't you dare touch yourself after I leave. I will know, even if it means sniffing your fingers."

I lean up on my elbows and raise a brow, challenging him.

"Guess I'll have to wash my hands, over and over and over . . ."

The muscles in his jaw ripple as he goes through a silent battle, possibly considering staying to follow through with his threat. Then, when the PA knocks for a third time, he gives up and leaves.

I lay back, finally breathing.

I'm screwed. Here I am surrendering to every demand from that frustrating man.

Maybe Mylan is my vice. One that I won't be giving up anytime soon.

Chapter 20 - Mylan

Telling Lana about Olivia, and how she broke me, was a relief—a weight lifted from my shoulders. Still, I worry that Jensen will find her and tell her all the dirty details of my addiction. About the nights I'd lose myself to the high and wake up in my own puke and piss, naked and pathetic.

I worry, but should I? Lana has a mind of her own—a strong fucking mind. She takes no shit from anyone, especially me. She wouldn't let Jensen sway her from . . .

From what exactly?

She's made it clear she doesn't want to talk about what's going to happen after I'm done filming. She must know I'm planning to ask her to come with me, back to L.A. to *be* with me. It's still early, so I can't push her. I can't scare her away.

Convincing her to take a chance on me is going to be the hardest part. Her life is here. Her past that never seems to stop haunting her is here. Leaving Arkansas would be . . . why would she leave? Why would she pick up her life for me?

Maybe if she loves me, but it's only been two weeks.

Do I even love her?

I know I can't stop thinking about her. That I want her around me all the time. That the thought of leaving her is . . . terrifying.

I never felt this way for Olivia, or Michelle, or any of my other failed relationships.

If that's not love, what is it?

You're an addict. You're addicted to her.

This is one addiction I will gladly lose myself to.

Lana's biggest hurdle when it comes to loving me is my age. She probably thinks I haven't begun living my life. That I have a future of endless possibilities. She probably assumes I would never leave my life in L.A., leave acting, for her.

Except, I would. I have enough money to last me a lifetime. I don't need to act. It was something I was forced into. Yes, I came to love it, but when you reach the brink of losing everything, you start to see things more clearly. I'm starting to see what's important in my life. Acting may not be it. Besides, I've lived more lifetimes in my twenty-five years than I deserved. I've traveled the world, met the president of the freaking United States, experienced once-in-a-lifetime spectacular moments like seeing penguins in the wild, building homes in third world countries, and learning how to make sushi from the world's greatest sushi chef in Japan.

I've experienced death, heartbreak, desperation, and failure. Now I'm ready for love and if that means staying here in Arkansas with her . . .

"You're pathetic," Michelle scoffs from the makeup chair beside me.

She waits for my reaction, but I ignore her, which pisses her off.

"I know you're thinking about that fat bitch. You're smiling like an idiot."

"Your jealousy is suffocating."

"I'm not jealous. I feel sorry for you."

"Like I give a shit."

"Haven't you read the articles? People are grossed out by your relationship with her."

My head jerks to Chelle and she smiles vindictively. She knew exactly what to say to piss me off.

"Yeah, they say she's too old, like, she could be your mother."

"That's ridiculous."

"They say she's only fucking you because you remind her of her dead fiancé."

"Shut the fuck up, Chelle."

She shrugs and goes back to her smartphone.

It's not true. For one, Lana told me I'm nothing like him, looks or personality-wise. Lana and I are connected *because* of Tyler but not because I *am* Tyler. Plus, we're controlling what the media is reporting. So, whatever bullshit Chelle is reading must be on fan blogs or sleazy websites that lack credibility.

"All done," Jenna, the makeup artist, says, and I'm out of the chair as if the surface burned my ass.

Chelle yells something after me but it has me walking away faster from her annoying voice. I stalk out of the makeup trailer back to set and turn the corner down the hallway, dodging anyone who tries to approach me or talk to me or even wave at me.

I have to get to her.

Sure enough, I find her talking to Jensen.

"Boss?" Bruno calls to me from behind. I look over my shoulder, and he's nearly jogging to keep up.

"It's fine. I'm fine."

"Uh huh."

My heart beats faster than my legs can move. I fist my hands at my sides, gearing up for a fight. Gearing up to defend myself from whatever bullshit Jensen is feeding her. One wrong word out of that asshole's mouth, and I'm going to explode.

Lana's laughter breaks through this wall of anxiety I've built around me. *You need this job. Lana needs you to get it right.* One simple thought of failing her, disappointing her, pushes down the anger boiling to the surface.

I calmly arrive at Lana's side. She turns to me, smiling, and I melt into a puddle. Okay, not really, but it felt like it. My fast-beating heart stutters and my entire body relaxes as Lana gently takes my hand with hers. She squeezes then brings it to her lips to kiss my knuckles.

I don't deserve her.

"Jensen was telling me—"

This is it. This is when the ball drops. This is when she leaves me.

"— about the pranks you used to pull on each other on set."

Wait, what?

Jensen laughs. "Mylan was a master prankster. I never saw it coming. I don't know how many times I walked out of the bathroom, pants down, ass showing because he'd fill the toilet bowl with fake cockroaches or cover it with Saran Wrap or slather the rim with Vaseline. I'd run out, too pissed to remember to pull up my pants, mooning everyone on set while cursing him out."

The corner of my lip turns up at those memories. They were the best times of my life—before I got sick with this fucking disease.

Jensen slaps me on the shoulder, pulling me back to reality. "You ready to start shooting, man?"

I blink at him as he turns to walk away. Who the hell is this man?

I give Lana a quick kiss before following Jensen out to my mark. "What's going on? Why are you being nice?" I ask the moment we're out of Lana's hearing range.

We're shooting a cafeteria scene today, so Jensen leads me to a table in the middle. His hand is on my back like he used to do when we'd enter a club—like when were friends—protective and supportive.

"What are you talking about?"

"Cut the bullshit, Jenny."

He narrows his eyes at the nickname I gave him when we were teens. He hates that nickname.

"Maybe I . . ." He glances around but no one is paying us any attention. The crew is busy setting up the scene. The rest of the cast is waiting behind the cameras until called to take their mark. "Maybe I was a little harsh. Judged the situation too fast. I see that you're actually trying this time."

"This time?"

"You know what I mean. You're, like, focused. Determined. I haven't seen you this motivated since before . . ." He shakes his head.

Lana watches us, concerned. I give her a wink, hoping that will ease her worry, but it only makes her scowl deepen.

"I think it's because of her." Jensen nods his chin at Lana.

"It's because she believes in me."

Jensen tenses, his hands fisting at his sides as I had done a minute earlier. "Yeah, well, I used to believe in you too. But you lost my faith when you stopped caring about whether you lived or died."

Jensen rakes his hand over the curls of his brown hair (for once not wearing that ugly beanie) then takes off his black-rimmed glasses.

"Mylan, I loved you. You were my best friend. I couldn't stand by and watch you kill yourself. I knew that would have happened eventually because no matter how many times you went to rehab, you'd go out to drink the same night you were released. I had to leave you because I couldn't save you."

Jensen's words break off and his eyes shine with tears. He won't let them fall because I don't think I've ever seen Jensen cry in the nine years I've known him.

"I'm sor—"

"If you say you're sorry, I'll kick your ass," Jensen says, and clears his throat. He's not angry. He actually smiles. Well, kinda. It's a sad smile. He puts his glasses back on. "What I'm trying to say is that I see the way you are with Lana—the way you look at her."

"How do I look at her?"

"Like you've finally found the hope stolen by this disease."

My eyes prickle, and I swallow down the threat of tears.

Jensen goes on. "I also talked to people around town, to Rebecca, even though I can't stand that woman, and everyone says you've been nothing but eager for this role. Eager to learn about Tyler and this town. People here love you."

He peers over my shoulder and nods. I follow his stare and notice the director of photography getting set up, which means we're about ready to start shooting.

"If it's her, if she's the reason you get clean and stay clean, then you better not let her go. And you better not fuck this up. Not with this one. She deserves better than that. Okay?"

So is that what he meant that day in the hotel lobby when he said not this one? He didn't want Lana to get hurt by *me*.

Jensen holds out his hand, and I do the same. He slaps my palm twice then turns and walks away. Not quite our secret handshake but it's something. A start. A step closer to repairing our friendship.

Bruno appears next to me. "Say the word and I'll charge him for upsetting you."

I bark out a laugh. I don't even tell him the saying is 'make him pay.' I wipe the tear that somehow rolled down my cheek. Me, crying? I hate crying. Fuck Jensen for making me not loathe him—for making me miss him and our friend-ship.

"You okay, brother?" Bruno nudges my shoulder.

Am I? For the first time in my life, I don't know if I'm okay. Because for the first time in my life, I have hope. Hope that my life isn't so fucked up. Hope that I hit rock bottom, and this is me climbing back to the surface.

This time is different.

Chapter 21 - Lana

G oing to set became easier. Everyone was so welcoming and informative. If I had questions, they answered them.

Despite the constant burn of grief at the back of my throat, not once did I let it take control. Instead, I found myself excited. I found myself enjoying seeing the story unfold before my eyes. A story I lived and seeing how the actors interpreted it, how the director choreographed it, was fascinating.

Beautiful.

It's been a month since filming began. A month of watching Mylan work his magic. He's pure art. The way he falls into the character and embraces it like a second personality. He's doing this role justice.

I soon realized that things were changed from the book either because it was easier to film, translated better from paper to film, or to have a bigger impact. As if telling the inspiring story of a young college football player who dies of cancer and spends his final days raising money to help others isn't a big enough impact.

The locker room scene where Tyler helps a teammate was changed to him helping a student in the cafeteria who didn't have enough food at home. So, movie-Tyler held a fundraiser to make sure that student never went hungry again.

The cliff scenes, when Tyler proposed to me and when we met as kids, also changed. For some reason, they didn't include him pushing me off the edge, which is the best part of how we met.

My favorite part.

If I'm honest, having that sweet moment erased from the big screen adaptation is disappointing. How will the fans react to this change and all the others? Rebecca said she had to make concessions in order to get the movie made. While she wasn't happy about those changes, she said she'll play along and show her support once the film is out. The production company hopes that will lessen any fallout. Rebecca also warned her fans on her social media pages that things will be different but quote, 'good different.'

Something I also learned about filming a movie is that it comes with a lot of downtime. Mylan told me he'd normally read a book or take a nap in between scenes. But with me there, we'd fuck or cuddle or talk about nothing while talking about everything; our favorite colors (me: blue, him: black), foods (me: donuts, him: pizza), books (me: The Kit Davenport series by Tate James, him: Dune by Frank Herbert), movies (me: Titanic, him: Dune).

We shared our love of music. I was shocked when he told me his favorite band was Queen. He mostly listens to classic rock, which explains why he chose Journey to sing that first night of Rock Star Karaoke.

While John Mayer is my all-time favorite artist, my favorite song is *We Belong* by Pat Benatar. The song embodies happy memories for me. Every time it came on the radio, my mother would stop what she was doing and turn up the volume. She'd come find me if I wasn't in the same room and then we'd have a dance party in the living room, twirling and jumping around until we were out of breath and sweating.

After telling Mylan that memory, he found the song on YouTube, turned up the volume on his phone, and we had an impromptu dance party in his trailer.

I love impromptu dance parties.

Mylan and I shared happy stories. Most of mine involved Tyler and Ginger.

I told Mylan about senior skip day in high school. Ginger, Tyler, and I drove to Memphis to walk around Beale Street. We stuffed ourselves with the best barbecue in the nation and snuck into a bar with our fake IDs. Tyler and Ginger got silly drunk while I stayed sober since I was the designated driver. I was always the designated driver, but that was by choice. After what happened to my parents, drinking just didn't appeal to me. Tyler wasn't much of a drinker either, especially during football season. The first time I ever consumed alcohol was in college. I hated the way it made me feel; out of control and sick to my stomach. People always found it ironic that I own a bar but don't drink.

Mylan told me about some of his favorite places he traveled. He showed me pictures and videos from his trips: the beaches of Bali, the ancient city of Marrakesh, the ghosts of New Orleans, the fairies of Scotland. I admitted how I'd never been out of the country and the only places I'd traveled were within driving distance of Silo, aside from my senior class trip to Disney World. I've lived such a guarded life, never allowing myself to follow my dreams.

Part of that was because that dream included Tyler. We both wanted to travel the world. We had planned to take the summer after college graduation to backpack through Europe, to wade in the crystal-clear waters of the Caribbean, to hunker down in an igloo in Alaska and watch the Northern Lights dance in the sky.

Then we'd return home and begin our lives together. I'd open my bar and Tyler would get a job mentoring troubled youth. We'd adopt or foster since I could no longer have children. Now that I'm older, the idea of having my own family gets further and further out of reach, because I never found anyone to begin that journey with.

Mylan and I talked about the happy memories, while avoiding conversations about our demons—our trauma that never seemed to relent.

One month.

It went by so fast. My days stayed busy, going to set in the morning then to Lilies at night to help, despite Ginger's griping at me that she and the staff had everything under control. I knew they did, but I still felt guilty for abandoning them.

"Spill," Ginger says, pulling me out of my thoughts. I'd been staring at the paperwork on the counter, absentmindedly chewing on my pencil. "You've got the look."

"You always say I have a 'guilty look' but never tell me what my face does to convey said guilty look."

She sets the last chair on the table-top so the overnight cleaning crew can come in to sweep and mop and walks over to where I'm leaning against the counter.

She boops my nose.

"Your nose scrunches up and twitches like a bunny. A mean bunny, but still."

I flip her off.

"The wrinkles around your mouth and between your brows also get more defined."

I gasp. "I do not have wrinkles." I take out my phone and throw on selfie mode to double check, frowning when I do, in fact, spot wrinkles.

Ginger bursts out laughing.

"Of course, you do, Lana Banana. You're old, like me."

"But you still look like you're in your twenties."

"Yeah, because Black don't crack."

"Jealous."

"What's bugging you?"

I sigh and set down my chewed-up pencil. Apparently, staring at the paperwork won't magically fill it out.

"I'm rethinking Jonesboro."

She rolls her eyes so hard I'm pretty sure I saw her shoulders roll too.

"We've talked about this."

"I know. But—"

"No buts. Lana, honey, we've had this worked out since the day that man walked through that door. I'll open the bar Sunday, Wednesday, and Thursday and Emily is going to close those days. She'll open Friday and Saturday, so I can be here at night when it's busy. She's been training for weeks now. She's ready. Plus, she's eager to boss people around."

I snort at that. I hired Emily a year ago. She's about ten years younger than Ginger and me. She left her stressful marketing job in Little Rock to move closer to her family in Silo. She bartended and waitressed in college, so she was an immediate hire. She's one of my best employees, so when she asked me about a managerial position, I was all for it.

"What about Monday and Tuesday?"

"Those are our least busy days. I keep telling you we should close on those days."

I open my mouth in horror, but Ginger cuts off my protest.

"Don't play dumb. Jesse manages Monday and Tuesday since we're both off. He'll *keep* working Monday and Tuesday, open to close. Stop looking for excuses and go!"

It's my turn to roll my eyes, which amuses her to no end.

"That's what I thought."

Ginger gives me a victorious look. She thinks she's won this battle.

"Let me present new evidence."

Ginger waves her hand in front of her. "Please approach the bench."

"Instead of staying up there the entire time, I'll only visit two days a week." Ginger blinks at me, waiting for me to explain. I sigh. "Mylan is the one who first suggested it and I think it's best. I'm worried about being on set every day, all day."

"You've been doing it for the past month. What's changed?" Realization hits and she narrows her eyes at me. "Are you worried about being on set or being around Mylan?"

"Both?"

"Banana," Ginger warns.

I hold out my hand, not to plead the fifth but to stop her whining, so I can explain.

"You know this is hard for me. If there's any hope for this ... relationship with Mylan to work out, then I need to take it slowly. *Slower*. Right now, it's intense. It's terrifying. This past month, I've had the option to leave and come here to the bar or to my apartment, my own space. I need a reprieve from the onslaught of painful memories tied with this movie, and I worry I won't have that there, on set with him, or in his trailer, or in his hotel. I don't want to get burnt out."

I also worry about how my not being there will affect Mylan's sobriety, but I have to trust him. I have to trust that he isn't relying on me.

Ginger stares at me, well, sort of. She's staring past me in think mode. She always disappears from reality when mulling something over. After at least a minute of hard thinking, she drops her shoulders in defeat. "The jury has reached a verdict."

She pauses (for dramatics).

"Reprieve granted." She opens her arms and I fall into them. "It's a good plan," she says in my hair. We hug for a while before she pulls away. "I'm proud of you."

I laugh, wiping away a lone tear.

"I'm serious. This is progress. Good progress."

I scrunch up my nose at her. "Then why do I have a sick feeling that it's all going to backfire?"

"Because love is a messy bitch."

I cough out another laugh and shake my head, returning to the paperwork I've been neglecting. I check the time on my phone. One in the morning.

"It's late. I'll finish up here. You go home."

Ginger's phone chirps at that moment, and she extracts it from her cleavage. She smiles at her phone, blushing.

"Good, because my ride is here."

She wiggles her eyebrows at me.

Before I can question who, though I should have known, Mylan and Bruno walk through the door. A door that should have been locked since we closed an hour ago. Ginger obviously knew these two were going to show up and left it unlocked.

"Hey babe!" Ginger squeals and nearly jumps into Bruno's arms. The two start making out in front of the door.

Ginger plans to visit Bruno on her days off. She hasn't admitted it to me yet, despite me asking, but I think she's falling for Bruno too. And by the massive grin on his face right now as she whispers likely naughty things in his ear, I'd say he feels the same way. However, I'm not sure if their love story will continue once filming is done because Ginger has her mother to care for. She could never leave Silo.

Mylan turns to me and opens his arms wide.

"I am not jumping into your arms," I muse.

He shrugs a shoulder and leaves his bodyguard and my best friend to their make out session. By the time Mylan leans onto the counter, picture perfect, looking like a model in one of those fashion magazines, Bruno and Ginger are stumbling out the front door of the bar. Ginger giggles as she locks up from outside then yelps, and I'm guessing Bruno is being very inappropriate with her.

I look away from the door and find a sea of blue staring back at me.

"Hi," Mylan says.

I blush and look down like I don't see his handsome face all the time. "I, uh, have to finish these receipts for the night, and I'll be ready to leave."

"Take your time." He smiles and rests his chin in his palm.

I try to concentrate on my work, but he's making it hard to do. Not once in the past five minutes has Mylan taken his eyes off me.

I slam my pencil down. "Are you going to stare at me the whole time?"

"I like to see you squirm."

My mind rewinds to the first time I was in his trailer—when he promised to punish me. He's yet to follow through on it. I brought it up once, and he said he wanted my punishment to be special, and we can't do that with long filming days and early call times. But now he's done filming here in Silo and filming at the college doesn't start for a few more days . . .

"I wanted to talk to you about Jonesboro." I don't look up from tallying the credit card slips.

Despite my lowered gaze, I still see Mylan lift his head and straighten his back. "I'm listening."

"I'm still going . . ."

"But?"

"But not the entire time."

"Donut—"

"I'll be there two days out of the week."

He stews over my confession with his mouth clamped shut, grinding his teeth before responding.

"You said you and Ginger worked out staffing."

"We did but I've been thinking . . ."

I proceed to tell him everything I confessed to Ginger—my concerns and my hopes about our relationship continuing beyond the end of filming.

"We need to spend time apart. I want to miss you. Because right now, I live, breathe, and consume you. Do you understand?"

A flash of hope crosses his face. It's the first time since that day in the trailer that I've given any indication of a future together.

"Okay."

"Okay?"

"Okay. I accept you coming to visit me twice a week if . . ."

I bite my lip. "If?"

"If you finally let me punish you."

Did he read my thoughts? How did he know I was just *thinking about this?*

"And what will I be punished for?"

"For telling me you'd be there the entire time then backing out."

I shift on my feet and try to ignore the heat flaring across my cheeks and chest.

"Mhm," Mylan hums. "Does that make you nervous, donut?"

"No," I say a little too quickly, which makes him smile wider than his bratty face will allow. "Not nervous . . . excited."

Why am I excited?

Probably because I read way too many smutty romance books. I never thought I'd find myself in a relationship that rivaled the bliss my favorite characters experience. I also discovered some kinks from reading those erotic books.

Like spanking, and praise, and being dominated.

Not that Mylan is a big dom. Are little doms a thing? Unless he's been holding back because of me—because he doesn't know what I can handle. To be honest, I don't know what I can handle either. The sex I had before him was vanilla as fuck.

The anticipation motivates me to finish paperwork in record speed and I'm tugging Mylan up the stairs to my apartment.

The moment I close the door and lock it, I blurt out, "So, do you, like, tie people up or . . ." My voice trails off the moment his smile turns cruel. Okay, clearly that was a dumb question.

"Oh, donut," he says through a sigh, approaching me as I lean back against the door. "Do you want me to tie you up?" His voice deep and full of desire.

"Um . . ."

He trails his fingers down the side of my face, to my neck and across my cleavage. Mylan's eyes rage with desire as he watches my heavy breathing, my heaving chest.

"I want you to spank me. Like you promised," I whisper.

He hums and leans in. I expect him to kiss me in the same spots his fingertips just touched. Instead, he huffs his breath along my jaw and my throat. I both love and hate when he does that. How he's touching me but *not*. That warm air is torture in the best way possible.

I arch away from the door, my stomach pressing up against Mylan's cock. It's hard and ready for me.

"I love this dress." He runs his fingers underneath the spaghetti straps of the simple white sundress with colorful flowers. "Do you love this dress?"

"It's all right. Not my favorite or anything." I shrug, and a growl rattles in Mylan's throat followed by him tearing the dress from my body with both of his strong hands. Literally ripping the fabric.

My heart kicks into action and my nipples rise.

What the fuck? Why the hell was that so hot?

"Oops," Mylan muses.

He's on me before I can curse him out for ruining my dress. His mouth claims a breast, sucking on my aching nipple. *He loves my breasts.* He laps his tongue and grazes his teeth over and over until I'm panting and wet.

Mylan's hand moves down my body, over all my stomach folds until he's slipping two fingers inside me.

I cry out, arching against him again. He pumps viciously, grinding his palm into my clit. He switches to my other breast, biting at my nipple before soothing it with his tongue. It's too much and not enough as my cunt clamps down on his fingers. I'm about to come.

He pulls out.

"No," I cry at the sudden absence. My pussy pulses, begging for something to grip on to.

"You'll come when I let you."

Oh. Okay he's that type of dominant?

He shoves his fingers in my mouth, the same ones that were just inside me.

"Suck."

Mylan groans when I do as he demands.

"See how good you taste, my little donut?"

He removes his fingers and takes my arm, pulling me away from the door. He walks us to my bed and stands me at the side. He lies down in front of me, leaning back on his elbows.

"Touch yourself."

I squeeze my legs together and Mylan tsks, tapping my ankles with the tip of his boot. "Keep those open. I want to see it dripping down your leg."

"Yes, sir," I taunt with a smirk.

"Donut," he warns.

Something comes over me and I start swaying my hips, despite there being no music. My hands are all over my body, my neck, my breast, twisting my nipples then moving my palms down my sides and over my stomach. I'm dancing for him, a personal dance like one you'd receive at a strip club. Except, I have no clothes to strip. Mylan knew I was braless and not wearing panties. He knew the only thing between him and my naked body was my dress.

So, he tore it to shreds.

Mylan's eyes ignite with need, with want, as he watches me. He bites his lip, then sweeps his tongue over the swollen bottom lip as I move my fingers down to my trimmed bush. I push them inside me and lock eyes with Mylan while I fuck myself. I use my other hand to keep caressing my body.

I pump faster but I need more, so I massage my clit while pinching my nipple harder. My orgasm builds from the friction and pressure. I'm on the edge of coming when Mylan stops me again.

"Not yet. I want to be the one to make you come."

"Brat," I murmur.

He heard me. I wanted him to hear me. I knew the moment I said the word he hates the most, he would explode. He leans forward to grab me by my arms and tosses me over his lap. How he's strong enough to hold me in place is beyond me, but he does.

I scream from the sting of his hand coming down on my bare ass.

"My bad little donut," he whispers on the top of my head. And he spanks me again and again, harder and harder with each whip of his hand. I moan and squirm and pant. "You like that?"

"Yes, please."

"Please, what, Lana?"

"More."

"More, what?"

Ugh why is he so frustrating?

"Fuck you," I say, and I'm rewarded with another slap, this one landing on my exposed pussy. I cry out, not expecting the harsh stimulation of my most sensitive area.

He plunges a finger inside me.

"You're soaked and ready, aren't you?"

I nod, biting my lip as Mylan slowly pushes in and out of me.

"You want to come?"

"God yes."

"No."

He stops fucking me with his fingers to rub the burning skin of my ass, soothing his punishment. It feels so fucking good.

He does that a few more seconds before picking me up off his lap and shoving me onto my back on the bed. He starts stripping—toeing off his boots, taking off his shirt, his pants, and his briefs. I appreciate his body, blanketing my gaze over his defined shoulders, the muscular chest, and down to his six-pack abs—abs that I'm drooling to touch. My eyes trail further down to find his dick, long and thick and pointing right at me.

He strokes himself and smiles, seeing my hunger for him. Then he's on the bed, crawling to me. Once close enough, he takes hold of my hair, tightening his grip, so he has full control of me. He kneels and brings my head down to his cock.

"Open."

I part my lips and he shoves his dick inside. I relax my throat, letting him go deep. He groans at how welcoming I am for him.

"I love the way your lips feel around my cock."

Then he fucks my mouth, rough and frantic and it makes my eyes water. I dig my nails into his thighs, breathing through my nose and swallowing so my throat constricts around him.

I move one hand to cup and massage his balls, and they lurch at my touch, tightening.

He's close, which surprises me when he pulls out. He lets go of my hair, and I savor the burn of how hard he was gripping the strands.

"Get on your stomach," Mylan orders and I do, loving this commanding side. Though, I can tell he's holding back. Not that I mind. I wanted a taste of domineering Mylan. Next time, I'll order the whole meal.

The moment I flip over, Mylan positions me so my head and chest are flat on the mattress, and my ass is in the air. The thick head of his dick nudges my entrance. He rubs it up and down, coating it with my arousal.

Then he slams into me, pushing my face into the mattress.

"Fuck, Mylan," I wheeze because it feels amazing at this angle.

He grips my ass, taking a handful like it's a handlebar, and he pounds into me. I'm moaning and screaming, reveling in the sound of our bodies clashing together. Mylan's palm claps down across my left cheek and I arch in response, not expecting that sudden pain.

"Your cunt is choking my cock so good right now, donut."

He smacks my right cheek this time, harder than the left side. He doesn't slow down. He finds a rhythm, punishing me then massaging the burning skin then spanking me again until my ass is on fire and I'm exactly as he predicted: soaked and begging for more.

He reaches an arm around my waist to rub my clit, keeping his thrusts ample, not relenting.

I buck at the rough touch and see stars as my orgasm explodes. Mylan pumps through my pussy walls tightening around him until he's coming too. Only then does he slow down.

He stays seated in me as we both catch our breath. He kisses my back, up the tattooed symbols along my spine. When he pulls out of me, I can feel his cum run down my leg. He cleans it up with his finger and puts it back inside of me.

Mylan collapses onto my bed on his back and I do the same, snuggling up against his side.

"Not sure why you considered that a punishment. I loved every single moment."

"Oh, donut," he says and kisses the top of my head. The small sentiment making my stomach flutter. "Just you wait."

Chapter 22 - Mylan

Lana fell asleep in my arms shortly after her first taste of my dominant side. I wouldn't say I'm a full-fledged Dom, nowhere close. Just enough to make my partner squirm and beg and fall to their knees before me. It's about control, especially when control is the one thing I'm bad at. When I'm sober, having that control in the bedroom is gratifying. I take pride in it.

If only I could redirect that control to other parts of my life.

I close my eyes trying to fall asleep, but Lana is snoring and it's annoying as hell but at the same time oh so adorable. Typically, noise doesn't bother me, being that my unimpressive superpower is falling asleep fast and anywhere, but tonight my head swims with scenarios.

What would my life look like with Lana by my side? Would she want kids? We'd have to adopt, obviously. I never wanted kids. I'd be a horrible father; too afraid I'd turn out like my own. But if Lana wants a family, I'd set aside my fears and strive to become the *best* father.

Would we become power philanthropists? Lana has inspired me to start my own organization. I already donate to plenty of charities, but what if I start a nonprofit to help people struggling like me?

Lana's head rests on my chest and I pet her hair. I'm pretty sure she's drooling on my bare chest, but I don't care. I lean down and kiss the top of her head, and she stirs.

"Tell me about your mother."

I freeze at Lana's words.

"I thought you were asleep," I whisper.

She hums and starts rubbing her palm up and down my stomach. The skin-to-skin contact is addicting. I need more so, I smooth my own palm along her upper arm, back and forth until she shivers.

"I dozed off. I used to have trouble sleeping."

"Really? When? You knock the fuck out when I'm around."

She lifts her head off my chest and smiles, biting her lip. I tug it out of her teeth.

"What?"

"After Tyler, I'd toss and turn with nightmares. Eighteen years of sleepless nights until you."

My breath catches in my throat. "Really? I helped?"

"You did." She kisses my chest before laying her head back down. I want to hear more about this. About how I help her sleep, but she's asking about my mother again. "You never talk about her. She's not . . ."

I shake my head, trying to form words. "No. She's not."

She doesn't say anything, waiting for me to explain. I've never talked about my mother with anyone. Not even Bruno. I told him where she is and why she's there but that's it. Eloise knows less than that. She probably thinks Marie Andrews is dead.

She almost died.

This part of my life has stayed out of the media, thanks to my amazing PR team. Even my Wikipedia page has few details, only mentioning my parents' names and my father's death fifteen years ago. No more information about him or my mother. *How* my PR team managed this still baffles me.

"I had her committed when I was sixteen," I finally answer. "I was emancipated and given power of attorney over her."

"What happened?"

The fact that Lana doesn't offer her condolences or her pity right away is refreshing. I hate being pitied. I understand people's need to sympathize, but it becomes exhausting. All I ever want is for someone to understand. Lana could be that for me. She's had enough trauma in her life to understand.

I swallow the lump in my throat. For the first time, I actually *want* to talk about my mother.

"My father was abusive. He started with verbal attacks, telling my mother how pathetic and useless she was. Or how she was the reason I didn't cast certain roles."

I pause to take a deep breath because this is where it all goes downhill.

"I was six years old the first time he hit her, only a year after they pushed me into acting. We were struggling since I hadn't booked a lot of roles and I needed a haircut for an audition. She couldn't afford taking me anywhere, and my father refused to give her money, so she tried cutting it herself. Man, she fucked it up. I ended up losing the role, but not because of the horrible haircut. I lost the role because I was nervous throughout the whole audition. I flubbed lines, or forgot them altogether, thinking about what would happen when my father saw the uneven hairline along my forehead. I mean, he'd yell at my mother for literally breathing the wrong way so what would he do about this?

"Before we returned home, my agent called to say I didn't get the role. My father had answered. He was so angry, and the moment we walked in the door, he took one look at me and that was it. He blamed my mother and cursed her out, screaming at the top of his lungs before backhanding her so hard, she hit her head on the wall and blacked out. I rushed over to try to wake her up. It took at least a minute. My father didn't even check on her. He retreated to the living room, drowning himself in a bottle of vodka. He didn't care if she lived or died by his hand."

Lana leans up on her elbow, holding her head with her palm. She's listening and not an ounce of judgment shows on that angelic face of hers.

"That wasn't the last time he hit her. Anytime he drank, he'd find something to get mad about. She never called police though. She'd always patch herself up and sleep off the injuries. She went to the hospital once, but they asked her too many questions, it spooked her. She made up some lame excuse that the hospitals bought because they were too busy to care or too overworked to pay attention to the signs.

"This went on until I turned ten. My father died a couple weeks later. My mom was the one to find him. He was passed out in his favorite chair, and she sat down to watch television. She thought he was taking a nap, which he did often in that chair. After he didn't wake up to demand she fetch him a drink, she realized that something was wrong.

"I couldn't understand why she was so devastated over his death. He was an abusive fuck. I don't know, I guess she loved him despite everything. In the six years following my father's death, my mother slowly lost her sanity. She blamed herself. She would always say if she didn't make him mad, if she didn't push him to drink, he'd still be alive. She blamed me a few times too.

"I endured six years of this. Her blaming me, blaming herself, her passing out on depression meds, sleeping for weeks at a time without checking in on me. It was a different kind of mental abuse because I was neglected by the one parent I loved.

"I worked as much as legally possible, so I wasn't around to see her gradually killing herself. She was in denial, and I was just a kid. I had no idea what to do. She refused to get help."

Sounds familiar. Is this how Jensen felt?

I push the thought away.

"I began the emancipation process on my sixteenth birthday when I had enough money saved and roles booked. The moment I had full legal control over my finances and my estate, I sent my mother away to a mental institute. A nice fucking one, where she's still living."

"Do you ever see her?" Lana asks.

I wince. "Not as often as I should. I try to visit around the holidays, on her birthday or on my birthday . . ."

"Your birthday is in September, right?"

I feign shock and hurt. "You don't know? I know *your* birthday."

"Oh yeah?"

"April twenty fourth. You turned forty shortly before I arrived."

"I don't remember telling you that."

"I Googled you."

Her eyes widen.

"What? You get to Google me, but I can't Google you?"

"Stop saying Google. You make it sound dirty."

I chuckle and kiss her forehead. "What's dirty is you not remembering my birthday. Also, you saw my I.D. that first night."

"Oh, you think you made that good of an impression?"

"Yes."

She slaps at my chest.

"September thirtieth," I answer.

"Oh right."

"I thought you didn't remember?"

"I just knew it was in September. Believe it or not, I didn't memorize everything about your life."

"I'm offended."

"Haven't you had stalkers in the past?"

"I still have stalkers, but they're not you. I'd love if you stalked me."

"You're such a weirdo."

"I'm your weirdo."

Silence stretches between us, and I worry that Lana fell back asleep. I should go to sleep too.

"Why do you do it?" Lana asks, her voice quiet and forlorn. "Why do you drink when it caused so much trauma in your life?"

"The booze is a problem only when I pair it with pills or other drugs."

"Do you really believe that?"

I suck in a sharp breath. I *do* believe that. "I can handle myself when I'm just drinking alcohol. The pain pills, the other shit I put in my body, it takes me away from reality. I turn to it when life gets to be too much."

"I read some articles about your past stints. Did they not offer you therapy?"

I snort. "Of course, they did. I guess I'm too fucked up for it to work."

"Or it didn't work because you didn't allow it. You weren't ready. You have to want to get better. You have to have something to live for."

My chest burns with guilt. With . . . regret. She's right. I can't tell her that, though. I'd have to tell her *why* this last stint was different. I change the subject.

"Tell me about the symbols tattooed on your spine." It's the one thing she hasn't shared with me. I only see the tattoos when we're naked, or when she wears a backless outfit, and before I can ask, her body distracts me and I'm touching and fucking her.

She sighs and my stomach tightens at the feel of her breath on my skin. "I know you're changing the subject because you don't want to talk about this anymore, and I'm going to let it slide."

"Because you do it to me all the time?"

I can't see her face, but she definitely rolled her eyes. She leans up and turns her back to me, swooshing her dark red hair out of the way. I run my palm up and down her back. I smile when she shivers and goosebumps surface along her arms.

"I got them on the tenth anniversary of Tyler's death. They're minimalist designs—a timeline of our life. From bottom to top: the water and sun represent the lake where Tyler and I met. The two faces kissing indicates our first kiss. The fireworks are from our senior trip to Disney World. The crowns are for when we were named Homecoming King and Queen, not only in high school but in college. The two interlocked rings for when he proposed. The two crosses for his death but it also symbolizes Tyler's Team. Finally, the tiger lily. To signify a new life. A new beginning. A life without him."

"They're beautiful." I slide my palm over the tattoos again. "The flowers on your arms are tiger lilies too?"

She twists back around, and I open my arm so she can return to my side.

"Yes. So are the flowers planted at the front of the bar and at my grandparents."

"They must be your favorite, especially since you named your bar Lilies."

"They are. My mother's too because of what they symbolized: rebirth. She always believed in second chances. And she was so optimistic. Even about the bad things in life. She would always say with every negative, a positive must occur. Yin and Yang. The universe is all about balance and if you're experiencing the bad, the good is soon to follow."

"What if all you've experienced is bad for twenty-five years?"

"Do you really think that Mylan?"

I shrug.

"You've had a lot of bad things happen to you but there's been plenty of good."

I'm having a hard time believing her. She must sense that because she starts listing them off.

"You've brought this world your wonderful talent. You're giving Tyler life again."

"My talent. Sure. That's all I'm good for."

"Are you kidding me?" She sits up and the restraint I have to not look at her tits is impressive. "I've read about all the charities you donate to. How you've paid off debts for some of the crew members of the productions you worked on without them even asking. Because you talk to them, you care enough to ask them questions about their life and their families. You hear about their struggles, and you don't think twice about stepping in to help. Also, didn't you literally go build homes in India for a few months after a devastating tsunami?"

I nod.

"You're always willing to greet your fans or help them when they reach out to you. You always listen when they tell you about how your movies have gotten them through hard times. You treat them like they matter."

My throat burns with an emotion I never let free. Pride. It's coming from Lana. She sounds so proud of me. It must be contagious.

"Your life is only beginning, Mylan. So much good is in store for you because, believe it or not, you're a *good* person."

A tear drops on my cheek. Another and another until I'm crying. This time, Lana is the one to kiss my tears away. She's so gentle with me.

I don't deserve you. I don't deserve you. I don't deserve you.

I must have been saying it out loud because Lana responds with *You do, you do, you do.*

Our bodies interlock in a mess of legs and arms. We hold each other, intertwined so tightly, not even a piece of paper could fit between us.

We both fall asleep like that.

Chapter 23- Lana

I'm angry at how fast these two months have gone by. Two months of driving to Jonesboro to visit Mylan and having just forty-eight hours with him each week. I tried to come on his days off, which were never consistent. One week he'd only have one day while the next they'd work him every single day. Some days they only needed him for four hours, while other days he was filming for eighteen.

If he had to be on set during one of my visits, we'd take advantage of the downtime in his trailer, making up for missed days by giving ourselves to each other. Then, after a long day on set, we'd return to his hotel room, fuck once more before collapsing into some of the best sleep either of us had ever experienced.

Two months and I'm exhausted. Mylan must be exhausted as well. The crazy filming hours are taking a toll on him because he's different from the first month of knowing him. I can't quite pinpoint what exactly has changed and every time I ask if he's okay, he says he's fine and just couldn't sleep without me.

I've been struggling without him as well.

Two months and I still don't know what will happen next. We've talked about it. He knows I want him in my life, and I know he wants me to go to L.A. with him but that's the one part holding me back from making this huge, life-changing decision. He's also made it clear that if I don't go to L.A., he will uproot everything to stay with me in Arkansas. How can I do that to him? He has so much life to live and I'm worried I'll hold him back. I worry he'll get bored with me. I worry about him falling back into his addiction. Concerns I've yet to discuss with him because what if he agrees and leaves me?

I know he wouldn't, but my irrational brain is trying to convince me of it.

Still, he hasn't pushed me for my answer. He *knows* how hard this is for me. He's so patient and sometimes I tell myself I don't deserve him.

"You come over here after abandoning us for three months and all you're going to do is stare at your food while it gets cold?" Gram grumbles, crossing her arms over her sagging boobs in her signature muumuu. Her voice startles me and I force myself back to the present.

"Sorry. I have a lot on my mind."

"If it's about that boy, then I hope you're thinking about your future with him."

"Et tu, Brute?"

"What's holding you back?"

"Leaving here."

"You can come back and visit. Hell, Pa and I need a vacation. We'll come visit you."

"I could stay, but then he'd stay. And I can't allow him to throw his life away."

"Throw it away? Lana, why on earth do you believe he'd be throwing away his life to stay here with you?"

"His career . . ."

"He's an actor. One who has a lot of money, right?"

"Well, yes—"

"So, he doesn't need to act full time. He could take on jobs whenever he wants. One a year and be gone, what? Three months at a time? You could go with him. Take some time off. Imagine all the adventures, Lana."

It makes so much sense, I can't argue. I don't say a word.

Gram opens her mouth to say something more, then snaps it shut. She stares at me for the longest thirty seconds of my life, saying more with those wise eyes than her words could ever convey.

"What's the real reason?"

"I . . . There's still a part of me that isn't ready. This grief—"

Gram's curse cuts off my words and I cover my mouth in shock because I rarely hear her drop the f-bomb.

"I'm going to tell you something and you better listen up, child," Gram begins, her thick country twang like molasses that cocoons my body, holding me captive and forcing me to listen. "There will always be pain with grief, but there's no reason to suffer from it. You've let Tyler's death haunt you for the past eighteen years. I understand it. When your mother died, I thought I would never be okay. Then one day, I was. Because I knew no matter where she was, she was at peace. Don't you think Tyler is at peace?"

"Yes, of course."

"Then why do you keep putting yourself through hell?" She shakes her head. "Tyler wouldn't want this for you. You should have moved on years ago."

I gasp at the harsh words, my eyes watering. "Don't you think I tried? The book and this movie? My grief keeps getting thrown back in my face. Moving on hasn't been an option."

"Bullshit."

"Gram?" I cry.

"Lana Banana, you're scared. I get that. You're worried that if you move on, you'll forget Tyler. That the love you had for him will be tarnished. You have to know that it won't."

My lip shakes as I let the tears fall. She's right and I hate it. I also can't forget Tyler's final words to me before he passed.

You have so much love to offer, Lana. Don't be greedy. Share it with someone special. Someone who deserves it.

Greedy.

A word Mylan likes to use. Your greedy kisses. Your greedy body begging for my touch. Your greedy cunt.

I've tried to share my love with other men but none of them were ever as special as Tyler. I keep telling myself Mylan is different.

He *is* different. He came into my life when I needed him the most. Now I'm ready to move on to the next step with him. I'm so scared but Gram is right. I can't let this fear hold me back any longer.

Today is the last day of filming—a night shoot. Call time is at sunset. They're shooting the football game. The one where Tyler collapsed. I'm picking Ginger up in a couple hours and we're driving there. We're going to be background actors in the crowd at the stadium. Jensen promised to place us near the front, so we'll be in plenty of the shots.

Then tomorrow night, after everyone gets some sleep, a wrap party will be held back here in Silo at the town's convention center.

I'll tell Mylan then.

I'll tell him I want to go back to L.A. with him. I want to go with him because I need a change in my life. I need to stop hiding and take those adventures Tyler and I had planned.

After tonight, there are still two weeks of production on a sound stage in Hollywood—the cancer scenes. Mylan can't lose weight or shave his head to appear sick, so to achieve this, he'll wear a green-screen suit paired with a ton of makeup.

Movie magic.

That will give me two weeks to figure out what I'm going to do with my bar. I need to talk to Ginger about this. Would she want to take over ownership? She's been hot and heavy with Bruno like I have been with Mylan, but she's already told me it has to end. She could never leave Silo, not while her mother, who has dementia, is still alive.

Giving Ginger my bar would be an honor. I know she'd take wonderful care of it. She'd continue my entrance ritual in an attempt to lower the number of drunk drivers on the roadways.

Yes, this is my plan. It's time for me to move on with my life, and if whatever this is between Mylan and I doesn't work out, then I had an adventure. I experienced another great love. I will always have Silo to return to. I'll always have my family and friends.

"That's more like it," Gram says. I glance up at her, not realizing I disappeared into my thoughts again. "You're smiling because you've decided, haven't you?"

I stand and give Gram a kiss on her cheek. I yell goodbye to Pa, who's dozing in his recliner in the living room, an old western blaring on the television, and he grumbles a goodbye. Then I leave and head to Ginger's house to pick her up.

Driving the three hours to Jonesboro is bittersweet this time. Almost as if it's the final trip. The one offering closure. Ginger, Tyler, and I used to make this drive every weekend. We'd leave campus Friday evening and return to Silo to visit our families, then return to Jonesboro on Sunday nights, blaring top 40 hits, and songs from the 80s and 90s.

Ginger insisted we take her car today saying my VW Bug is a piece of shit and she doesn't want to listen to the Spice Girls' Spice album on repeat. Ginger's Camry is still at least fifteen years old, but it has air conditioning and an upgraded stereo system with Bluetooth. We connect her phone to a nostalgia channel so we can rock out to all the songs we listened to in high school and college.

We're fired up, not only excited about being extras in the movie, but because I told Ginger my plan. She responded with a high-pitched squeal, telling me how it would mean the world to her to be able to take over running Lilies.

We arrive to campus as the sun sets. The sky ignites in a wonderful ombre of cotton candy colors. It's hot but the decent breeze will offer some relief when we're sitting in the metal stands for the next several hours.

A lot has changed since the last time I was here, which was close to ten years ago. More dull gray buildings have been erected, but the boring architecture is livened up with trees and colorful flowers. The landscaping is the best part of the campus, almost offering a serene environment for the students to counter the stresses of classes, tests, and planning a future.

After driving past all the buildings, we finally reach the football stadium, located off campus, half a mile away. We park in an area sectioned off for crew members, next to rows of the same white trailers I saw at Silo Springs High School, designated for the cast, or used to store filming equipment.

We're greeted by a beefy security guard giving off The Rock vibes who escorts us to set. We pass by white tents erected to house more equipment. There's also a tent for food and drinks with a neon green paper sign reading *Craft Services.*

Past the tents, background actors line up in groups, waiting to be herded into the stands. They spot us and start waving, calling my name and some even yelling Ginger's name. We smile, wave back, and beg Beefy Security Guy to let us go over there for selfies and autographs. He shakes his head no, saying something about orders to bring us directly to Mylan Andrews.

Five minutes later, we arrive at the holding area where Mylan and other cast members are waiting to begin filming the first scene. Michelle Miller takes one look at Ginger and me approaching and snarls, turning on her heel to leave.

Good riddance.

Next to the holding area is Jensen's tent, where important crew members whose titles I can't remember huddle to go over the shot list. Jensen offers us a smile and a nod but appears too busy to come over to chat.

Mylan scoops me up in his arms the moment I reach him, and I yelp when he swings me around. I'm more surprised that he was able to lift my two hundred-some pound ass off the ground than the actual spinning around part. He sets me down after a few twirls and kisses me hungrily before taking my hand and leading me to a row of flimsy director chairs.

Ginger and Bruno are full-fledge making out, and I cough loud enough that they break apart. She flips me off but joins me with a smiling Bruno following.

I step aside and wave my hand at a director's seat with Ginger's name on it.

"I get my own chair?" she squeals.

Mylan smiles, tugging me against his side. "Lana already had one, so I asked the props department to make yours the moment I found out you were going to be an extra tonight."

"You did this for me, Mylan Andrews?" Ginger asks, her voice a pitch higher. She brings him in for a hug, which also includes me. Then Bruno is wrapping his long, strong arms around the three of us.

"Isn't this heartwarming?" Rebecca purrs as she walks into the tent.

We break apart and Ginger scowls. "Becca."

"Ging," Rebecca answers, her tone matching my best friend's. The two are working on being civil around each other but they still have a ways to go. I told Ginger she's actually been nice during this whole filming process.

To be fair, Rebecca never hated Ginger. Ginger also admitted that not including her friendship with Tyler and me in the book stung, but she ultimately understood and accepted Rebecca's reasoning. Her dislike for Rebecca came during the years of constant calls, texts, and e-mails during the long process of getting the book turned into a movie. Ginger saw how it hindered my progress in grieving Tyler.

How it stopped me from moving on. She felt Becca pushed me too hard.

Rebecca only wanted me to be involved because it was my life and love story. I *did* want to be involved. Then it started to weigh down on me. Still, I felt obligated to stick with it.

Until I could no longer hold myself together. Until the constant reminder of his death finally broke me.

Telling Rebecca I no longer wanted to help devastated her. She couldn't understand and interpreted my leaving the project—as she called it—as an attack on her personally. She'd said some cruel things, and *that* is why my best friend started hating her. Ginger's hate was stronger than mine because I understood how abandoning the process left Rebecca alone in her own grief. I felt guilty but, in the end, I had my own mental health to worry about.

Rebecca apologized a few weeks later for the things she said but the damage to our relationship was done. Now, we're repairing that relationship and reconnecting through the filming of Tyler's legacy.

Ginger tries out her director's chair. She struggles to sit in it, like I did that first time, but the moment her ass hits the seat, she beams and pulls out her phone. She starts taking selfies, breaking out her duck lips and winking at the camera. "Babe." She summons Bruno over. "Take a picture of me from the back. Make sure you can see my name."

Rebecca shakes her head at Ginger and turns to me. "Final day. How are you feeling about everything?"

I smile, genuinely. "It's been wonderful. I'm glad I got to be part of the process. And I'm sorry—"

Rebecca holds up a hand. "It's all water under the bridge." She focuses her attention on Mylan, patting him on the shoulder. "As for you, thank you for doing this role justice."

"Of course." Mylan blushes. I haven't seen Mylan blush often, but I have to say, it's the most adorable thing in the world. Adorable to me but uncomfortable to Mylan. He turns away from Rebecca's praise and says to me, "I have to get ready. See you in about an hour."

He gives me a long, deep kiss that leaves *me* blushing as he jogs away with Bruno trailing. I spot Eloise sitting on a black and silver storage box, scrolling through her phone. She snaps up her head as Mylan approaches. He stops to say something to her, and she barks out a laugh that has me smiling.

They're a family: Bruno, Eloise, and Mylan. I hope Mylan realizes that. He always talks about not having a family, but he does. One that is about to include me.

"You two getting serious?" Rebecca asks, sitting next to me.

I shrug.

"Yes," Ginger answers for me.

"I think . . . I mean, I know . . ."

"She's going to go back to L.A. with him," Ginger blurts out, and I give her a scowl. She sticks her tongue out at me.

Rebecca leans back in shock before offering me a smile. "I think that's great Lana. I do." She takes one look at my face and holds up a hand. "Do not feel bad about this for my sake."

Damn. Is my guilt face that obvious?

"I know you loved my brother deeply, and because of that, your grief will never go away. But what's great about love is how it heals broken hearts. Love can make grief's pain bearable. If Mylan is the one to offer that to you, then you have my blessing. And my parents' blessing. Hell, you had their blessing the day you brought that man over to their house. They adored him."

I laugh and sob at the same time and Rebecca gracefully stands from her flimsy chair to give me a hug. It's brief because she knows the longer she holds me, the more I'll cry. She rubs my arms and sits back down.

"I would hug you too, Lana, but if I get out of this chair, I'm never getting my fat ass back in it." Rebecca and I burst into a fit of giggles at Ginger's words.

Jensen walks over at that moment to a group of giggling grown women. He raises those perfectly groomed brows at us, possibly questioning our sanity, and says hi to me then Ginger.

"Becky," Jensen grumbles, refusing to look Rebecca's way.

"Jenny," she counters.

He curses and mumbles something about Mylan telling people about that stupid nickname. He continues to ignore Rebecca and turns back to Ginger and me. "We're ready for you to take your place in the crowd."

"Oh em gee, Banana," Ginger shrieks. "I'm going to be famous!"

Jensen lets out a nervous laugh. This man strikes me as an introvert working in an extroverted field. Or maybe he's not used to energetic personalities like Ginger's.

Jensen nods my way. "Thank you for doing this. The fans were hoping for a cameo by the real Lana Young." He scans the set. "All my PAs are busy wrangling the background actors, there's a lot tonight, so I'll take you two over to your marks if you want to follow me."

He turns and walks away, pausing at a nearby tent to say something to a crew member.

Before following, I lean in to Rebecca. "How very sweet of him."

She snorts and crosses her arms. "He's nice to everyone but me."

"I think it's because he likes you." I smile and wink then leave to let that sink in with her.

Rebecca's not a serial single lady like me. She's had a few long-term relationships. She dated NFL players, actors, a politician once, and regular ole Joe's. Why she's single now is beyond me. However, the sexual tension between her and Jensen is palpable.

Jensen weaves us through all the equipment and busy bodies. He hands us off to the person in charge of placing background actors in the stands. They sit us exactly where Jensen said we'd be.

Front and center.

I pull two battery-operated fans out of my purse and hand one to Ginger. We're filming in the summer, but the home-coming game was played in late September when the nights start to chill, so we're wearing long sleeves. Some people are holding light jackets, too, which I assume they'll put on right before we start filming. I'm sweating bullets. I can't imagine how uncomfortable they'll be.

It takes another thirty minutes before the production team is ready. A lanky white man with his long white hair in a low ponytail stands at the bottom of the stairs and yells commands into a bullhorn.

"Clap, cheer, look excited! But don't make any noise! That will be added in later. And don't forget to make conversation with the people around you. Quiet conversation."

"We're mimes now?" Ginger snorts.

"Apparently."

Once the man is certain we understand our instructions, he leaves. I spot Mylan running onto the field with the rest of the cast. He stops to talk to Jensen and after about a minute, they both look our way.

Mylan flashes me his wonderfully white teeth then blows me a kiss. I catch it and store it in my purse. He winks and puts on his helmet.

Ginger bumps my shoulder with hers. "You okay?"

"I am. What about you?" I noticed how wide her eyes got when Mylan ran out.

"I'm not going to lie; he looks like Tyler in that uniform. It's creepy." She laughs and shudders.

I lean my head on her shoulder and she rests her head on mine. We stay like that until minutes later when the production crew starts belting out commands.

Mylan and his movie-teammates huddle and Jensen yells Action! A boom mic hovers as they say their lines but we're too far away to hear the words.

They do the huddle scene over and over again before moving on to action shots of the game. After at least a dozen takes of that, possibly more since I wasn't counting, the crew resets and they shoot the exact same thing but at a different angle.

Five hours of fake yelling, quiet cheering, and miming our conversations, I'm exhausted. They announce a lunch break, which I take with Mylan, Ginger, Bruno, and Rebecca. We sit near the crafty tent at one of the many tables lined up for the cast and crew. Eloise pops in to snap some photos for social media then runs off to flirt with a tiny redheaded crew member who likely works in the props department based off the rolls of tape and a Fanny pack around her waist.

We take our seats back in the stadium after lunch (I ate some marinara pasta dish with sausage and Mylan had a light meal—grilled chicken and veggies—since he has to run up and down the field for the next several hours).

My heart starts racing and I find Ginger's hand, taking hold and squeezing hard.

"Ow, bitch." I loosen my grip.

"Sorry but look." I nod my chin at the end-zone.

Ginger follows my line of sight, confused for a moment until it sinks in.

"Oh," she whispers. "They're ready to film the collapse."

"Yeah." I let out a shaky breath.

When Tyler collapsed that horrible night, Ginger was as much of a mess as I was. How she was able to drive us to the hospital is beyond me.

After thirty minutes of getting the background actors in place, and the shots finalized, filming begins.

The first time Mylan collapses, I hold my breath.

When Michelle Miller runs out to the field and falls to his side, my tears begin to well.

When movie-Rebecca tries to tug movie-me away, my tears fall.

When the ambulance arrives and the movie-medics load Mylan into the back, something strange happens.

I stop. I stop crying. My chest stops hurting. My throat stops aching. And . . . I'm okay. Going to set for three months became easier, but I knew this scene would be the hardest. I knew it would be a test.

A test that I passed because I'm okay.

Jensen yells cut and the crew resets, the actors return to their marks and then they shoot it all over again. Then again and again at least twenty more times.

Each time, I watch the memory of the worst day of my life.

Each time, my grief retreats further down to that box I plan to keep it in.

This memory has now been captured on the big screen to last a lifetime.

Tyler's story is now complete.

Chapter 24 - Mylan

That's a wrap.

I probably collapsed on that field a hundred times tonight. After each fall, I'd turn to the crowd the moment Jensen yelled cut to see how Lana was coping. She was sitting too far away, so I asked Jensen to check on her. He returned a few takes later to say she was handling it like a rock star.

I meet Lana on the field after she exited the stands, and I give her a big sweaty hug that she gripes at me for being gross and smelly, but she still refuses to let go after we lose ourselves in our kisses.

It's late, well past two a.m. and I still have to give a couple wrap interviews for the onset documentary crew who films the behind-the-scenes footage.

I ask Lana if she wants to stay but she's struggling to keep her eyes open, so I send her back to the hotel with my room key. By the time I'm walking through the doors, she's fast asleep. I shower then crawl into bed, spooning Lana and wrapping my arm around her chest. I inhale her clean scent, her vanilla and berry body spray, and kiss her neck before I, too, surrender to my exhaustion.

We wake up late afternoon and eat breakfast in bed, thankful the hotel staff granted my special request for afternoon pancakes, eggs, and sausage. Once our bellies are full and teeth brushed, we make love.

I savor her body, dreading that this will be the last time I'm inside her. I fear that I'll never hear those small moans and gasps of pleasure. I anticipate that she'll take her love away and leave me alone like everyone else.

She knows I want her to come back to L.A. with me. She knows I would stay here for her. But she has yet to make the decision. It's far too important for me to push her.

If I asked her to make it too early, would she choose neither? I didn't chance it. Tonight, that changes. If she doesn't say anything first, then I will ask. I won't leave without her answer. Who am I kidding? I won't leave without her. I will stay here if she'll have me.

Another reason I haven't pushed her is because there are things about me that she still doesn't know. Things that might scare her away. Things I need to confess. Things I haven't told her yet in fear of ruining this blissful time with her.

The three-hour drive back to Silo is quiet, just me, Lana, and the driver. Ginger and Bruno follow in Ginger's Camry. I hold Lana's hand, caressing my thumb over hers and try to ignore the anticipation thick in the air.

Ginger and Bruno veer off to Ginger's house for her to get ready, and I drop Lana off so she can change and fix her face (her words, not mine, because her face is perfect). I told her I'd stay while she got ready, but she refused, saying I'd only distract her, and we'd end up fucking and make us late to the party.

True.

She didn't even want me outside waiting in the car, instead telling me to go and be social. What she really meant was go find Jensen because she wants us to repair our friendship.

My driver pulls up to the small convention hall where the city is allowing us to hold our wrap party. Lana donated the alcohol and Jerry and the Jerry Boys will perform. The old-fashioned diner Lana once took me to donated the food.

I'm one of the first to arrive. Eloise is running late, checking in to the hotel room she booked for tonight. I'll be staying with Lana, and Bruno with Ginger. Those two aren't here yet either. I'm not concerned about needing protection because there are two security guards at the door. They'll keep out any fans or media.

The band sets up in a corner and the wait staff puts the final touches on the food. I'm stressed beyond belief and need something to take the edge off. I wander over to the table of liquor bottles.

Three months since I was released from rehab, and I lasted a little over a month this time. *Confession number one.*

One month is the longest I've been sober since I began my downward spiral. I tried so hard not to drink. It started with one glass after a long day of filming. A lonely night of missing Lana. I had called and texted her that night, but she didn't answer. She must have been asleep. Of course, she was asleep. Yet, my anxiety began boiling. Doubt clouded my brain.

What if she's not asleep, and she's not answering because she doesn't want to talk to you?

What if she's not answering because it's over and she doesn't know how to tell you?

I needed to escape the toxic thoughts. I slipped out of my room, called an Uber because Jonesboro is in a dry county, and had the driver take me to the closest liquor store. I bought a bottle of whiskey.

The month I was with Lana, my addiction shifted to her. Without her, the need to calm my demons became unbearable.

So, I drank.

There I was alone in my hotel room with a full bottle of liquor and no one there to stop me. Not like that day on set when I nearly lashed out at Jensen, when my anger was mounting, and I was seconds from losing my temper. I'd been stopped by Lana's laughter, by the mere sight of her.

She wasn't there to stop me the night I decided to pour myself a glass.

Just one glass.

One glass one time quickly became one glass every other night, then one glass every night. I only stopped drinking on the days Lana came to visit. When everything was right again.

The more I drank, the more thoughts of disappointing Lana plagued my body. But the problem with addiction is it doesn't give a shit about guilt or regret.

Fuck, why am I like this?

I take a red plastic cup from the stack on the liquor table and pour some whiskey into it.

I swish the brown liquid around, contemplating if I need it. I don't. I *want* it. In one fast gulp, the drink is gone. I pour another and down that one just as fast.

By the time people are filing in, I have a good buzz. I'm relaxed. I'm ready for whatever Lana has for me. I mentally prepare myself to tell her I slipped, that I've been drinking. I'll tell her everything is fine. I can stop. She can trust me. She has to. If she's ready to begin a life with me, she has to trust I'll always be honest. That I'll always be around.

Except, I haven't been honest. I should have told her the moment I had the first drink two months ago.

This is a minor setback.

I'm finishing my fifth cup when Bruno and Ginger arrive. I greet them, managing to keep myself from swaying on my feet.

Shit. I went too far this time. I had one too many.

I lost control.

Bruno and Ginger are so wrapped up in each other, saying their final goodbyes because their hot summer fling will be ending after tonight, they don't notice I'm tipsy and on my way to drunk.

"Lana says she'll be here in ten minutes," Ginger says and giggles as Bruno smooches along her neck.

I respond by holding up my cup (as far as they know, it's water), and the two head off to a corner for privacy.

Panic nips at my nerves. I'm going to be drunk by the time Lana gets here. The minute she sees me, she'll know. It doesn't matter how many pieces of gum I shove into my mouth; she'll taste it on my kisses.

A chorus of chirps and dings fill the air of the small room. People take out their phones to check whatever alert was pushed from whatever news organization they subscribe to.

My own phone buzzes, and that's when I know the alert is about me. Because the only alerts I subscribe to are ones mentioning my name—and my addiction. I take my phone out of my pocket and glance at the screen.

Confession number two.

The room goes silent, chatter coming to a stop. The band is still setting up, oblivious to what's happening. All eyes turn on me, full of horror and pity.

I back up, slowly, until the backs of my legs hit the table holding the booze. A wave of déjà vu washes over me. Except, this time, Lana isn't here to walk me into a picnic table, and I'm certainly not backing her up to her bed.

This is me returning to rock bottom.

I turn and storm out of the room, dizzy from the booze and adrenaline coursing through my body. Once outside, I search for my driver, who parked the SUV in the first row. He's in the car, taking a nap when I open his door.

"Get out."

My booming voice jerks him awake. He's confused but he gets out. I drop down into the seat and slam the door shut. By the time the driver realizes I'm stealing his car, it's too late.

I'm gone.

I'm heading to Lana's.

Chapter 25 - Lana

I'm buckling the strap of my sandal when I hear a muffled boom followed by a faint rumble.

What the hell?

Did a transformer go out? It's happened before in the summer but it's not that hot out tonight. I walk over to the window facing the street in front of my bar and pause.

Mylan's driver's car.

No.

It can't be.

I waste no time and rush out my door, down the stairs, and over to the black suburban. The front end is smashed and the white sign that sits near the road to promote specials and bands for Lilies is a twisted mess.

I run over to the driver's side window, which is rolled down, and I gasp.

"Mylan?"

He stirs at my voice. His head lifting from the now deflating airbag. A small cut on his forehead bleeds.

"Lana?" He palms his forehead and opens the door, struggling to step out of the SUV. He falls the moment his feet hit the ground.

I crouch down to help him up and he takes my face in his hands.

"I love you, donut." My heart flutters because it's the first time he's said those words to me, and maybe I would have said it back if it weren't for the strong odor of booze.

He's drunk.

I stand, forcing Mylan's hold on me to drop. His shoulders droop and his head hangs.

He's fucking drunk.

My phone buzzes in my pocket, still on silent from being on set yesterday. I never turned the ringer back on because I didn't want anyone interrupting my time with Mylan. I forgot the ringer was off until now as someone frantically tries to get a hold of me.

An overwhelming sense of dread consumes me as I pull my phone out of my dress pocket and scan through the texts and missed calls from Ginger, Bruno, and Eloise.

The three are pulling up to the crash scene now, piled in Ginger's car.

"What the hell is happening?" I ask Mylan. He looks up from the ground through glazed eyes. His skin is clammy and pale.

"Lana, please, don't read the article."

"What article?" I don't let him answer. I go back through the texts, skipping the ones from my friend, Mylan's bodyguard, and his assistant. Instead, I select the one sent to me by the gossip queen of Silo Springs: Cara Calloway.

Mylan begs *please don't, please don't, please don't,* as I click on the link she sent.

My stomach dips.

Mylan Andrews' Brush With Death

Written by: Angela Borrows, *Entertainment Now*

Sources confirm to Entertainment Now that the troubled actor's latest stint in rehab was due to an intentional overdose. Mylan Andrews was rushed to the hospital after his assistant, Eloise Granger, found him unconscious in the living room of his Beverly Hills home. Sources tell us several empty bottles of pain pills and an empty bottle of whiskey were found next to Andrews's body. Paramedics arrived on the scene to a frantic Granger performing life-saving measures. According to the police report we obtained, Andrews wouldn't have survived had Granger not given him CPR.

I stop reading because I can no longer see through the tears. Ginger and Bruno stand nearby, not daring to say a word. Eloise is next to them, her eyes and cheeks glisten with tears.

By some miracle, there's not a paparazzi in sight. I assume they're all gone now that filming is done or maybe they found out where the wrap party is being held and are there now.

My eyes return to Mylan who is still on the ground, his back against the tire of the SUV. "You tried to kill yourself?"

He sighs and leans his head back, closing his eyes. "Yes."

It's all he says. I wait for him to explain. He's not going to.

Eloise walks over to Mylan and hands him a water. He drinks it. All of it.

"Why?" I demand once he tosses the empty bottle the ground.

He stands, wavers, and plants a hand on the vehicle to keep himself upright. "Can we go somewhere else to talk about this?" He glances to our friends. Their heads are lowered, sad and disappointed.

"No. They need to hear it too."

He sighs, defeat weighing down on him. "Because I thought that was my only option. I thought I had let my life get so out of control, there was no hope left for me." The water, or perhaps the serious situation at hand, must have sobered him up fast. His speech isn't as slurred or incoherent. "I was losing jobs, no one would hire me. I fucked it all up and my career was over. I was a disappointment. And the people in my life, Bruno and Eloise, I was about to lose them. They were on the brink of quitting."

"Not true," Bruno says at the same time Eloise blurts out, "Bullshit."

Mylan purses his lips at them.

"Still, it wasn't fair to them. I thought if I . . . ended things . . . everyone would be better off."

"And now? Do you feel the same?"

"No. Of course not. I . . ." He moves closer to me, and I step back. The hurt that crosses his face stings.

"It's always going to be like this, isn't it?"

"No, Lana, this is nothing."

"Nothing? Mylan, you *drank*. You drank and crashed a car into my sign. And after knowing what happened to my parents—"

A sob cuts off my words.

"It won't happen again, I promise."

"You can't make promises you never plan to keep."

I cross my arms over my stomach. I was prepared to give this man my future. I was prepared to begin a life with him. How foolish was I to believe he was ready for that?

How did he get out after only thirty days? He needed to stay longer. I'm sure he worked his celebrity magic to stop them from keeping him.

"You fucked up. I told you the moment you fucked up, I'm out. And this," I point to the wrecked car, "this is unforgivable. You need help."

His face contorts with a few emotions. Fear, pain, anger. He sticks with anger.

"I need help? What about you? You think you're better than me because you have your life together. But do you? Do you really? Because I'm not the one who can't move on. You're living in the past."

My skin lights up in fury. "You're only saying those things because you're wasted and feeling hopeless. Do you think being cruel to push me away will protect you?"

He sobs and moves towards me too fast. I'm not able to stop him from wrapping his strong arms around me. He cries into my neck, fisting the fabric of my dress.

"I'm sorry. I'm sorry. I didn't mean it. Please. Please. Please. I'll get better. I'll get better for you."

"That's the problem, Mylan. You need to want to get better for yourself."

I let him cry for a few minutes, his tears soaking the exposed skin of my shoulder.

After a minute, at least, the sobbing subsides and he pulls away, hiccupping to catch his breath. "What if I'm too broken? What if I can't be fixed?" he whispers.

"You're not too broken. And you can be fixed." I palm his cheek.

"You'll never forgive me for this."

You fucked up. I told you the moment you fucked up, I'm out ... This is unforgivable.

I wince as my words repeat in my head. I shouldn't have said them. I was angry, and he's so vulnerable right now. Still, he needs to take responsibility.

"You can earn my forgiveness, Mylan, by getting help."

Pain, guilt, defeat.

He doesn't believe in himself. He doesn't believe he can get better to earn my forgiveness. He's giving up, and if I don't tell him now, I'll lose him.

"When Tyler died, I'd have moments in my life where something great would happen and my first thought was to tell him. Then I remembered he was gone. I had a lot of those moments because Tyler was supposed to be my forever. He was supposed to be there for graduation. He was supposed to be there when I opened the bar that I'd been talking about opening since I understood alcohol claimed my parents' lives.

"Now? Mylan, now that person is you. You are the one I want to tell these things to. You're the one I want to experience once-in-a-lifetime spectacular moments with, because I love you."

I hear a gasp to my right, probably Ginger.

Mylan wraps his fingers around my wrist to pull my hand away from his cheek. He drops it and takes a step back.

Shit.

It didn't work. He's shutting down. Building walls. It's almost as if something clicked into place inside his head. As if my words triggered . . . something.

"I can never be Tyler Taylor."

I suck in a sharp breath. "I'm . . . I'm not asking you to be."

"I can never give you the love you had with him."

"But I want *your* love."

"You don't deserve this. *Me*. You don't deserve this disease."

"Mylan, how can you—"

"I need to go." He turns his head to Eloise. "Call my accountant. Have him send Lana the money for the sign and tell him to pay the car company for the damage."

I step to Mylan and grab his arm. A flash of weakness crosses his face before he puts on a mask of defiance.

"What are you doing?"

"I'm letting you go."

"Like hell you are."

His clenched jaw loosens, his bottom lip shakes. "Lana, can't you see? Can't you see I'm in denial about my alcoholism and my addiction? You love me and I love you, but I realize now how much I rely on you. I drank because you weren't there to stop me."

"But I'm here now. I want to help. I want to support you. I'm here and I'll stop you."

"That's not your responsibility. I should be able to stop myself." He rubs his hands over his face, swaying slightly on his feet. "You are both my weakness and my strength. I do want to get better but in order for me to do that, I need a clean break because what I'm doing now . . . it's not working. I have to do this on my own."

"You don't. We're here for you."

"Please," he whispers. "If it doesn't work this time . . . If I . . ."

He can't say the words.

If I die.

I drop my hand and Mylan backs away slowly before turning around to head towards Ginger's car.

"You're wrong, Mylan Andrews. I *do* deserve you, disease and all. Don't you think for one minute that you're letting me go forever. I gave you my heart and you know how hard that was for me. So, it's yours. It'll be yours when you're better. When you're ready. Understand?"

He pauses at the passenger side door and nods, then he gets inside the car.

I watch as Bruno whispers to Ginger and she answers whatever he said with a hug and kiss on the cheek. With Bruno behind the wheel of Ginger's Camry, Mylan in the front seat, and Eloise in back, I watch as they drive away.

Chapter 26 – Mylan

T he car is silent as we head to the regional airport twenty miles outside Silo. Bruno drives, his hands tight on the steering wheel, turning his knuckles white. Eloise is in the back and every once in a while, she sniffles.

A phone rings and Eloise mumbles a hello upon answering. She gives a few "okay" answers, then hangs up.

"The plane will be ready in ten minutes. How much longer, Bruno?"

"GPS says fifteen minutes."

"Okay," Eloise whispers. More silence and I almost can't take it. "What about our stuff?"

"I'll send a courier to get it."

By the time we're pulling onto the tarmac to board my jet, the air of sadness in the car is near suffocating. Bruno barely puts Ginger's Camry in park and I'm jumping out. I know Bruno and Eloise follow when two more car doors slam shut.

"I'm not going." Eloise's strained voice stops me halfway up the plane's stairs. I turn to face her and she's *crying*.

Shit.

"I can't."

"I understand. I'm sorry, Eloise."

"Fuck you, Mylan." Her words slap me. "How could you do this? Again? After I . . ."

I walk back down the stairs until I'm an arm's length away from her.

"I saved your life."

"I know."

"You told me you'd stop. You *promised* me."

"I know."

"So why?"

"I don't have an answer for you, Eloise. Other than I'm sick."

She cries into her hands, and I step closer to pull her into a hug. I rub her back as she sobs into my shoulder. This is my fault. I let her down. I'm the reason for the worst day of her life. No one should ever be put into a position to play God. I'm only here because Eloise brought me back to life.

"This time will be different."

"How?" Eloise demands. "Why should we believe you?"

"Because I'm going away for longer this time. Before I left Forest Ridge this last stint, they urged me to go to a year-long recovery program. I refused because of my pride. Because I thought it wouldn't help, and I'd get better on my own."

Eloise scoffs.

"I know. What a fool I was. Dummkopf." *Idiot.* "But now I understand. Now I'm ready. Now I have this family who I constantly hurt, and I hate myself for repeatedly doing that."

Bruno rubs the back of his neck. His eyes are shining with tears. I can't remember ever seeing Bruno cry. "Now you have a family? You realize we have *been* your family for a long time, right? That we've cared about you as a friend and a brother for a very long time. You know that, right?"

I bite my lip because as much as I wanted that, I never let myself believe it. I didn't think I deserved it.

"Mylan," Bruno sighs and drops his arms to his sides. *Mylan.* He called me by my name. He never does that. "Yes, you are my boss, but protecting you stopped being a job the moment you treated me like family. You showed me your heart."

"Cheesy," Eloise snorts.

"Huh? No, I do not want cheese. What are you talking about?"

"Never mind, Bruno. Keep going."

"You stopped being a boss when you paid my family's debts. You saved their lives because they owed a lot of money to some very bad people. Then you moved them to a new home far away from those people, set up a state-of-the-art security system to protect them, and even hired 24/7 guards."

"I had the money, so . . ."

"Yes, you did, but Mylan, it's not just about the money. If it was just about the money, if you didn't care, you wouldn't ask me how Mutter and Vater are settling in at their new home in their new town. How Vater's steel sculptures are selling. I know you bought them all anonymously, triple his asking price."

He knew about that?

"You talk to them on the phone despite not knowing a word of German. You went above and beyond for *me*. Bosses don't do that. Family does."

Bruno lays a heavy hand on my shoulder, and I'm crying and then he's pulling me into a hug. We part and I turn to Eloise.

She holds up her hands. "I already reached my crying quota for the year, so don't expect me to get all mushy like the big guy."

I laugh. "I'd expect nothing less."

She bites her lip, which lets me know she *does* have something to say to me. "When I came out to my parents, you were there for me."

I nod. My jaw tightens remembering the devastation on Eloise's face when she returned to L.A. after a visit home for her cousin's wedding.

"Midwest Christian parents find out their only child is a raging lesbian, and they disown her. Shocker."

She pauses, offering me a sad smile.

"I'd only been your assistant for six months, but you didn't hesitate to give me time off."

"Which you didn't take."

"Because you were my escape. You let me vent, let me cry, let me get stupid drunk. I never had siblings but, on that day, almost two years ago, I gained a brother and you've been supportive of me ever since as I slowly repair my relationship with my parents. My parents who were too quick to cast me aside, and you were faster to pick up my pieces. Bosses don't do that. Family does. So, yeah, you're our family asshole."

"I'm your asshole," I say and cringe. "No, wait, that sounded bad."

Eloise laughs and wipes a tear. Look at us, three emotionally closed off assholes crying on the tarmac in the middle of nowhere.

"So, what happens now?" Eloise asks.

I sigh, blowing out a long stream of breath to prepare myself for my next words. "I'm relieving you both of your positions."

"What?" they say in unison.

"I'll pay your salary while I'm in recovery. After that, you are welcome to come back and work for me, but I wouldn't blame you if you didn't."

Neither of them speaks, though I can see how badly they want to argue or fight me on this. Still, they don't.

"Do you really have to let us all go?" Eloise says.

"It's the only thing I haven't tried. I have to hope it's the one thing that will work."

Chapter 27 - Lana

*D*onut *and the Brat.*

I lost count of how many times I traced over the carving of our nicknames on the wooden counter of the bar where Mylan used to sit. He must have snuck in and carved it when he dropped me off before heading to the wrap party. It was fresh and big enough that I spotted it the moment I walked by.

That was a year ago.

He cut everyone off. Even Bruno. Even Eloise. Especially me.

Bruno and Eloise would at least receive an email from him once a month telling them he was alive and doing well.

That he was getting help.

I'm not going to lie, he broke me. I cried for weeks when my texts stopped delivering. My calls also stopped going through because he either blocked me or disconnected his number. His social media went dark. People thought he died. His PR team assured the world that he wasn't dead and was at a year-long rehabilitation program—location unknown.

Weeks before the Labor Day weekend release of *Tyler's Team,* everyone anticipated his return. Jensen and the production company were assured that Mylan would be there for the press junkets and the red carpet.

He never showed for the press junkets. Those interviews began weeks ago, and Mylan is still M.I.A.

Now it's the morning of the big Hollywood premiere. I won't be there because Mylan cut me off, he let me go.

I told him my heart was his when he got better. It's been a year, and he's yet to claim it. That's my answer. He doesn't want my heart. Which means he won't want to see me, if he even shows himself, and to be honest, I can't let him see how broken I am without him.

Ginger and Bruno ended their hot summer fling, despite Bruno no longer having the job of protecting Mylan. He could have moved here to be with Ginger, but he said he had to take care of family things in Germany. Four months ago, he called to offer his condolences for Ginger's mother Gracey passing away. They talked for hours, catching up about life. I'm confident the two will end up together again because not a day goes by that Ginger doesn't somehow bring Bruno up in the conversation.

My life went on, just with a piece of it missing. A piece that I will never get back. Another hole that can never be filled, like the hole left by Tyler.

I'm doing last minute checks before opening the bar when Ginger barges in.

"Turn on the TV," she orders, out of breath. She slams her purse on the counter.

Rude.

I find the remote underneath some paperwork and hand it to Ginger. She turns on the TV then flips through channels.

"What's going on?"

She waves me over. "Just watch."

She turns up the volume. A commercial ends, and the opening to one of those morning television programs plays. A beautiful Black woman wearing a fashionable suit I could never pull off, appears on the screen.

"A year after falling off the radar to work on his addiction, Mylan Andrews is back."

My heart lurches, and I step closer to the TV.

"His new movie, *Tyler's Team*, premieres tonight in Hollywood and he's here now to talk about what we can expect. Before we discuss the movie, you wanted to update everyone on your recovery?"

"Yes. Thank you, Ariah." Mylan shyly dips his head before looking at the camera. He shifts in his seat. He's nervous as hell. "For the past year, I've been at a live-in recovery center in Northern California, taking a break from my life so I could treat my disease. I've been healing, mentally and physically."

He gulps and picks up a glass of water on the table next to him. He takes a sip and continues.

"I've been sober for a year and a week now."

"How wonderful, Mylan. Congratulations," the anchor says, gently placing her hand on his knuckles. A pang of jealous passes through me, which is ridiculous, so I quickly push it away.

"I've also reconnected with my mother. You don't know much about her because I never allowed her story to be in the media. She's a victim of domestic abuse. *I'm* a victim of domestic abuse. I was verbally and mentally abused by my father, but it was worse for my mother. He berated her, beat her, damaged her. When he died from his alcoholism, my mother went into a deep depression. It got bad enough that I had to have her committed.

"I wasn't a very good son. I never called to check on her and I hardly visited. It was too painful. During my recovery, I learned to face the pains of my past. I was ready to make amends. I began seeing her once a month, then every other week until now, once a week. Her institution was only a town away from my treatment center, so it made it easier to reconnect."

The studio is silent, stunned, as Mylan talks about his tragic life.

"We still have a lot to work on when it comes to our relationship, but I'm happy to say that her mental health is improving. She was lonely. She had no one. No hope. Now she has me back in her life. Now she has someone to live for again. She has a family again."

Mylan lets out a long breath.

"That article that came out about what I did ... it was true. I almost killed myself. I no longer wanted to be a burden to the people who somehow remained in my life. You see, I wasn't afraid of dying. I'm still not afraid of dying, but that's something I'm still working on. What *has* changed is that I'm afraid of what my death would do to those who care about me. Over a year ago, I thought that was no one.

"People saw my addiction. My failed rehab stints. They saw who I was in film and television. But behind the interviews, the red carpets . . . beyond the bright lights, I was this man with darkness. Trauma. I let it fester and refused to allow rehab to help me. Because I was scared. I was scared to face my demons. Until I met *her*. My light. A beautiful angel who had her own darkness and trauma. She didn't allow it to claim her. Not like it did me. She was the one who broke through the walls I built. She was the one who finally made my stubborn ass realize that this disease wasn't worth dying over. My assistant was the one who kept my heart beating, but it was Lana who breathed life back into me."

Mylan turns to the camera.

"You saved me, Lana Young. You saved my life, and I can never thank you enough for that."

You saved me.

Mylan's words echo in my head. They repeat until etched in my brain. I'll never forget those words.

My ears ring, and I'm not listening to the rest of the interview. Then Ginger shakes my arm, and the noise comes back at full force. Mylan is still talking directly to the camera.

He's still talking to me.

"Lana, you deserved a love as great as Tyler's but I wasn't able to give that to you. Not then. Because I had lost myself to my addiction. I only *knew* myself through my addiction. Then I met you and fell for you. You made me a better person. Better, but not healed. So, I cut you off. I had to. I had to let you go in order to find myself again."

"I still don't understand why I couldn't be there for you during your recovery," I cry at the TV.

"I know you wanted to be there for me," Mylan continues.

"Oh my God," I whisper, my heart thundering against my chest.

"You, Bruno, Eloise, Ginger, all wanted to help me. I understand that."

Ginger screams at her name being mentioned.

"But what if my rehabilitation didn't work again? Three times before and I still managed to fuck it up." Mylan pauses to apologize for cursing on live television. "Second chances shouldn't be endless yet here I was again, getting another opportunity to make it right. I knew if I would have allowed you to come with me on this journey, you would have been a distraction. I don't mean that as a bad thing. I *want* you to be a distraction. I just couldn't allow it while I was getting better. I needed my focus to be on my recovery. So I could be there for you one hundred percent.

"I did what I had to. What I believe was right whether you agree or not. I cut you off because I would have rather you hated me while I tried to get better again than fail, or die, knowing you loved me."

"I never hated you. And I still love you."

"What I'm trying to say is that I did it on my own. I had to show you, myself, that I could face my triggers and battle my demons. I had to step out of my comfort zone because that was the only way I could beat this disease.

"I'm not saying that I'm fully healed. I'll always be an addict, an alcoholic, but I now understand how to control it. I have control over *all* aspects of my life now. Remember what I told you about control?"

My face heats. I nod at the TV, which is silly since he can't see or hear me.

"You told me a year ago that your heart was mine. You said I could have it once I'm better. I understand I no longer deserve it . . ."

I'm crying. Full-on ugly face crying. "You do deserve it. It's yours."

"Tonight is the premiere. I heard you weren't going to be there. I hope that's not true. Because I love you and I need you. I need my donut. If you will allow it, if you still want to give me your heart . . ."

I should be embarrassed with him saying his nickname for me in front of millions of people watching around the country, but I'm not because *he loves me.* He *still* loves me.

Ginger turns off the TV and slams the remote on the bar. I whine because his interview wasn't over yet.

"Go pack."

"Ging," I begin to protest but she points her hands, in the form of a gun, at me.

I gasp. "You're holding me hostage?"

She hasn't pulled the hostage card in ages. We plead the fifth all the time, we present new evidence and reopen cases, but rarely do we take each other hostage. A hostage situation is only needed when either of us is being stupid or need some sense talked into us.

"Walk your ass upstairs and pack your bags. Fly out to that man who just cut open his heart on national TV and let it bleed. He loves you. He needs you."

"What if we don't get a flight this late? What if we don't make it in time?"

She fires an imaginary shot. I clutch my chest where the pretend bullet struck. "Brutal, Ging!"

She blows the end of her finger gun and secures it in her invisible holster.

"Go. We *will* get a flight."

"We?"

She scoffs. "You think you're going to L.A. without me?"

Chapter 28 – Mylan

I pace my living room. She's not going to show. It's an hour before the premiere and no one's told me if Lana is on her way.

I could call her. I still have her number written on the receipt she gave me that one day. I changed my own number and got a new phone, so this paper that I keep in my wallet is all I have of her. It's the only way to get in touch. Still, I don't. Because this is her decision.

Okay, it's not the *only* way to contact her.

I could log on to social media and check to see if she's been spotted. I could ask Bruno to text Ginger. He would do it too. Again, I don't because *this is her decision.*

Eloise decided not to come back as my assistant because she's perusing a photography career, taking classes at New York Film Academy's Los Angeles campus. I basically had to beg her to come tonight as my friend. I showed up at her downtown loft and handed her the letter I wrote her during recovery. She read it, cried, then punched me in the shoulder for making her cry.

Now she's lounging on the couch next to Bruno, feet planted on the coffee table, watching me pace.

"If you don't sit down, I'm going to kick you in the shin and give you a reason to sit down."

I stop to glare at her. "She's not going to show up."

"She will. Stop worrying."

Eloise is not concerned one bit. I start pacing again, resulting in an exasperated sigh from her. "Just end your suffering and call her. Or have Bruno call Ginger. I bet even Jensen could get a hold of Lana."

I throw up my arms in defeat. My relationship with Jensen is still on the mend. After my little stunt crashing the car, he tried to have me fired. The production company wouldn't even consider it. We only had two weeks of filming left in L.A. and firing me would have meant recasting Tyler's character and reshooting the entire damn movie. So, I was allowed to keep the role, assuring the studio I would be clean for those two weeks (I was). I also had to give them proof I was getting help once filming was finished.

Jensen was pissed, and only spoke to me if it had something to do with the scene.

It was two weeks of agony.

Two weeks wallowing in what I did to Lana. Watching her face fall when I broke her heart nearly had me changing my mind.

Cutting her off was the right decision for me. I started with Lana because severing her from my life was the hardest. Then when I left for treatment, I released Bruno and Eloise from duty, promising to pay their salary for a year.

Part of my recovery was writing a letter to everyone I'd wronged. Eloise got hers in person, but I also sent one to Jensen. I apologized for everything I put him through, explained that I understood his reason for dropping out of my life. There was a lot more groveling. He didn't write back for a while. Months. Then one day, his letter arrived. His response: We're good.

Asshole.

It still made me smile with relief because growing up that's what he'd always text me after every disagreement we'd have. Big or small, physical or verbal.

We're good.

I wrote everyone a letter except for Lana because she deserved so much more. She deserved a very public apology, and that was the only reason I did the interview this morning.

Eloise stands, hands on her hip. "Look, she's not going to show up here at your house. If she's coming, she'll go straight to the theater. Stop wearing a path in the carpet and let's go. Traffic is bad, so we're about to be late."

I comb my fingers through my hair, not caring if I mess it up. I button my black Armani jacket, adjust the black skinny tie, and nod.

"I can't believe you're wearing that dress shirt," she snorts and walks out of the room.

My anxiety doesn't ease once inside the limo. I drum my fingers on my shaking knees. My nervous ticks are bad enough that Eloise actually kicks my shin for real this time, and I flip her off. She rolls her eyes and hands me a bottle of water. I drink it all. I'm sweating. My heart races.

Is this what it feels like to die?

Wait, I know what that feels like. No, this is worse.

Eloise was right about traffic. It takes us about forty-five minutes to arrive to Grauman's Chinese Theatre in Hollywood. We sit in a line of limos, waiting to be dropped off at the foot of the red carpet laid out for celebrity arrivals. That takes another ten minutes, and I'm surprised I haven't lost my mind yet.

The moment the door to the limo opens, bright lights flash. Paparazzi snap away and microphones point toward me, yelling questions I'm not paying attention to as my eyes scan the crowd, trying to find her.

She's not here.

"She could be inside," Eloise offers and gestures for me to start walking.

I don't get far because my PR team said I had to stop to answer questions since I skipped all the press junkets. I'm asked about my sobriety, my next project, about Lana. Questions I don't answer and, instead, I talk about my excitement for the film finally being out.

Once I'm done with red carpet interviews, it's time for the movie to start. Inside the theater, I push past people in line, and emerge in the seating area to search the audience.

"She's not here, buddy," Jensen says, appearing beside me and clasping a hand on my shoulder.

I shake Jensen's hand off me the moment I spot Rebecca. She sees me coming, full force, and frowns at the determined look I surely have on my face.

"I haven't heard from her."

I stop, a few feet away. "How does no one know if she's coming or not?" I growl and the hum of chatter falters as people stare our way.

"I'm sorry. I tried calling, but it's going straight to her voicemail."

"What about Ginger?"

"I don't have her number."

I walk away, not caring how rude it is. I go up to Bruno. "Please. Tell me."

He sighs and reaches into his pocket to extract his phone. He types out a text and waits. Nothing happens and before I can demand he call Ginger, the lights flicker.

The movie is about to start.

Fuck.

This is it. She's not coming. She would have been here by now if she was coming.

I wallow in self-pity during the entire movie, not paying attention. It must have been good because everyone around me laughs and cries. Except for Bruno and Eloise. He's showing her his phone and the two of them smile. I can't remember the last time seeing them smile like that. No, I do. It was in Silo when we all hung out.

I poke Bruno's arm then point at the phone. He shakes his head, and I sink back into my seat, crossing my arms

The movie ends and the audience erupts into cheers. Then they stand and I'm getting bombarded with accolades. I'm overwhelmed, but at least I'm distracted from thoughts of *her*.

We file out of the theater, Eloise and Bruno leading me to the waiting limo. The shutters of cameras click rapidly, flashes near blinding as paparazzi yell more questions that I tune out. The world around me disappears as I wallow in pity. I hate when people pity me, yet here I am, the biggest offender.

"I don't want to go to the premiere party," I tell Bruno and Eloise the moment we're inside the limo.

"Too bad, you're going," Eloise answers, smirking. She doesn't see the scowl I'm sending her way because she's frantically typing on her phone.

I lean my head back on the cushioned headrest and close my eyes. I'm too tired to fight with her.

It takes us about twenty minutes to reach the Hollywood Hills. The party is being held at a mansion owned by one of the *Tyler's Team* producers. The guard at the tall black metal gate checks our names on a clipboard and nods, pushing a button to let us in. The driver takes a twisting cement driveway up a steep incline until reaching a two-story, mid-century modern home, painted white with black shingles and trimmings.

I barely register the interior as I walk in with Eloise guiding me by the elbow. Bruno is on alert behind me, but I'm zoned out. A zombie. My heart, dead and growing cold.

"It's going to be okay, Mylan," Eloise says next to my ear since the music is too loud. A DJ on an elevated platform in the living room bobs his head and shoulders as he manipulates the two pop songs and merges them together.

"I need some air," I manage to say.

Bruno hands me a bottle of water. "Here."

I nod to him and take the water, finding the door that exits to an expansive backyard. Fairy lights are hung around the pool and cabana. Lit tiki torches are spaced throughout. Everyone must be inside enjoying the food, music, and booze because I'm all alone out here.

Alone.

Even now, in this moment of lost hope, when I'd normally want to snort a drug and drink to forget or numb myself, the thought of having either makes me sick.

I set the unopened water bottle on a table and walk to the pool, standing with my hands in my pockets, my back to the mansion. Lights illuminate the pool's basin, the water making tiny ripples from a slight breeze. It's peaceful here, only the songs of tree crickets play. The music inside is low enough not to interrupt their concert. A plane soars overhead, and I look up to the stars, shining bright in the cloudless sky. Not even smog taints the clear night here.

I close my eyes and listen to the world around me, contemplating what happens next. What will I do without her?

Music starts playing and I wonder if someone opened the door to come outside. No. The sound is too small, too near.

It's behind me.

The song is familiar. Not a recent song. One from the eighties. I danced to this song before. In my trailer in Arkansas during an impromptu dance party.

Then someone starts singing.

I slowly turn around.

Not someone. *Her.*

Lana is here. She's breathtaking, wearing a dark green sleeveless gown. The plunging neck offers a glimpse of her ample cleavage, only covered by a sheer veil of fabric. Her long dark red hair cascades over her shoulders in luscious curls.

In her hand, held up high, is her cell phone. *We Belong* by Pat Benatar, her favorite song, plays on the screen. It's a karaoke version.

She's singing it to me.

She sings about belonging to the light and thunder.

Words we've both fallen under.

She sings to me about whatever we deny or embrace, for worse or for better.

We belong together.

She's stepped close enough that I could reach out and touch her. I need to touch her. Before I can, she turns off the video and slips her phone in the pocket of her dress.

"Sorry I'm late. We got on the earliest flight available."

I'd been holding my breath, waiting for her to speak. I let it out, shakily.

She points her thumb over her shoulder. "I was going to ask the DJ for a mic and have him play this song in there.

I was going to make this grand gesture, a cheesy, Lifetime movie-worthy gesture, and sing to you. But I saw you walk in and immediately disappear out here."

"You were going to sing in front of a bunch of strangers?"

"Yes."

"For me?"

"For you."

"But you have stage fright."

"Yes, I probably would have thrown up."

I laugh, a quick burst that hurt my throat because I can't remember the last time I laughed like that. No, I do. It was with her.

"Someone once told me to face my fears, or I'd miss out on some spectacular moments in life."

"Whoever said that must be brilliant."

She nods, biting her lip. The simple gesture sparks an explosion within me. Whatever feelings that laid dormant for her reignite and pour from my body. I reach out and grab her, tugging her to me, then I wrap my arm around her waist. My other hand moves up to her face, tracing her jaw with my fingertip. She lets out a breathy moan. A moan I've longed to hear for over a year.

"I've missed you," I say.

"I've missed you, more," she challenges, and I claim her mouth, biting her bottom lip to show her that she's wrong, and *I'm* the one who missed her more.

When we pull away, she pauses, noticing my dress shirt. "Lilies?"

"For a new beginning."

Tears fill her eyes, and she palms my cheek. "I love you. I think I have since the day you started calling me donut."

I lean my forehead against hers. "Liar."

"You're right."

I tilt back, surprised she admitted it.

"It was after 'just a hug.'"

"I love you so freaking much," I say and kiss her again. The world around us resumes—the sounds of the bugs, the planes flying overhead, and the muffled music playing inside at the party.

She pulls back. "No one told you I was coming?"

"Nope."

"Good. They weren't supposed to."

"Oh, that's cruel."

Lana takes my hand and kisses my knuckles. I'm already contemplating how to punish her for not telling me she was going to be here. Though, I'm the one who deserves to be punished.

The thought excites me.

Epilogue – Lana

Two years later

The doorbell rings as I'm setting down a tray of donuts on the white cloth-covered table. I scan the spread, crossing my arms and nod.

Perfect.

Lilies decorate the spaces between the food prepared by our personal chef. It's still overwhelming having household staff. Two years of people doing things I used to do myself: cleaning, preparing the meals, serving guests at dinner parties, answering the freaking door.

"Lana Banana," Ginger sings as she enters the home. Our tiny butler, Gina, yes, I have a butler now, nods her black bobbed head to me and runs off to hide until the next guest arrives. "I brought banana pudding!"

"How clever of you," I grumble as I hold out my hands to take the dish. Except, Ginger places it in the outstretched palms of a server.

Bruno lingers long enough to say hello to me then wanders off to find Mylan, who's upstairs working on his speech for tomorrow night's fundraiser for his new charity, Beyond the Bright Lights. The nonprofit offers additional resources to people in the weeks, months, and years after rehab to help them stay on track.

As for me, I gave my bar to my employees. Well, not all of them. Only the ones who wanted a claim in ownership. There are four of them who now run it together, carrying on my entrance ritual and discounted cab rides.

Now, I solely work for the Tyler's Team organization. I'd stepped back as co-creator after the book came out due to all the publicity but for the past year, I've been more involved. I even do on-camera media interviews now.

Mylan and I also took a break from our lives to travel the first year of our relationship. We visited all the places I dreamed about. Hawaii, London, Ireland, Italy, Paris, Tokyo, Australia (where I got bit by a vicious spider and had to go to the emergency room for a steroid shot in my ass to stop the poison from spreading to my heart.) Traveling with a celebrity was easier than I thought it would be. There were times when the paparazzi found us, but for the most part, no one bothered us. Sometimes we'd venture out in disguises, especially if we were going to a crowded area in big cities.

The disguise idea also helped when we returned to Los Angeles. We'd turn it into a game. Who could come up with the most ridiculous outfit/wig combination? Mylan usually won. His favorite persona was 70s porn star with the horrible mustache and a mullet.

We'd dress up and head out into Hollywood, or to the Santa Monica pier, or anywhere crowded to see how long we could go before being discovered. It worked for months until we started going to karaoke once a week. People figured it out. Then they got in on the game. Like *Where's Waldo* or *Where in the World is Carmen San Diego*. Social media accounts were made with pictures of us out and about in our costumes.

"Everything looks wonderful, Lana," Marie Andrews says, walking into the room. Mylan's mother is steadily coming back to life. Her dry, thinning black hair grows fuller every day. She's gaining weight, her pale skin now tanned by the warm Southern California sun. She's no longer living in the institution in Northern California and stays in the guest house behind the Malibu home Mylan and I bought together last year.

Our home.

"Thank you for helping me decorate!"

The doorbell rings again and before I can answer, Gina appears out of nowhere (I swear) and tugs the door open.

"Who are you?" Pa's gravelly voice shouts followed by Gram saying, "That's Lana and Mylan's butler! I told you they had a butler!"

Ginger giggles, and I shake my head as my grandparents waddle their way into the expansive living area. The furniture is vintage, with an antique red couch and matching red chairs, and a white wooden coffee table on top the dark hardwood floors. Mylan picked out the artwork, minimalist drawings inspired by the timeline of how we met. Like the minimalist tattoos that line my spine.

"Ain't this fancy!" Gram says with nothing but awe in her voice as she inspects the living area. It's the first time they've visited us because it took two years for us to convince Pa to fly on a plane.

"I don't like it," Pa grumbles.

"I don't like you!" Gram counters.

"Why don't you two grab something to eat? I've got mac and cheese, some Memphis barbecue, cornbread. Pa, there's some grilled chicken and salad, and other healthy things for you."

"I'm on vacation. I'm eating whatever the hell I want!"

Pa and Gram stop to say hello to Ginger and Mylan's mother before wandering off, bitching to each other non-stop. My heart swells. Their love is one I envy. I can only hope my love for Mylan grows to that level of bickering when we reach that age.

Though, I'll reach old age before him.

"And why are you feeling guilty?" Mylan whispers against my neck, wrapping his arms around me from behind.

"How'd you know?"

He points at the mirror across from us. My scowl and his smirking face stare back. "Whatever."

"Whatever? Donut, you know I hate that word. Are you wanting to be punished today?"

"Listen, brat," I begin, and he bites me! Not hard. A love bite. Still, he knows how much I melt into a horny mess when he does that.

"I hate that nickname too," Mylan breathes on my neck and kisses the place he just bit. I close my eyes and stifle a moan.

"Maybe I don't like *my* nickname."

"Liar."

"I told you. Calling a fat girl donut? Cliché and offensive."

"And *I* told *you* the reason I call you donut." He moves his hot breath up my throat to my jaw, causing that moan I was holding back to escape.

"Get a room!" a familiar voice calls out.

I peel myself out of Mylan's strong hold and whip around to find Jensen at the entrance to the living area. Mylan moves to him, and they greet each other with their so-called secret handshake—three palm slaps, two fist bumps, a fist to the chest over the heart. Jensen smiles then adjusts his black-rimmed glasses and folds his arms over his wide, flannel-covered chest. That man hasn't changed one bit.

Which is why I'm surprised to see a certain woman walking in right behind him.

"Wow. Did you two come together?"

"Ugh, no," Rebecca blanches. She tosses her long light brown hair over her shoulder and crosses her arms, laughably matching Jensen's pose.

"Wrong. She *came* with me but we're not *here* together," Jensen answers with a cruel smile that makes Rebecca blush.

Interesting.

Rebecca clears her throat. "Um, yeah, the driver picking me up from the airport got a flat tire and they didn't have another person to send right away. I was going to call an Uber but this one," Rebecca explains, pointing her thumb at Jensen, "saw me waiting and insisted I ride with him."

"What a nice young man," Gram beams.

"That's just what he wants you to think," Rebecca adds.

"You know nothing about me," Jensen snarls.

I take my attention away from the man and woman who clearly have a thing for each other, but pretend they don't, and I scan the room. My friends and family laugh and eat and enjoy life together. My throat burns with tears, and I don't think I've ever been happier.

We're only missing . . .

Before I can finish the thought, the front door bursts open and Eloise barges in, not even knocking or ringing the bell. Gina peeks her head around the corner, spots Eloise and scowls then goes back into hiding. "Did I miss anything?!"

"Yes, your manners," Bruno laughs, and Eloise flips him off.

She adjusts the expensive-looking camera she always has hanging around her neck these days. "Sorry, I'm late. My photoshoot was *wild*. The models they hired for the magazine spread apparently hate each other and they kept arguing. It took forever to get the right shots. I was so tired after all that, I needed a coffee and while I was in line, I met this cute girl—"

"Oh, so *that's* why you're late," Mylan muses.

Eloise flips him off too. We're immature. All of us, I swear.

"Anyway, I'm here now. Let's get this little shindig started."

"Be right back," Mylan says quietly against my ear. He kisses my cheek and leaves to get our surprise.

I clear my throat. "I'm so happy you all could make it today."

"You forced us to be here," Jensen snorts.

"Yeah, basically threatened us if we didn't show up," Eloise adds.

I ignore them and keep talking. "Anyway, what I was *trying* to say is that we have some exciting news—"

"Oh em gee!" Ginger squeals. "Are you and Mylan engaged?!"

I narrow my eyes at her. "No."

Rebecca gasps. "Are you two adopting a child?!"

"What? No." I rub my temples. "Can y'all let me finish?"

"Oh, she's angry-angry," Ginger snorts. "Did you hear how thick her twang got?"

"Ugh, Mylan, will you just come out here already?"

Mylan rounds the corner, out of the hallway, carrying an adorable fluffy golden retriever puppy.

A collective 'aww' sounds from our friends and they huddle around Mylan to pet the pooch and get slobbery kisses from it.

"You got a puppy?!" Ginger croons.

"*Lana* got me a puppy. We've had him for a month now." Mylan smiles at the animal and smothers it with kisses. We're calling him Banana. Not my idea, but it was the first word that popped out of Mylan's mouth. The way his face fell—and I swear hearts flashed in his eyes when I surprised him with the puppy—I couldn't deny him anything he wanted. Even borrowing my nickname to name the dog.

"Is this really what you invited us all out here for?" Ginger scrunches up her nose, chewing her gum loudly.

"Yeah, I flew in from a book signing in Chicago," Rebecca adds.

"And I skipped the last day of press for my new movie," Jensen scowls.

I sigh heavily and roll my eyes at my privileged friends. "Actually, there's more." I wave a hand at Mylan for him to take over.

He stands awkwardly, arms behind his back. It makes his T-shirt stretch across his vast, muscular chest and suddenly I want to kick everyone out so I can take my man to the bedroom.

"We're here to celebrate my three years of sobriety."

"Hell yeah, Boss!"

"Bruno, you haven't been my bodyguard in over a year. Stop calling me boss. You're your own boss with an extremely successful personal security company that you run with Ginger."

Bruno frowns and Ginger gets on her tiptoes to kiss him on his cheek.

"If you ever decide to get back into acting, you better call me to hire a full-time bodyguard."

"I promise."

"Everyone has been anxious for your return," Jensen says. "I mean, you *are* an Oscar winner now."

"We're *both* Oscar winners, thanks to *Tyler's Team*."

"Okay, enough with the ass kissing," Rebecca scoffs. "Mylan, that's amazing. We're so proud of you."

"Thank you, Rebecca." Mylan takes a sip of his water and smiles. "But we're also here for something else."

"I knew it!" Ginger takes a step forward, away from Bruno. "You *are* getting engaged!"

"No, Ging," Bruno says, getting on one knee. "You are." Then the big man blushes. "If you'll have me, that is."

The loudest squeal I thought wasn't humanly possible rips from Ginger's mouth.

"Of course, I will!"

Bruno slips the massive rock on Ginger's shaking hand and scoops her up in a hug, swinging her around and around before setting her down and smothering her with kisses. She rushes over to me to show me the ring—a gorgeous two-carat, pear-shaped diamond with a silver band.

"I'm so happy for you!" I say and Ginger hugs me, then narrows her eyes at Mylan. He holds up his hands.

"Don't look at me that way. I've proposed to Lana twice now."

"Banana!" Ginger screams and Banana, the puppy, barks. Mylan and I laugh at the confusion on our friends and family's faces because we haven't told anyone his name yet.

"Maybe someday," I say.

Ginger rolls her eyes then saunters off to show Gram, Pa, Mylan's mother, and Eloise the ring. She also happily shows Rebecca. The two became friends over the past couple of years. We've all become close. Our little friend group turned into a *family*. Our busy lives make it hard to hang out. This is the first time I've managed to get everyone together in at least a year.

Mylan turns to me and wraps his palm around the side of my neck. He slides his thumb under my chin to tilt up my face. *Still* my favorite thing he does.

"Someday? Really?"

I shrug and Mylan clenches his jaw, his nostrils flaring.

"Did I ever tell you how much I *hate* when you shrug at me?"

"Oh yeah? What are you going to do about it?"

"Donut," he warns and proceeds to whisper sweet threats into my ear.

For the first time since Tyler, my life has finally reached a point of certainty. A point where I know who I am, who I love, and how my future will look.

A future with Mylan.

The End

What's Next?

Curious about Jensen & Rebecca?

Beyond the Fame is the woman who makes me question *everything*.

My name is Rebecca Taylor and I'm not okay. I'm 39-years-old and my life has been a whirlwind of heartbreak, beginning with the death of my brother when I was 18-years-old. I grieved my best friend by writing a book about his life and that book was turned into a movie. That's when I met him. Jensen Boliver, the movie's director. He's younger than me, controlling and infuriating. For four years, I've denied my attraction to him because every time he shows an ounce of compassion, he takes it away and shuts down.

Now we're in Hawaii for our friends' wedding. The hotel has lost my reservation... and Jensen shows up with a solution. "You can stay in my suite."

My name is Jensen Boliver and I'm not okay. I'm a 30-year-old plus-size man who's been told my entire life that I should hate myself and my body. Then I met her. Rebecca Taylor. She's beautiful, intense, and makes me feel things I've convinced myself I didn't deserve. Every time we cross paths, our attraction to each other grows. Last year, we both caved. She let me have a taste, but we weren't ready. Now we're in Hawaii for our friends' wedding and the hotel has lost her reservation.

Good thing my suite has a spare room.

Get Beyond the Fame on Amazon

Thank You

Did you enjoy Lana & Mylan's story? Please consider leaving a review!

Goodreads

Amazon

Acknowledgments

I'd like to thank my amazing alpha readers—three superhero moms who offered their time amid their busy schedules to read this story in its roughest form. Xan Garcia, Stephanie Patton, and Maranda Perdue. Thank you for always being real with me and not holding back with your critiques.

To my beta readers—Kristyn Habick, Maggie Linton, Jen Brutger, and Gabrielle Amthor—you were my final eyes before this story was sent to the editor. Thank you for pointing out any final inconsistencies.

To my editor Jenny at Owl Eyes Proofs & Edits—I'm so sorry about all the commas you had to add!

A very special shoutout to Mitzie Gibson with Bold Bodies Collective. Thank you for connecting with me on TikTok to shoot the beautiful cover. Thank you for your mission to change the world's unrealistic body and beauty standards by photographing bodies of all sizes and inspiring acceptance. Thank you to Hazel Hellcat and David Kurti for being the perfect embodiments of my characters, Lana Young and Mylan Andrews.

To Kate at Y'all That Graphic - thank you for taking me on for last minute to revamp the covers. They look fantastic!

And finally, to my readers. You are the reason I keep writing. Thank you for all your support. To the ones who've been with me from the very beginning, I see you. I appreciate you.

This book is for the big girls who need reminding that you are worth it and you do deserve love.

Also By Settle Myer

If you love action & adventure, badass women with superpowers, diverse characters, found family, and fated mates—check out my sci-fi romance trilogy. Book 1 is a clean romance with some cursing and violence, but books 2 & 3 have a sprinkle of spice in them.

Trinity Found

Trinity Returns

Trinity Rises

About The Author

Settle Myer lives in New York City with her two cats, Zombie & Michonne. She's currently a TV News Producer who hopes to one day leave a world of death, disaster, and politics to write about worlds with plenty of forbidden romance, badass women with superpowers fighting violent villains. She loves all things zombies, cats, karaoke, and tattoos... but not necessarily in that order.

Social Media

Check out her website and sign up for her newsletter for updates on new books, discounts, and sneak peeks!

https://www.settlemyerauthor.com/
Follow her on social media:
TikTok: tiktok.com/@settlemyerauthor
Instagram: https://www.instagram.com/settlemyerauthor/
Facebook: Settle Myer Author
Join her readers group on Facebook. Search Settle Myer's Stars and be part of the discussion with fellow fans. Settle posts fun facts from her books, characters, and more!
Twitter: https://twitter.com/Settle_Myer

Made in the USA
Middletown, DE
25 April 2024